THE BONE WOMAN

The Farmer's Market Mysteries

Bushel Full of Murder
Merry Market Murder
A Killer Maize
Red Hot Deadly Peppers
Crops and Robbers
Fruit of All Evil
Farm Fresh Murder

The Country Cooking School Mysteries

If Onions Could Spring Leeks
If Catfish Had Nine Lives
If Bread Could Rise to the Occasion
If Mashed Potatoes Could Dance
If Fried Chicken Could Fly

The Dangerous Type Mysteries

Comic Sans Murder
Bookman Dead Style
To Helvetica and Back

The Scottish Bookshop Mysteries

Written in Stone
The Poison Pen
Fateful Words
The Burning Pages
Deadly Editions
The Stolen Letter
The Loch Ness Papers
Lost Books and Old Bones
Of Books and Bagpipes
A Christmas Tartan
The Cracked Spine

The Alaska Wild Mysteries

Perfect Storm
Lost Hours
Winter's End
Dark Night
Cold Wind
Thin Ice

The Broken Rope Novellas

Like Seeing a Ghost

THE BONE WOMAN

A NOVEL

PAIGE SHELTON

CROOKED LANE

NEW YORK

Books should be disposed of and recycled according to local requirements.
All paper materials used are FSC compliant.

This is a work of fiction. All of the names, characters, organizations, places and events portrayed in this novel are either products of the author's imagination or are used fictitiously. Any resemblance to real or actual events, locales, or persons, living or dead, is entirely coincidental.

Published in the United States by Crooked Lane Books, an imprint of The Quick Brown Fox & Company LLC.

Crooked Lane Books and its logo are trademarks of The Quick Brown Fox & Company LLC.

Library of Congress Catalog-in-Publication data available upon request.

ISBN (hardcover): 979-8-89242-716-6
ISBN (paperback): 979-8-89242-717-3
ISBN (ebook): 979-8-89242-718-0

Cover design theBookDesigners

Printed in the United States.

www.crookedlanebooks.com

Crooked Lane Books
34 West 27th St., 10th Floor
New York, NY 10001

First Edition: October 2026

The authorized representative in the EU for product safety and compliance is eucomply OÜPärnu mnt 139b-14, 11317 Tallinn, Estonia, hello@eucompliancepartner.com, +33757690241

10 9 8 7 6 5 4 3 2 1

This one has to be for my husband,
Charlie, who is always ready to be my
research partner in crime. Fictionally, of
course. This one took us to the middle of
nowhere Arizona, where he calmly took care
of a flat tire as my crazy imagination
conjured a million ways we could die out
there. Love you.

CHAPTER

1

THE DESERT SWALLOWS things. Bones. Bodies. Memories. They can disappear forever. Or they can resurface when you least expect.

I knew how to sift through the desert's ingredients, how to find things that most people couldn't. I'd been born there, made of it, according to my father, Wilmot Dylan. He'd said as much when I was a child sitting atop a table next to his workbench as he went out about his trade.

I remembered a knock on the front door early one long ago morning, as one had come many mornings. That day, I'd pulled myself from my small bedroom and crept out to the museum, its walls and corners filled with the feathers, fur, and fangs of animals that were once alive but no longer. No one was as good as Wilmot Dylan had been in emulating that life in taxidermized form.

It hadn't been strange to me. It had been home.

That day, someone had brought in a mountain lion. Later, after he'd chilled the carcass, Wilmot got to work creating the mount for the customer. I'd watched him, fascinated, too young at the age of six to have been introduced to the hatred and disgust that some people felt about my father's livelihood. Too old to remember any sort of existence before the one we, just the two of us, occupied.

"You know," Wilmot had said, "there was a time, oh, I think fifty years ago or so, hunting mountain lions was illegal. It would have been wrong to work on this beautiful creature's body if it had been poached." His dark, serious eyes were framed with crow's feet, scorched deep by the sun. At thirty-three years old, I had those same eyes now. The sun always carves its way in.

"I know, Papa," I'd said.

"What do you think, little one, would I have taken an animal killed illegally?"

"No."

"Hmm."

He'd always claimed that he and I had been formed by swirls of dust devils—tornados of dirt that could spin all the way up to the sky. He used that story mostly when I asked about my dead mother, Catalina Shaw Dylan. He'd never said the exact words, but it always seemed he was trying to tell me that she had been made of softer stuff than he and I, something not devilish.

"Papa, can I have that one?" I'd pointed.

"The femur bone?"

"Yes." And then I'd whispered words that had seemed magical to me: "A mountain lion's femur."

Who wouldn't want something like that?

"Are you building a skeleton, Hazel?"

"I . . . like the bones, Papa."

He'd laughed then, a noise filled with real glee. "You are a chip off the old block, little bit. Okay then. You clean it, and it's yours."

I had nodded and then turned my attention back to my father's hands as he worked quickly, expertly.

Almost thirty years had passed since that day—it was so long ago that I was always surprised when the memory resurfaced. But it was one of the clear ones I still had of my father, who disappeared seven years later, when I was thirteen, probably swallowed by the thing that had made us, and the place the sheriff had brought me out to this morning—the desert. That was the day I'd earned not only Wilmot's approving laugh but also that femur.

Now, I tipped my cowboy hat to shade my eyes better as I looked out into a tangle of cactus and dirt patterned by the wind, though no devils were currently present, at least of the dust variety. I pushed away the memory and worked to keep cool, somewhat literally but mostly figuratively—the morning summer air was too warm, hinting at what was sure to be another typical southern Arizona scorcher, but it was still bearable enough.

"I've never seen anything like it," Sheriff Benji Calloway muttered behind me. His voice was as dry as the air.

"Yeah," I said distractedly. I was still trying to digest the scene.

Like the man with the mountain lion all those years ago, the sheriff had pounded on my door right before sunrise. "You in there, Hazel?"

Used to the occasional middle of the night interruption, either someone with a fresh kill who didn't know I hadn't continued my father's trade or someone wanting to haze me for the same misconception, I'd opened my eyes quickly.

I'd roused myself from the bigger of the two small bedrooms I'd moved into on the second floor after Wilmot wasn't there to occupy it anymore, threw on some clothes, and opened the nightstand drawer. My gun was there but not the folding knife that I carried in my back pocket most of the time. Where was it? It came to me a moment later—I thought I'd left it on the patio the night before. I didn't want to take the time to look for it now, so I grabbed the gun and made my way down to the gallery, the place that was still visited sometimes, coins and dollar bills left behind for the chance to take a look at the most lifelike dead animals in the state of Arizona, maybe the whole western United States. Once I recognized the voice, I set the gun on the donation table and answered the door.

"I need you to see something." Sheriff Calloway stood there in civilian clothes but with his gun holstered at his waist.

"What?"

He shook his head slowly. "I'm not sure I can describe it."

I inspected his face for hints. Maybe it was the way the rising sun's rays shadowed half of it, but I thought there was nothing there but fear and terror. He usually had a better poker face.

"Okay. Let me grab my hat and boots."

Part of the life of bones that I lived included helping law enforcement, but the sheriff was more tightly strung than I'd ever seen before. I'd known Sheriff Calloway my whole life, and I sensed that he was about to jump out of his skin.

The fifteen-minute ride out into the middle of almost nowhere, the stretch of desert we called The Wild that was between the town and the Tumacácori Mountains, had been silent and bumpy, the truck's shocks hating the trip even more than my lower back. We'd gone east, toward the mountains and the Vulture Caves, over terrain crowded with tumbleweed and cactus as well as the occasional camper trailer, parked out there so the inhabitants might be left alone to live off the grid, or just because it seemed like a good place to throw one away. The desert chewed on those before swallowing them.

The small town of Black Vulture was once a semi-thriving mining town. Now, though it wasn't quite a strong wind away from disappearing forever, the remaining buildings were worse for the wear, chipped stucco and paint, faded signage, most of the remaining windows cracked or punctuated by some random bullet that, so far, hadn't hit human flesh. The businesses that remained were kept afloat by the locals as well as two nearby large corporations.

The downtown was shaped like a north to south S. My lab that used to be my father's studio, the place where I examined bones and deciphered their stories, was located at the bottom curve. It was boxed together with the small museum gallery and my upstairs living space. My walled-in patio backed up to The Wild—some might say encroached upon it as I often had to shoo away snakes, scorpions, and the occasional tarantula. A building with three spaces sat at a northward angle from my place. One of those spaces held the diner, but the other two were considered uninhabitable, though they did sometimes offer shelter to squatters or desert creatures who'd run out of other options.

West of town and on the other side of Interstate 19 were the big corporations—a biosphere where the University of Arizona conducted survival studies, and the Institute for Otherworldly Populations, where those inside spent their time staring either at their computer screens or up to the sky in search of alien life. We kept it simple and just called it The Institute. Though some who worked at The Institute lived in town, most of them drove the forty-five-minute commute back and forth from Tucson.

The county sheriff's office was about a mile south of town and located in a single-wide trailer that had been reinforced with wood walls painted a reddish brown. It was an eyesore, even from the interstate, but it did have a large air conditioner. Manned by Sheriff Calloway and two deputies, they were more prepared to fight crime than the two-person police crew who worked out of an old five-space strip mall at the top of the S.

We were ruled by, lived by, and some even died by, the desert, a place where everything, plants and animals alike, wanted to kill you for your water. Now, as Calloway and I stood in the thick of it and as my eyes landed on something so familiar and foreign at the same time, it was impossible not to think that that place made of all those devils had won this round.

However, whoever had placed the abomination amid the needles and sagebrush was human, no doubt, though made of evil, that was certain.

At first glance, I realized that there was a chance that what I was seeing wasn't real, not made of the genuine thing, but now I was pretty sure it was, and my stomach was airy, my tongue dry.

"I need to get closer," I said.

"Let's go."

We closed most of the gap.

"Jesus," I uttered.

"Yeah. Is it real?" Calloway asked.

I let my eyes graze over the skeleton. "Yes, I think so. Look at the coarse texture, the foramina—"

"Foramina?"

I nodded. "The holes. So things like nerves and blood vessels can move from one area to the next. People who create fake bones don't usually take the time to add the foramina."

I'd worked with thousands of bones, but the stories they told could still unsettle me.

"I need to get even closer," I said.

Wilmot had always been adamant about separating life from death, animal from hide, body from spirit, and bone from flesh.

My father's religion hadn't resided inside a church building or any sort of book, but according to him, the obvious difference between life and death was enough. His respect for both had been all encompassing and had left behind a reputation I still didn't quite understand.

However, it was natural for me to separate the two like I'd been taught, but this skeleton was undoubtably meant to shock.

I wanted to cringe, draw back, maybe even run away. But this was my job.

The bones had been posed, using wire, sticks, pieces of wood, and probably other things that I didn't notice right off. It had taken a lot of work—without the connective tissues, the bones wouldn't stay together on their own, keep their form. A red scarf had been tied around the neck—representing blood was my first guess. The bones were bright against the other building materials. It seemed they had been thoroughly cleaned, but I'd need a closer look. They were a stark white and—I leaned in for a sniff. "They've been bleached."

"Recently?"

"Well, I still smell the chemicals, so I can narrow it down a bit, but maybe not exactly."

"Bleach took off the . . ."

"Defleshed the bones? Maybe. There's some pitting probably from bleach." I tilted my head upward. "Full sun this time of year could help with decomposition too." I squinted at the bones again. "Look how white they are. Clean. Yeah, they were soaked in bleach probably. I don't see any sign of leftover tissue, no pieces of ligaments, tendons, cartilage. Just the cleaned bones."

There was no blood either, but the scarf, rippling in the gentle wind, was a convincing enough representation.

The handiwork was . . . impressive.

Our boots grinding into the brittle earth again, we circled around the skeleton. Our path wasn't easy as we had to veer around jumping cactus. The jumping wasn't real, but the needles from the sloughed-off stems didn't hurt any less because of it.

The sheriff asked, "What do you think?"

I startled and then I hesitated. I'd been asked that question more than a few times. My immersion into the life my father had set in motion for me, as well as my own curiosity that had taken me away from Black Vulture for a time to study more deeply, had qualified me to offer all sorts of opinions regarding bones and crime scenes, but not without some consideration first. As I looked into the sheriff's eyes today, confirming they were, indeed, pinched in fear, I knew he wanted something fast. He had no idea what this was about. In fact, I didn't either, but I knew some things he didn't.

I looked at the ends of the humerus bones, the ones that made up the top parts of the arms. I skimmed the others too, knowing all of this would require a closer look.

"Okay, well, I can say with reasonable surety that the limbs were disarticulated–cut off–before being put in bleach. I spot knife knicks at the ends of the bones, but whoever did the cutting kept it at the joints, I think." I squinted and moved my head in again. "They don't appear to have been too impatient." I stepped back around to the front. I glanced into the empty eye sockets, the open mouth. "Teeth are there. That could help with ID."

"Cause of death?"

I shook my head. "I'm not seeing the hyoid bone." I put my fingers to the top part of my throat. "It's a horseshoe shaped bone that usually gets damaged when someone is strangled. This might mean the victim was, indeed, strangled, and the hyoid was damaged, so it wasn't included to give us that clue. But I don't know. I can't give you a COD right now."

"Okay. Anything else?"

There was something else in Calloway's tone now. I studied the skeleton again. The pose was familiar—on all fours, the carefully placed arms, the way the finger bones, attached to wires, curled inward, the mouth forced open, making the exposed teeth seem bared in a howl.

My pulse was beating in my ears. "It's been posed to look like a coyote, its throat cut and bleeding."

"That's what I thought too. A mount."

"This isn't taxidermy," I said quickly.

"I know."

"Who found it?"

"A hiker coming back to town. He passed this way two days ago and it wasn't here then." The sheriff paused. "You have a coyote in your museum, don't you?"

I nodded, but my eyes returned to the skeleton. "Two. One is posed very much like this. Sheriff, this wasn't easy to do. I can't . . . quite grasp how unwieldy it must have been, how much time it took. The bones might have been defleshed quickly, but this . . . sculpture was work."

"Right. The perpetrator or perpetrators might have known . . . I don't know, about taxidermy, typical poses maybe."

"Maybe."

A long, silent pause later, he said, "Are you in touch with any taxidermists?"

"There are still quite a few out there, lots of them not on the books, not legal. Taxidermists who take poached animals make much more money than those who don't."

"Do you know who around here is doing it, legally or not?"

"There's a guy in Tucson—"

"Closer than forty miles."

I squinted at him under the brim of my old black felt cowboy hat. He was getting at something. I didn't think he was accusing me of anything, but maybe he was. "Are you asking me if I had something to do with this?"

"No, Hazel, but . . ." He sighed. "All right. Look at its left hand."

I hesitated, went down on all fours, and leaned in, the scent of bleach now even stronger. My eyes went to the left hand.

Stuck in between the first and second fingers that had been curled under to make them closer to the size of a coyote's paw, was a separate phalanx—the singular term for a finger bone. *Phalanges* was plural. It wasn't easy to immediately identify which phalanx you were looking at. The middle ones attached to the tips and were smaller than the proximal ones, the ones attached to the metacarpals, the hand bones. But it was probably a good guess to think we were seeing a middle phalanx, maybe from a middle finger, a digitus medius.

"Shit," I said quietly.

"Yeah," she sheriff said. "Wilmot carried one of those bones around with him."

Decades earlier, my father discovered a mostly complete human skeleton out in the middle of nowhere, maybe not far from where we currently were. He'd told me that he'd been too tempted not to take a bone for himself. The one he chose was the middle finger's middle phalanx. Then he notified the authorities about the skeleton, a male whose identity has never been determined, as far as I knew.

I'd never told anyone about the theft, but over the years word had gotten out. My father had been a talker, and he'd probably shared his "secret" with far too many people.

His story was part of how I had been given my nickname. My fascination with bones, my real collection (all legally obtained), my profession, and then my father's strange habit of carrying around the bone, rolling it between his fingers like a magician's quarter, had led to me being called the Bone Woman.

I didn't hate it.

I looked back at the sheriff and squinted. "You don't think . . ."

"Your father, Hazel . . . there were rumors, things he did. Different sorts of things. Did you listen to Minnie's podcast?"

My jaw clenched as I felt myself go into defense mode. "No. What things? Sheriff, this could just be the perpetrator giving us the finger." Other than the one theft and the nature of his job, I wasn't aware of a slew of other controversy.

A local, Minnie Chavez, had been producing a true-crime podcast for a long time. She'd done a series about Wilmot and him going missing, but I had not listened to it. I hadn't listened to any of Minnie's podcasts.

"I was just . . . maybe the podcast would help with remembering," Calloway said.

I didn't have amnesia really, but I hadn't ever been able to remember clearly some of the days right before and right after my father's disappearance. Shock had had its way with me. I didn't need therapy to understand that some sort of denial was at play, but that didn't stop me or other people from questioning me every now and then, wondering if anything new had come back to me. Nothing had. I wasn't the only one who wanted answers regarding what might have happened to Wilmot.

I considered those days one of the desert's biggest heists. The least it could have done was let me keep all my memories. But life did go on, and I had too much to do to dwell on that loss. I didn't have any desire to "fix" it, whatever that might mean, particularly after so much time had passed. That didn't stop Calloway from continually doing his job—investigating, questioning.

"What specifically do you think I need to remember?" I asked.

The sheriff sighed and continued, "Have you heard from Wilmot? Recently maybe?"

My knee-jerk answer was "No," but as the moments ticked by and the sun rose a little higher, I couldn't deny the fact that the skeleton's pose and the extra bone stuck in between the fingers, just might be some sort of message that Wilmot could have concocted. Or perhaps someone was sending a message about him, maybe even via his remains.

Had the desert spit up my father, and if so, had he become some sort of psychopathic killer, or perhaps a victim of one? Were these his bones? Why would someone pose them this way?

I glared at the sheriff. I hoped he didn't see my doubt or maybe it was confusion. No matter what this all turned out to be, I knew I had to redirect any light of suspicion until I could figure out for myself what might be going on.

"No, of course not." I nodded back at the sculpture. "You think this could be him?"

"Could be anybody," he said, his voice scratchy, desert dry. "Thanks for taking a first look. I've called Tucson too."

I nodded. "The bones'll go up to Tucson?"

"Probably. I don't think we can take them to your lab first. That's too much . . . moving things around."

"I can make the trip up there if need be."

As a consultant, I took on individual jobs throughout the entire world, though mostly the southwest. I was also on retainer with the state of Arizona, so those cases were my priority. I was available at their request and if my schedule permitted.

"Thanks." Calloway paused. "But can you tell me anything else right now?"

I didn't want him to read the personal things twisting around inside me, so I turned back to the bones. Photographs can be key to any crime scene, but I hadn't thought to bring my digital SLR, and Calloway hadn't thought to suggest it. I didn't want to waste time going back to get it, give the Tucson people a bigger head start, so I grabbed my phone from my back pocket and started snapping pictures.

"Not yet, but I'll keep looking."

"Good enough. Thank you, Hazel.

I ignored the tinge of sympathy in his tone. I just needed to focus on the work, the task at hand, not try to superimpose some old image of my father over the sculpture in the desert.

I hoped it wasn't him, but I would figure out the story these bones had to tell. That's what I did, and I was very good at it.

His eyes propelled open, and he gasped. His sleep had been bloated with bad dreams, distorted images from the things he'd done. He hadn't considered that his efforts would be burned into his brain, that they would hunt for and haunt him, even as he closed his eyes.

He'd expected the beginnings of a cleansing of sorts, freedom from the binds that had tormented him for years.

He'd had no choice. If he hadn't finally done what he'd done, he'd have surely lost his mind. He couldn't have waited much longer, so when the opportunity presented itself, he moved quickly.

The killing had been the easy part. It was the other things, cutting up the corpse, stripping the bones free of the flesh—getting rid of the tendons, organs, blood—and then posing the bones. It had been so much work.

He'd known what to do, though. He'd studied. He'd bettered himself, transformed into a new man. He'd done everything right to prepare. He told himself not to let it bother him, that no matter how arduous it might get, he was on the right path. He hadn't counted on the dreams, the nightmares. He'd have to make it through.

Thankfully, there was only one task left.

Well, there was only one important *task left. He could rightfully continue, but after going through all the work, he could only commit to one more.*

A break first, though. Besides, time would serve multiple purposes. He could rest. He could work on erasing the dreams. He could contribute to misleading the authorities. He could ingratiate himself with the community.

But no matter what, he was going to finish what had been set in motion over twenty-five years earlier.

CHAPTER 2

SHERIFF CALLOWAY DROPPED me off downtown and then steered his truck back toward the scene, where investigators from Tucson were going to be arriving at any minute.

I would write up what I'd seen or what I might find as I took a closer look at the pictures I'd taken. Calloway would let the lab in Tucson know that I would be coming by. I understood that the reason Sheriff Calloway had taken me out to the scene was more about Wilmot than my expertise, and though I didn't want him feeling sorry for me, I was glad he'd gotten me out of bed.

"I need you to help with a possible message. I also want you on your toes, looking for your father or signs of him. Once the techs are done with the bones, particularly the extra finger bone, I'll get you the results if you don't get them first yourself, see if that shines a light on anything. Dental records are going to be our best hope right now, but that extra bone . . ." he'd said.

Yeah, that digitus medius. Wilmot's had been with him when he left, either of his own accord or not.

A cold dread filled me as the sheriff's truck disappeared into a cloud of stirred-up dust. I hadn't realized how much safer I'd felt with him nearby. I was rattled by the bone sculpture.

I looked out to the distant desert at familiar sights, things I tried to see with fresh eyes today. A nonproducing pecan farm was made with perfectly matched and manicured rows. The mountains, frequently topped off by snow in the winter, sometimes in spring as the temperatures made their run toward three digits in Black Vulture. A gathering of a group of almost matching tiny houses, at one time barracks where miners used to live when they were working, now occupied by those who chose to reside in Black Vulture. My eyes went toward the Tumacácori mountains again, the Vulture Caves, a place that had been fodder for all kinds of local and evil fairytales, villains made of bats and blood-drinking killers. My father had loved hiking out to those caves. He'd been fascinated by the bats in the caves and their nightly exodus on their way to eat from the plentiful bounty of insects in and around The Wild.

"You out there, Wilmot? Pop?" I muttered as I scanned.

He could be anywhere. He was probably nowhere, but the idea I'd always held on to, the thing that had lain even more groundwork as to who I'd become and had sent me out on too many desert excursions to count, was that his bones must be somewhere.

There were ways to destroy them, hide them, but like the strange bone between the skeleton's fingers, the one I'd assigned the label of digitus medius whether or not that would prove to be true, there was usually something left over or overlooked. I squeezed my eyes shut tight as the sculpture and its coyote taxidermy-like pose came back to my mind.

There was no way not to be shaken by what had been staged. If someone had taken the time to create it, it must *mean* something.

A noise that sounded like a mix of foot stomps and deep voiced groans forced my eyes open again. Colors, movement, and scents came at me all at once, and before I could understand what was happening, I was knocked down on my back on the cracked and uneven walkway.

The fall took the wind out of me, but I still managed to exclaim something like "Hey!" as my frantic hands worked double-time to push the man off me.

Putrid scents, body odor and other wild things, reached my nose, but I didn't take the time to analyze the scent soup. My eyes finally focused on a dirty face and black rotted teeth with even darker gaps showing through a grimace. The man, his hair color hidden by a knit cap, could have been in his twenties or in his eighties—his face was too dirty to tell, and his eyes were red and rheumy.

His breath was worse than everything else.

"Get off me." I tried to roll or buck him off, but he was strong enough to pin me, at least for a few seconds.

"Hazel Dylan, you will pay for the sins of your father," he said, his face way too close to mine.

There were other words that might have gotten my attention, but those rocked my soul and stilled my struggle. "What?"

"Hey!" A voice came from behind my head. "Get off her!"

The man atop me, too agile to be too old, I decided, dismounted me, and in a stumble-run, took off down the walkway and then around the building.

"Are you okay?" A man stood next to me, offering a hand.

I nodded and took the help, hoisting myself up all the way before hurrying along the path my attacker had taken.

"Hey!" the man who'd helped me said again.

The few seconds it took to stand were somehow enough for the other man to disappear down the side of the building that held the diner. I ran through and looked toward a road that led to more houses and a northerly view of the desert, different from the direction I'd been looking in just a few moments earlier.

The man who'd helped me stopped next to me and followed my gaze with his. I scanned the post office and then back at the desert again.

"I don't see anybody," he said a long moment later.

There wasn't even any stirred-up dust.

"Damn it," I said.

"Are you okay?"

I finally looked at him. I had no idea who he was, and when that happened, the person was either passing through on their way to or from Mexico, a visitor for the biodome, or someone who worked at The Institute. It was stereotyping, but this guy, his buttoned-up dress shirt, ironed khakis, black, thick-framed glasses, and short haircut told me he was from The Institute.

"Who are you?" I asked, suspicion lining my words, like it would with most any stranger, but even more so after the morning I'd had.

"I, uh, I'm Sonny Riley. I work at The Institute." He put his hand out for me to shake.

I frowned at it and almost asked him where he'd been the past couple of nights. Except it wasn't my place to question anyone regarding the skeleton sculpture, even strangers who seemed to appear out of nowhere when I was being attacked by someone who'd mentioned my father.

Things were layering uncomfortably, coincidentally. But sometimes, that's just what happened.

Sonny pulled his hand back, seeming to see silent questions under my furrowed eyebrows. I had no idea where my hat had gone. I remembered that I'd left my gun in the museum and hadn't tracked down my knife before leaving with Calloway. He offered what he probably thought were appropriate answers. "I was at the counter in the diner. I saw the guy come at you."

I gave it another few beats before I said, "Do you have any idea who he was?"

He shook his head. "No clue. Are you okay? Hurt anywhere?"

"I'm fine."

"Good. Let's go inside, grab you a glass of water or something."

I needed to call the sheriff. I reached for my phone in my back pocket, but it wasn't there. It must have fallen out in the struggle. "Shit."

I stepped around Sonny and made my way back around the buildings.

I grabbed my phone from the walkway and swiped my finger over a screen that was now more cracked than it had been before, leaving a trail of blood as it came to life.

"You are hurt," Sonny said as he stood next to me again.

I wanted him to go away. I tried to scroll to the sheriff's phone number, but the blood that was coming from a gash on my finger was smearing the screen to opaque.

"Here, use mine." Sonny fumbled in his pocket for his phone and handed it to me.

But before I could take it, he pulled it back a little. "Listen, you're hurt, and we need to see how badly. Come on, let's get inside."

I looked up at his face, not sure if I wanted to punch it or take his phone and throw it as far as my arm could manage. If the twitch at his left eye was any indication, he was tracking my anger. He cleared his throat and said, "Please."

I shook my head at the "magic word."

I was twenty steps away from my home, but I didn't want this stranger to know where I lived. So I stepped around him and made my way through the diner's front door, lit with a neon "ner," because the first two letters didn't work.

Not surprisingly, Sonny followed.

CHAPTER

3

THE GASH IN my index finger needed stitches, but the one doctor who came through town wouldn't be there until a week or so. I could drive closer to Tucson and visit a nurse practitioner I knew or make the trip all the way to Tucson for urgent care.

I took the option that included Dixie, a diner waitress, and Doug, a diner cook, putting on clean gloves and performing a little needle-less surgery. Dixie held the gash closed while Doug taped it up with some butterfly bandages found in the diner's first aid kit.

"This isn't smart," Doug said as he put on his glasses and peered closely at the cut and his handiwork. "You need stitches."

Dixie snapped off her gloves and said, "I think it'll be okay. We drowned that thing in hydrogen peroxide. Bacteria will not come calling, and you have good steady hands, Doug. The scar won't be bad, honey."

Dixie had eleven children. It would take an arterial bleed or unconsciousness to worry her. In fact, she might meet unconsciousness with "Give it a few minutes."

Outfitted with torn vinyl booths and rocky tables and chairs, the diner had been around forever as far as I knew. It was the only restaurant around these days, unless you traveled about ten miles toward Tucson for a freeway exit of fast food and homemade pie. I didn't mind the trip when I was craving a thick crust pizza, a greasy burger, or a slice of banana cream. But most of the time, not being fond of cooking anything that couldn't be warmed in my countertop toaster, I ate at the diner. Lots of us did. It brought in plenty of money, and a remodel or even a facelift to the place would not only ruin its charm but also show up every other establishment in town. Keeping it a little bedraggled matched the rest of us, its customers, and made us comfortable.

"Hey," the diner's youngest waitress, Trish, came through to the back room where we'd convened. "I found some superglue."

"Good girl," Dixie said. "Give it to me."

"Superglue? Like over-the-counter superglue?" I asked.

Dixie took the tube from Trish. "Perfect. It hasn't been opened yet. We'll glue the cut shut. Doug can lift off the bandages one at a time. We'll have it closed up tight. Shoot, you might not have any scar."

I examined their handiwork and was impressed enough. "It's closed pretty well, Dix. I think we'll just stick with this."

Dixie seemed disappointed but shrugged a moment later. "Suit yourself." She put the tube of superglue into her uniform's apron and stood. Her hand went to the small of her back as she took another moment to straighten.

Not only had she raised eleven children, she'd done most of it on her own, working at the diner for years. Three of her kids had graduated from the University of Arizona. Every time someone asked her if she was ever going to retire, she'd tell them how many more she had to go before a "life of leisure" was possible.

Eight might be her current tally, but her son Griffen was a senior in high school this coming year and would graduate with honors if he knew what was good for him.

Doug was the only male who worked in the diner. He claimed to enjoy working with the "girls." However, jobs weren't easy to come by in Black Vulture. So even if he didn't like it, he'd find a way to put up with his female coworkers.

"Hey, Hazel," Trish said. "I've spotted some official cars heading out to the desert. Crime stuff. Do you know what's going on?"

"I don't have any details," I said without hesitation.

Trish nodded and bit her bottom lip. She turned and gazed in the direction of the employees' small lockers, battered and peeling from years of use.

"What's up, Trish?" I asked.

Her attention snapped back in my direction. She shook her head. "Joey hasn't answered my texts since yesterday. He might just be being an ass, but I guess I'm a little worried."

Dixie sent me a look before she turned to Trish. "He's done this before, honey. Like some stray animal, he'll come sniffin' back for you when he gets hungry enough."

"That's not nice, Dixie," Trisha said.

"I know." She frowned at Trisha.

A long beat later, the younger woman deflated. "I know. He's done this before."

"Yes, he has."

I couldn't help but dig a little—unofficially. "I'm sure he's fine too, Trisha, but do you have any new or unusual reason to be concerned about him?"

She frowned at my authoritative tone and then thought for a moment. "Well, I'm not sure . . ."

She had all our attention now.

"What does that mean?" I asked.

"He was . . . strange the other day."

"Strange how?" Dixie asked.

"Sad about something, but he wouldn't tell me what."

I knew Joey about as well as I knew most of the people around Black Vulture. He was in trouble more than he wasn't, though it did seem he'd grown up some since dating Trisha. Those of us who'd met both him and Trisha were in Trisha's court and hoped she'd decide he wasn't her forever guy, but, sigh, the heart wanted what it wanted.

"He'll get back to you." I would let Calloway know what she'd said even if it didn't matter.

I'd considered calling the sheriff before having my finger attended to, but how important could my problem be when he was working with Tucson authorities on something that was undoubtedly a higher priority? I'd text him in a minute, let him know I'd like to talk to him when he was available.

I hoped for quick answers from Tucson, and I didn't want to put any speed bumps in anyone's way.

"You're probably right," Trish said weakly.

"What in the hell is going on?" Virgie, the diner's owner, pushed through the door. Four feet something, Virgie was tiny with a giant voice, and teased gray hair that was closer to Jesus than any of the rest of her would ever be. "What is everyone doing back here?"

"Sorry," Trisha said as she made her way around the boss.

"We were fixing up Hazel's finger," Dixie said.

"Fixing? Was there blood? In here?"

"Seemed more appropriate than the dining room," Dixie said.

Virgie wasn't fond of backtalk. She wasn't an unkind person, and she ran a clean and tight ship. The only one who could get away with anything that might be considered disrespectful was Dixie, but Dixie was just being Dixie. Virgie, unbeknownst to

Dixie, tolerated whatever Dixie dished out since the whole town would revolt if their favorite waitress was fired.

"Get your asses back out here. And you," Virgie looked at me, "don't you dare bleed in my restaurant."

I nodded and followed the others out to the dining room, again patting my back pocket and wondering where my phone had gone. The diner staff who'd been taking care of me had all dispersed to their tasks.

I thought about returning to the break room to search for the phone, but what was his name . . . ? Sonny. Sonny waved it at me as he sat on the stool at the other end of the counter. Then he pointed at my hat, also on the counter.

I sighed and then made my way toward him.

"It's cracked, but I cleaned off the blood." He handed me the phone.

"You did? Why?"

"I didn't think you'd want a bloody phone."

He didn't understand the depth of my question, which, had I wanted to expound upon it, would have been something like "Who cleans blood off any phone that isn't theirs?" But I didn't.

"Right." I sat on the stool next to him and took the phone. "Thank you. And thanks for coming out to help me. And gathering my hat."

"You're welcome. How's the finger?"

I held it up so he could see the waitress and cook's work.

"Nice," he said.

"They mentioned superglue, but this seemed good enough."

"Superglue might help."

"I'll see how it goes."

Sonny nodded. "I think I was the only one to see anything. I'm sorry I didn't get a better look at the guy." He paused. "I could smell him, though."

"Me too."

"I called the police."

"Why?" I demanded.

Sonny frowned for a moment. "Because I witnessed a crime and I'm a good citizen?"

I tried to squelch the growl in my throat, but I wasn't ever good at that.

"What?" he asked.

"How long ago did you call?"

"Right after they took you back to wherever they performed the patch-up."

"That was," I glanced at the time on a big analog clock on the wall behind the counter, "probably about thirty minutes ago."

"Sounds about right."

"The police are located about one minute away, and there's been no response yet."

"Oh. Yeah. Well, it was the right thing to do, and . . . well, I did just leave a voicemail message. No one answered."

"I will text the sheriff, but I'll track down a local officer too," I acquiesced.

"I wouldn't have thought to call the county sheriff."

I nodded, not sharing the morning's events with him just like I hadn't with anyone else.

The local police were as close to useless as police officers could get. I didn't blame them fully. Lazy has a way of begetting lazier, and at some point, you must not be able to pull yourself out of the stagnancy that came with being a Black Vulture police officer.

"I met the new police chief yesterday," Sonny said.

"We have a new police chief? I mean, I didn't even know we had someone with that title. I thought we just had a couple guys posing as officers."

He nodded. "Well, he said he was new."

"I hadn't heard."

"Yes. He was very serious."

"Name?"

"I couldn't tell you. He came out to The Institute. Someone had knocked over a saguaro out front. They're protected, aren't they? Saguaro, I mean."

"That's kind of a myth. They're no more special than any other cactus, but knocking one over on private property without approval would be against the law." I paused, my eyes swinging toward the front door. No one who looked like a police chief was on his way in. "Maybe I'll go introduce myself."

In fact, considering the morning's tour out to the desert and the sheriff's command to keep him notified regarding Wilmot contacting me (this wasn't that, but Wilmot was still in the mix), the sheriff did need to know about the man who'd accosted me. In an ideal world, the local police would be more pertinent to some guy knocking me over on the Black Vulture sidewalk. Would a new police chief be better than what we had previously?

Sonny nodded again. "Want some water? Something to eat?"

"No thanks."

"Seriously, are you okay? Are you . . . shaken up?"

It was an interesting choice of words. My eyebrows furrowed. I probably should be more bothered, but I was used to a little tumult. Vandalism to the museum, cases I worked on. I spent a lot of time dealing with, if not bad things, things that might, indeed, bother many civilians.

"I'm—"

A bloodcurdling scream filled the diner.

We all jumped and turned toward the noise.

Trisha was behind the counter, at the far end, near the coffee machines. One hand was over her mouth as she held her phone with the other, something I knew Virgie didn't allow—no phones on shift! Trish looked up and around. Her eyes were bright, pooling with tears and fear.

"A body's been found! No!" she squealed. Her eyes landed on mine—everyone in town thought of me as some sort of law enforcement officer. I wasn't, not even close, but I hung out with that ilk more than most. Her mouth formed words though she didn't say them aloud: "Is it Joey?"

I scooted off the stool and held back the shrug I felt in my shoulders.

Hell if I knew.

But I'd sure find out.

CHAPTER

4

I THANKED SONNY AGAIN and grabbed my hat from the counter. My phone was clean, but a part of me wondered if the blood that had covered it had been all mine. Was there a chance it could have been analyzed, and the man who'd attacked me potentially identified?

It was too late now.

I kept my old Jeep parked next to my property on a graveled plot of land that did the job well enough, but the only shelter came from a tall mesquite tree that dropped seed pods onto the exposed interior all year long.

Once I cleared away today's gathering of pods, I hopped in and steered my way to the top of the S, where an old building housed the local police, next to a butcher shop that had been one of the first businesses in town and had garnered a reputation that brought in customers from all over the state. BV Butchery carried only "the finest" cuts of meat from the nearby working ranches. Today, a short line of four people snaked out from the front door, but I'd seen it go all the way around the building during sales.

Last I knew, Black Vulture's force consisted of two part-time officers, Steve and Caleb, one of whom always carried a cell phone with him in case of emergencies. I didn't think either of them had received much training, if any.

Black Vulture had seen its fair share of snake removals and petty theft, but there wasn't enough crime to keep the local officers as busy as the county sheriff. I couldn't imagine that we'd somehow acquired a real police chief, and I was hoping to get the details.

The main doors to the building were tucked under an old decorative stucco arch that had probably been put there for the sole purpose of adding some shade. In a half-moon arc, inside the dark lobby were four more glass doors. Three were dark—I didn't think there had been any occupants inside those spots for years. The fourth one was bright with fluorescent light. "Black Vulture Police" had been painted on the glass.

I pulled on the door and made my way into the familiar space. Nothing much had changed since the last time I'd been there, but I didn't see any people. With four desks, two of them messy with storage, and a break room in the back, the place was utilitarian and gray. Lots of gray. It always smelled like coffee.

"Hello?" I called.

After a beat or two, the distinct sound of a toilet flushing came from the back. When I heard a door open, I repeated, "Hello."

"Oh, hello," a man said as he looked up and noticed me. He was drying his hands on paper towel that he deposited in a gray garbage can as he made his way toward me. "Yes, can I help you?"

A little older than me I thought, his face held a scrutinous frown as he walked, but he was a pleasant-looking man. Just over six feet probably, he wore an official uniform and appeared to be in decent shape. His hair was short, and his brown eyes were bright and curious.

His hard gaze made me wonder if I'd respectfully taken off my hat. I had. I'd left it in the Jeep.

"My name is Hazel Dylan. I live—"

"Yeah. I know you, Hazel. Wilmot Dylan's daughter?"

"Yes." I watched him for some sort of clue. Was he about to rail against taxidermy or tell me my father had done great work? I got both. He did neither.

"I heard about you. Your dad." He extended his hand. "I'm Knox Verro, the new police chief."

"Nice to meet you." We shook.

"How can I help you, Hazel?" The frown remained in place, but his eyes told me that he was listening. He put his hands on his hips.

"I . . . uh, was attacked up by the diner."

"Attacked?"

I nodded. "I think you have a voicemail."

He frowned at the phone on the desk and then looked at me again. "Are you okay?"

I held up my wrapped finger. "I'm fine, but . . . have you heard what was found out in the desert?"

"The skeleton? Yes."

"I probably wouldn't be reporting the attack if I didn't wonder about its potential tie to . . . the other things, I guess. I'm really okay."

"You should always report an attack. Come sit down. Let's write it up."

Chief Verro was a smart man. He knew how to ask questions and what to put in a police report. He told me that no one else had come in, at least recently, with a complaint about a man who looked like the one I described. He seemed to know his way around being a law enforcement officer. It was refreshing.

"My other officer won't be in today, but I'll talk to her about this guy, see if she's heard anything," he said after we'd gone over the specifics a few times. "Are you sure you're okay?"

"I'm fine. Her? She?"

Verro nodded, but still frowned.

"I'm sorry I sound surprised. The last time I was here, there were two male officers hanging out playing solitaire on their computers. Now we have a police chief and a female officer?"

Verro nodded. "Yes, we do. So, Steve and Caleb?"

"Yeah."

"They've been relieved of their duties. Not my call. I might have given them a chance, but the city manager, Virginia Walthrop, told me she wanted a fresh start when she hired me."

"Wait. Virgie, the diner's owner, is the city manager?"

"Well, I don't know. Petite woman? She didn't introduce herself as Virgie."

"Big hair?"

"Sounds about right. No one told me she also owns the diner. I still have a lot to learn."

"Apparently, I do too. I didn't know she . . . I, uh. Well, welcome to Black Vulture."

"Thank you." Verro looked at me like he knew the questions that were now running through my mind. He could have ignored them, but I was glad he didn't.

"The city council got some sort of infusion of money because of a new tax law that applies to the extraterrestrial place, The Institute. I really don't know the details, but here I am. Steve and Caleb are gone, and I've hired Jenna Griffen to help me out. Between you and me, she'd probably be the better chief, but I didn't hesitate when Ms. Walthrop offered me the position."

Jenna's name didn't sound familiar. "Are either of you from around here?"

"I'm from Prescott. Jenna moved here not long ago, but I'm not sure where she came from."

"And you chose to come to Black Vulture?" I cleared my throat, trying to skip over the surprise.

"I took the position of chief because I thought it might be good for my career, but I like Black Vulture just fine."

I did too, but I often thought that was only because it was the place where all the bad stuff had happened to me; the town and I had trauma bonded.

"Congratulations then," I said.

Verro nodded. "I hear you help us out around here sometimes."

"I do."

"But you aren't a forensic anthropologist?"

"I am not. I'm a consultant. I'm also the daughter of a taxidermist, and I spent a lot of time in Tucson with a mentor, learning about bones. My background is unusual."

"How does that work?"

I smiled. "My mentor, Dr. Fulgi, is well known throughout the . . . well, the world. Because of my time with her and her recommendations, lots of people want to hear my conclusions."

"Interesting."

I nodded. I was used to people doubting me, and I didn't spend time defending myself. If someone needed me, the proof would be in the pudding. I'd already proved myself plenty of times.

I said, "May I ask if you know if there's any ID on the skeleton found out in The Wild this morning?"

"Not yet, but it's been transported up to Tucson." He paused. "Calloway told me to give you full access to anything I hear."

I was happy about that. "Have you heard anything else?"

"Only that the scene has been cleared."

There was something else in his tone. I asked, "You didn't get to take a look?"

"I was not called until afterwards."

"Calloway's good. Maybe it was a simple oversight. Talk to him."

"I did."

"Good. How long have you been here, Chief?" I asked. "Not only did I have no idea that Virgie was the city manager, but I also didn't know about these changes. Maybe Calloway was catching up too."

"Today is my twelfth day on the job. Griffen's eighth."

"Okay. People are going to be happy you're here, but it might take a little time. How do you feel about snakes and tarantulas?"

A hint of a smile played at his serious frown. "I'd rather not meet either, but I'm prepared if I do. And Steve and Caleb and their families aren't thrilled."

"They'll get over it." Though I wondered if they would. Jobs were hard to come by around here. "Thanks for taking my statement."

"We'll see if we can find out anything about the man who assaulted you."

I looked at the bandaged finger. "I'll be all right."

He nodded. "I see that."

Verro seemed like a fine officer of the law, probably better than Black Vulture had ever seen, but I wasn't ready to share everything with him. I had another place I wanted to visit, and taking the new police chief with me might not be a bad idea. Except I felt like I might be betraying Trisha if I asked him to join me at her boyfriend's trailer.

"Would you mind calling or texting me if you hear anything more?" I asked as I stood.

"How about a deal?"

"Okay?"

"You do the same. You call me if you hear something more. I'm not sure I'll be first on anyone's list yet. If you'd give me the consideration, I'd appreciate it, and I'd reciprocate."

"Done."

We shook again before I was on my way.

CHAPTER

5

I WAS CAREFUL OF the injury on my finger, double wrapped in some duct tape I'd found under the Jeep's back seat to keep the gauze in place. And my lower back twinged on the journey out to Joey's place along the unpaved roads toward the outskirts of Black Vulture. It was a bumpy ride to say the least.

And hot, but that wasn't unusual.

I never seemed to get around to putting the doors back on my old Jeep Wrangler. Even in the middle of the worst heat or on the freeway to Tucson, I hadn't taken the time. Along with the seed pods, it and I were always covered in a little dust, my shoulder-length hair always some level of windblown even with a ponytail and my hat.

But until funding for more paved highways came through, the roads were going to continue to be a challenge. We had a police chief now, though, so maybe more upgrades were on the way.

I made a disgruntled noise as I went through a rut that would take out a lesser vehicle's suspension before I stopped, rested my arms on the steering wheel, and squinted at the sight ahead. It was always disturbing, even if you'd seen it before, even if you knew it was simply a part of Black Vulture.

All those bones . . .

Trisha's scream had led to more questions than answers. She'd shown me the social media post put up by one of her friends.

EEEEW, a body's been found not far from where I live. Gross, gross, gross.

A skeleton wasn't a body, but semantics maybe. Trisha pointed out where her friend lived—about a quarter mile away from the skeleton's pose, which might be considered close enough for her to think the skeleton was a body. I asked Trisha to attempt a phone call to her friend, which she did, but was greeted by a message saying that the voicemail was full.

Was there a body out there too or was the skeleton the only horrifying recent discovery, and Trisha's friend just didn't have the correct details?

I'd texted Calloway the question but hadn't heard back. He had his hands full enough probably.

I also wondered about Joey's seeming disappearance—enough to take a closer look.

Trisha's boyfriend, Joey Smoot, lived in a trailer his grandfather had owned for at least fifty years. I might not like Joey, but his grandfather, Jerry, had been close to Wilmot, and when he'd disappeared, Jerry had been one of the locals who'd contributed to "taking care" of me. He'd even offered me a room in the three-bedroom single-wide. I'd declined.

Lots of people around Black Vulture had offered me a place to stay, but somehow, I'd been fine. My father had left plenty of money in his account to keep my bills paid and food in my stomach for a long time. In fact, I'd been surprised by the amount. Our building, though not fancy, was long paid off. I didn't need to do much but take care of myself and clean everything, which I'd been doing for a while by then anyway.

The family court judge who'd ruled on my case had listened to me and my desire to continue living where and the way I had. While locals were there to tell the court that I could live with them, they'd also supported my wishes. The judge had ordered that social workers "check on me" until I turned eighteen. I'd had only a handful of visits over those five years. Folks like Dixie and Sheriff Calloway had made sure I was taken care of. It had worked out okay.

Twenty years ago, Jerry Smoot had driven to his meth head daughter's trailer and gathered Joey. Rumor was that he hadn't even bothered to explain himself, just took the toddler and brought him back to his place. Further rumors stated that his daughter hadn't even noticed, never said a word.

She'd died ten years ago, up in Phoenix, in some abandoned building in a rough part of town. No one had been surprised, but I'd witnessed Jerry in real mourning for his daughter. If anyone understood grief over someone who'd lived with bad or unconventional decisions, it was me. I'd brought a bottle of whiskey out to the trailer. We'd sat in lawn chairs and got drunk as we discussed the family members you can't choose and looked up at the blanket of stars, thinking that the answers to all our questions were out there somewhere but weren't finding their way to us. The whiskey helped us not care too much.

That had been my last trip out to his place, though I'd seen him in town enough. He'd stopped by the museum a time or two, just to "check on me." It hadn't mattered that I was years beyond eighteen.

While Jerry was a friend, I didn't like Joey at all. But despite being a jerk to Trisha sometimes, he wasn't into drugs, the things that Jerry called his "breaking point."

The reason Jerry and my father first hit it off all those years ago was their common tie to remains, bones specifically when it came to Jerry.

Over Jerry's life and as he'd parked his trailer out in the middle of the desert, he'd become as enamored by bones as I had, though his interest showed itself in a different way.

The night we'd shared the bottle of rye and shed a few tears, Jerry told me that his obsession had begun with the skeleton of a dead rat. Like other folks out here, he thrived off the desert, its sights, sounds, and wildlife. He started most every morning with a walk "into the thick." A walking stick, forged from the insides of a long-ago downed saguaro cactus, helping him along as he zigged and zagged around dangerous and deadly plants and animals.

Jerry and his rat bones had been the beginning of a years-long collection, one that had turned into a mound of bones in the spaces behind and next to the trailer. If you could get past the gruesome part, it was interesting. At least I thought so.

The last time I'd taken a closer look at the piles was just before sunset that night of grief. My eyes had scanned, but I'd been sure they hadn't landed on anything human. Femur bones could be tricky, but the bone I'd picked up to take a closer look had been equine. I put it back.

I put the Jeep back into first and closed the distance toward the trailer, noticing quickly that the front door was open. I silenced the engine and listened for a long moment.

All I heard was the wind. I always thought it sounded like it came from another world just to whistle through all this dust.

"Jerry?" I called. "Joey? You guys in there?"

A distant hawk's caw was the only response. After meeting Verro, I'd run back home and gathered the knife I did, indeed, find on the patio. Then, because of how far out into the middle of nothing I was headed, I went back inside and got my gun. I frowned as I grabbed it from the passenger seat and climbed out of the Jeep. I held the weapon at my side, pointed downward, and made my way to the door, announcing my arrival the whole way.

Open doors, though always a little odd, weren't necessarily as unsettling out here as they might be in a heavily populated suburb. Maybe the trailer just needed aired out.

I'd tried to call Jerry, his phone taking me directly to voicemail as if it had been turned off. Again, this wasn't completely strange. Jerry had never had a landline, and he often forgot about his cell phone, choosing to make the drive into town if he wanted to talk to someone.

I called out again before I leaned carefully into the front doorway. "Hello?"

Once I could see inside, I could tell that no one, dead or alive, was in living room or small attached kitchen. The space was messy, with a crocheted blanket over the back of the threadbare couch, a few empty beer cans here and there.

Empty shotgun shells lined up like broken soldiers on the scratched coffee table. Supplies—gunpowder and tools—were scattered about. I knew Jerry liked to reload shells, but I had no idea if Joey did the same. Jerry shot clay pigeons in the space behind the bones in the back. Wilmot used to join him back in the day.

I turned my attention toward the narrow hallway, grateful that I hadn't met with any sort of disturbing scents.

"Jer? Joey?"

The whole place seemed to move and groan with my footfalls. It was an old trailer. Carefully, I peered into the bathroom and then the three bedrooms. No beds were made, and clothes were strewn here and there, but the place wasn't filthy.

There was no one there.

I didn't suspect that the skeleton sculpture was Joey's bones, but Trisha insisted that he'd never ghosted her for this long. Joey was probably just somewhere being a jerk. I wondered more about where Jerry's bones were and if they were still protecting his organs as he breathed in oxygen.

I walked back to the living room and crouched by the coffee table. I inspected the shells and their supplies more closely, but they didn't tell me anything.

I sighed. Other than the door being open, there wasn't anything strange here. Even the door might mean nothing.

Using the back of a receipt I found in my pocket and a pen on the kitchen counter, I left a note.

Call me—Hazel.

I closed the door on my way toward the piles of bones.

"Jesus," I muttered as I came around the corner of the trailer.

The piles had grown, but I wasn't going to take the time to sift through them for anything suspicious. Whatever was going on in Black Vulture, I had to believe that the Smoots didn't have anything to do with it. Well, I hoped.

If whoever created the sculpture somehow gathered the bones from these piles, any remaining human bones weren't obvious. I scanned hard.

Jerry took remains from the desert. He boiled them, cleaning off whatever might still be attached to them, before he put them out in the piles. He used some of them to create jewelry that he sold from a shelf in the grocery store. There wasn't a big call for necklaces made of things like lizard skulls, but he had customers, some of them loyal and repeat.

"Keeps the vultures away," he'd say when asked about cleaning the bones.

My life had been comprised of a bunch of strange episodes and my father's unusual occupation, so I wasn't easily rattled. However, the quantity of bones behind Jerry's trailer, even with no human ones obvious, was off-putting today. I wondered if it was the number or the growth of the piles that left me feeling guilty for not coming out to visit Jerry in so long. It was a marker of the time at least, and a lot of time had passed.

Jerry was, at his most rooted level, a good guy, a law-abiding citizen, until he had no other choice. If child protective services had done something to save his grandson, he wouldn't have needed to gather the boy himself.

Fresh carcasses were supposed to be reported. Endangered species and dinosaur fossils also required calls to Fish and Game or law enforcement, but he'd only taken bones he'd come across.

There was a time when the police hassled him for his collections, but not for long and not with much gusto. Gathering animal bones from the desert wasn't against the law. I wondered what Verro might think and do, and was glad I hadn't asked him to come with me. He'd see the piles on his own at some point.

I wished one of the Smoots would drive onto the property while I was there, if only to check them off my list of suspects and/or victims.

I'd driven out there to search for Joey, but I'd also hoped to see Jerry too. I didn't want to include either of them on any list, but Jerry had known Wilmot well. He could have posed the bones into whatever he wanted—he had both the skill and the patience. He would know that my first thought would be that the sculpture looked like an animal from the museum. He would know how in some way Wilmot's name would come up because of the extra phalanx.

Mine too. The Bone Woman had her own fair share of critics.

With one last, quick glance over Jerry's collections, I turned and took a step toward the Jeep. Something flashed in the corner of my eye. I whipped my attention back around and stood still as I lifted the gun.

A coyote was making his way around the pile of bones at the end of the trailer. He stopped and stared at me. I thought about the knife in my pocket and that fact that this was one of the reasons so many of us carried one—danger at almost every turn out here. I didn't reach for it, though, and I lowered the weapon.

I loved the brutality of the desert life. The need to survive was ever present, kill or be killed.

But I had deemed myself an observer only. I'd vowed to never become a hunter. I could kill a scorpion but probably never a coyote. I'd never wanted to, but I was aware enough to understand that perhaps I was making myself pay some penance. Sins of the father and all, or more specifically, sins of his clients, but neither they nor Wilmot looked at their deeds that way, so it was only me self-castigating.

I stood there and let the coyote decide what he wanted to do. I wasn't going to run away.

Both of us made of the desert, I was sure my father and I shared the same end—it and its creatures would decide what was to be done with us. They'd probably already sealed Wilmot's fate.

Today, the coyote, whose eyes were locked on mine, wasn't up for a hunt. Shortly, he turned and ran toward the horizon and the lowering sun.

I watched him go, then got back into the Jeep and headed home.

CHAPTER

6

I FLIPPED THE LIGHTS on inside my lab, the space that had once been Wilmot's studio. This place had seen lots of blood but none from my time. I worked only with bones that wouldn't bleed anymore. But Wilmot had drained creatures. Though I didn't think about them often, I remembered those days, and I remembered thinking that everything my father did was interesting. It had all been long ago. I could look back as if the little girl hadn't been me, but some other innocent child who simply idolized her father.

I hadn't considered that I needed to forgive myself for then. But even when I remembered that the little Hazel had been me, it had been easy to see my life through the lens of an observer who could understand why that little girl was so intrigued by what went on inside the studio.

This evening, as I looked around the lab, I tried to remember more, maybe something that might give some sort of clue or hint about the bone sculpture. But nothing new came to me. It was all the same old, same old. And from a long time ago.

My lab wasn't as sterile as it had been when it was Wilmot's studio. I had shelves filled with boxes—bones as well as equipment and books inside them. The tools of my trade were different from my father's, the floor drain unused for decades.

I closed my eyes and set my hands flat on the steel anatomy table, letting its coolness seep through my flesh, hoping the touch would fill in the voids or push my mind a little further than just the edges of those fuzzy images from the days around his disappearance.

Nothing.

I opened my eyes and grabbed the bottle of beer I'd set on the corner of the table. I stepped toward the door, but stopped again. I turned and made my way to a box. I dug through it and found the item I'd been looking for. A wireless camera, one that was attached to an application on my phone. I plugged it in to charge, made my way out of the lab, and then through the museum to the sliding glass door and out to the patio.

I'd think about where to put the camera.

The space on the patio was made for one, unless two people liked each other enough to be crowded. One small table sat next to one chaise that had seen better days. I'd purchased the chaise from a box store up in Tucson the summer before, but what the desert creatures and plants didn't destroy, the hot Arizona sun ate away. I'd have to get a new chaise soon.

Concrete block walls surrounded the patio. There was no door to the other side, no way out except over the wall.

I lay back on the chaise and looked up at the sky. Like many communities in Arizona, Black Vulture was a dark-sky town, and we kept all outdoor lighting to a minimum so as not to interfere with the views of the night skies.

My eyes acclimated quickly, and I searched for my favorite constellations as I let questions from the day play through my mind of their own accord. Maybe something would solidify.

I never heard wings, but rustles from the landing always made me sit up and search the palo verde limbs from the tree on the other side of the patio wall. The tree encroached onto my property and helped with morning shade.

The Wild was back there, and for a reason I didn't understand, one of its creatures had become one of my frequent visitors.

I searched the tree, finally seeing the glimmer of the owl's eyes as light from the quarter moon shone off them. In a minute or so, I'd be able to see the whole creature.

"Hey there, Jack," I said.

He stared at me. My voice never bothered him.

Arizona horned owls were impressive—brilliant hunters, and big, they could reach two feet. Like other nearby horned owls, Jack probably nested in a Saguaro cactus. Clearly, he ate well, seemed healthy.

I had no idea why he'd landed in that tree just over a year ago, and I didn't understand why he kept coming back. I saw him three times a week, at least. When I wasn't out on the patio, he'd hoot to get my attention. I'd look out and tell him hello, which was the communication he seemed to be looking for.

He never stuck around for long, just enough to check in, hoot out some other message that was probably not meant for me but for some lady owl out there, and then fly away until next time.

A horned owl also filled a corner of the museum, its wings spread wide and secured to the ceiling with transparent string, its glass eyes aimed toward the front door. I'd never asked my father, but I wondered if he'd done that on purpose to set visitors back onto their heels.

I'd witnessed a few gasps over the years.

I wondered if Jack might somehow be related to the taxidermized animal in the museum, and he'd come back to claim his ancestry.

That was ridiculous, of course, but I truly had no idea why he visited me so often.

I took a long pull of the beer and then held the bottle with both hands.

"What's going on out there, Jack? You see anything suspicious?"

He blinked and stared at me.

"I wish I could ask you to survey and report back. We could use you, or a drone maybe."

I considered that idea, wondering what the Tucson people might be up to and if they'd thought about a drone search. I'd ask at some point, but it seemed obvious.

I'd spent many an evening talking through an assignment as Jack listened briefly. He'd helped me work out a few things, just by staring or blinking, but mostly I enjoyed his company. Those eyes, watching me or as he turned his head to look behind him. It was a myth that they could do a full swivel, but they could most definitely check their six. It was always a treat when he hooted, the white patch of feathers on his neck rolling with the rich noise.

I swigged the beer again and stood to walk toward him. He never got spooked, but I'd never reached out, tried to touch him. He'd never flown at me or been scared away.

"Seriously, what do you think is going on out there, Jack?" I asked, and then I lowered my voice and whispered the question I always asked him, "Have you seen my father?"

He blinked.

The noises that came next melded together—snaps, rustles, and then a *thunk* on the concrete patio floor. It happened quickly. I flinched and lifted my arm as my instincts keyed in on something coming in my direction, but I still managed to see Jack take flight. I was pretty sure he hadn't been hit.

I snapped my attention to the thing that had landed on the patio, crouching to pick it up.

There was nothing special about the rock—it was heavy, a little smaller than a baseball, though deadly if someone's aim was precise.

I stood again and hurried to the six-foot wall, stepping up onto an old overturned planter that hadn't seen anything green inside it for decades. I could see over and into The Wild, but I didn't spot Jack. I didn't see anyone or much of anything except the outlines of the desert terrain, silhouettes against the mountains in the distance. Was that a light near the cave openings? I squinted, but the yellow flash I thought I'd seen didn't come again. Besides, the rock hadn't come from that far away. Someone a lot closer had thrown it.

"Hey, who's out there?" I called.

My phone's flashlight wouldn't help much, and I didn't want to take the time to go inside for something stronger. I wasn't going to hop the wall and search, particularly at night. Or ever, really. The landscape was too rough.

I listened for a long time but didn't hear voices or movement. I didn't hear anything but the wind, not even the screech of an owl, one who might have become angered by a rock being thrown in his direction.

"Sorry, buddy," I said, hoping Jack would come back soon.

I considered calling either Verro or Calloway to tell them about the rock, but short of searching The Wild, there was nothing they could do. They'd probably conclude that it had been some kids out there up to no good.

I hadn't been that kind of teenager, mostly because I hadn't been much of a joiner. I'd been too busy figuring everything else out. I shook away the willies, and then shook my head, needing to let go of the entire day and get some rest. I clutched the beer bottle in one hand and the rock in the other as I made my way back to the museum.

Once inside, I looked out through the sliding glass door and mumbled, "Kids."

But I wasn't so sure I was right.

I double-checked that the doors were locked before I went to bed.

He knew it had been a gutsy move, but the rock had been right there by his foot and he'd heard her talking to that owl. That was creepy.

He'd been hiding there for a long time, hoping to spy on her. He'd been still for so long. When the owl had swooped in and landed in the tree, it was all he could do not to make some noise. It had been an amazing sight, one he'd never seen before, even back when he first lived in Black Vulture.

His memories of the wildness of the place, the creatures, the primitive land were tainted. Until he'd seen that owl, he hadn't realized the parts of him that had missed it. It hadn't been all bad even if it had held the worst parts of his life.

When he moved his foot just a little bit, the owl turned and looked right at him, his eyes shiny from the bright moon. It had been both alarming and cool as shit.

Was that creature going to give him away? He needed to get out of there, but there was no way to do that without making noise that the owl would certainly hear. Maybe she would too.

He threw the rock, hoping for distraction. He hadn't aimed for the owl, but he did want to get its attention. He didn't care much if he hit her, but he hadn't been trying to do that either.

When the rock was gone, he took off down the trails, one he'd found, one he'd forged himself to make a direct route to her place. It had been work.

From a better distance, he hid behind a clutch of cacti and watched as she peered over the wall. When she called out, he wanted to step out and tell her who he was and why he was there, that she was fully in his sights. But he'd kept quiet. It wasn't time yet.

When she disappeared again, he made his way out of there. But he'd be back soon enough.

CHAPTER

7

As they usually are, my dreams were strange and symbolic. They were also bloody, which wasn't quite as normal.

I'd gone to bed shortly after taking care of the camera and then a call with Calloway, who was pleased that I'd reported the assault to the new police chief. Calloway suspected the man who attacked me was just someone who hadn't liked my father's ways, who probably thought I should have gotten rid of the mounts, not allowed anyone into the museum, not that visitors were pouring in anyway. He probably wasn't the one who'd built and left the sculpture.

I didn't tell him about the rock coming over the wall, but besides kids up to no good, there was a chance that someone who wasn't fond of Wilmot had thrown it. Someone looking to defend animal rights who wanted to make a point. Maybe the attack and the rock had come from the same person. Everyone was looking for him. Time would probably tell.

I'd silently debated aiming the camera out toward The Wild or somewhere out front. Out front had won, but I thought I might order another one for the back.

I'd never been physically assaulted because of my father before yesterday, if that's what that had truly been about. I'd been yelled at, my property had been damaged, but no one had touched me. No one had thrown anything at me either.

It wasn't a huge leap to think that the violence I'd experienced was making my dreams bloody.

I wished they'd give me some answers too.

I didn't tell Calloway about my visit to the Smoots, but I did confirm with him that a body hadn't been found in the desert, that news of the skeleton had spread fast, the hiker who'd found it having posted on social media before even calling the police. Trisha's friend had been posting about the skeleton, calling it a body.

Welcome to the modern, overly informed, and unreliable world of information.

Calloway had no leads on any of the mysteries. Nothing. But he wanted me to join him at his office around noon. He had someone he wanted me to meet, and we were all going to drive up to Tucson together. I wondered who it might be, but he had to end the call before he could tell me more.

It was another knock on the museum door that pulled me from the nighttime images that left me foggy-headed and thirsty. I sat up in bed, shook my head, and glanced at the time. It was seven-thirty, and if it wasn't the police or my attacker, someone probably wanted to see the museum.

"Hang on," I called, considering yelling "We're not open," but I was awake enough. Besides, my coffee pot was calling, and I had a model that wouldn't brew itself.

I didn't post museum hours. In fact, people walking through it after Wilmot wasn't around anymore had been an accident at first. I let in some curious visitors when they knocked on the closed door. Word had spread, and more people had stopped by. I answered when it was convenient for me.

I put myself together as much as I was willing. I opened the nightstand drawer and considered the weapons. Knife or gun? I grabbed the knife and tucked it in my back pocket before making my way downstairs.

I peered out the door, my eyes blinking with the brightness. Oh. Him. What was his name? *Sonny* . . . I finally thought to myself before I opened the door.

"What?" I asked.

"Good morning."

"Not yet."

"Right. Sorry to bother you so early."

"Okay. What's going on?"

Not to be deterred, Sonny fought a smile before he pushed up his glasses.

"I wondered if you'd like to have breakfast at the diner with me?" He paused. "I'll buy."

No, I didn't want to have breakfast with him, anywhere. In fact, I didn't want to have breakfast at all until at least another hour had passed and caffeine had done a couple laps through my system, paving the way for food, like digestion was supposed to work. I was so thrown off by the whole encounter that all I could do for a moment was cross my arms in front of myself and squint at the man standing on my cracked stoop.

"Right," he said again. "Well, the new police chief and another officer are over there, having breakfast. I don't know, it seemed like a good opportunity for you to meet them."

"Well." I glanced toward the diner. I squinted and frowned at Sonny again. "I met the chief yesterday but not the new officer. I like your plan, I guess. I'll buy my own breakfast though."

"I accept."

I shook my head at him. "Meet you there."

"I'll wait." Sonny cleared his throat and reached for his wallet, gathering some bills. "In fact, could I wait inside? I'd love to see the museum."

Ah. Maybe he'd just wanted to see the museum and was using everything else as an excuse to do so.

"Sure."

I turned and made my way back up to the apartment as I heard him come in and close the door behind him.

I smiled to myself when I heard him gasp.

"Wow . . ." he said a moment later.

"If you haven't already, you'll hear stories," I called.

He didn't respond.

I'd showered the night before, but I made sure the jeans and T-shirt I grabbed were clean and free of holes.

I had one dress and one suit, used only when I was asked to attend big meetings where official people would be gathering to discuss something important. Anything like that was usually held in Tucson, but the people I would see later today wouldn't require a fancy getup.

I put the knife in my pocket, but left my cowboy hat on the nightstand, the gun in it, and made my way back downstairs.

Sonny was peering closely at a mountain lion.

I studied him as he inspected the mount. He seemed genuinely curious. I cleared my throat.

He jumped. "Oh. I . . . this place is completely . . . intriguing and terrifying."

I nodded. I'd heard that many times over the years.

Sonny looked at me with almost the same intensity he'd been giving the lion. It made me uncomfortable.

He broke the moment by waving a hand. "This is kind of amazing. I mean, it's not my thing, but I can see the talent and skill involved."

"My father was good at his job."

Talent, good intentions didn't always mean things were being done correctly. I'd never felt like Wilmot's taxidermy was wrong, but he was probably seen as a strange and demented man at times.

"Should we go?" I headed out the door.

"Of course. I'd love to spend more time looking at this, though. May I come back?"

"Yes."

People had called the collection everything from peaceful to fascinating to scary as hell. I'd been told that the movie *Psycho* had nothing on the displays. I'd never watched it.

To me, though the things inside it might have rattled me a time or two, this room was, at its most basic, the culmination of my father's work. After he'd disappeared, not much of anything had made sense like it had before. Once he'd been gone a while, I tried to throw the mounts away, taking them out to the dumpster behind the diner. My motives had been twofold. I'd wanted to move on, but anger had been real too. I was very mad for a long time. I still am sometimes. If he left on his own, how could he? If he didn't leave on his own, why couldn't we find where he'd gone or what was left of him?

However, I'd gone back out to the dumpster and hauled them out, putting the mounts as they'd been.

They would always be a part of my life, but I had made my own reputation, one bone at a time.

Sonny watched as I turned the key and pocketed it. I was one of the few people in Black Vulture to lock my front door. When my father left, it had been one of the things I'd made sure I did to be safe, though not without an internal battle first, a sense of control at last.

What if Wilmot came home and the door was locked? Once I let a rush of panic pass with the crazy thought that he would just leave again if he couldn't get inside immediately, and after I let in those first curious customers, I found the control.

It had become a fixation for me. Like I'd heard some people worried about turning off their dryers or unplugging their curling irons, I often wondered if I'd remembered to lock the door. For the most part, I had, but that didn't stop me from dwelling on it sometimes.

"How's your finger?" he asked as we set out the short distance to the diner.

I'd cleaned the wound and rewrapped it the night before, using more gauze and medical grade tape instead of the duct variety.

I held it up. "Not infected and I doubt I'll have much of a scar."

"That's good." He smiled as he reached for the diner's door, pulling it wide.

I had an urge to ask him why he was smiling so much. I figured that would make me look like a jerk. I really did need some coffee.

"Thanks." I went through.

He followed and then stood next to me as we looked around the jam-packed place.

"Take a seat if you can find one," Dixie called. "Coffee will be on the way."

Before we could make a move toward a couple of stools at the counter, Trisha, coffeepot in hand, hurried in our direction.

"What's going on?" she asked me. "Could the body be Joey's?"

The noise in the place precluded anyone else from hearing her panicked words and tone. I put my hand on her arm.

"It wasn't a body, Trish. It's a skeleton, bones cleaned. You saw Joey recently enough that, reasonably, it can be concluded that it's not him."

"Where is he?"

"I don't know."

I didn't tell her about my visit to the Smoots, but I wondered if she'd taken the same trip.

"Trisha!" a customer called "More coffee when you get a minute?"

"Let me know if you hear anything," she said before she hurried off.

"A skeleton?" Sonny asked.

I looked at him. "You hadn't heard?"

"Nope."

"You're not on social media?"

Sonny laughed. "I'm not on anything."

Suddenly, I saw him with new, less critical eyes.

"A skeleton posed as a coyote was found out in the desert."

Sonny frowned. "A real human skeleton or a coyote skeleton?"

"Human."

"That sounds terrifying."

"It's not good."

He looked at me a long moment before he nodded toward a booth against the wall. "The police are over there. Want me to grab a couple stools while you go say hello?"

"That works. And coffee."

"I hear you. Food?"

"I don't know yet."

"Got it."

As Sonny made his way toward the counter, I set my sights on the customers in booth three.

When Verro saw me making my way, he waved me over.

"Hazel, good morning. This is Officer Jenna Griffen. Jenna, this is Hazel Dylan."

She nodded as she wiped her mouth with a napkin. "It's nice to meet you." She scooted in a little but didn't smile. She inspected me with curious eyes. "Have a seat."

"I don't want to interrupt," I lied.

"Not at all," Verro said.

I sat. I didn't recognize her. I'd never heard of a family with the last name Griffen in town. Her features were pretty but sharp, made more so by the severe bun she wore. Immediately, I decided that she was even more no-nonsense than Verro.

"I'm sorry for what you went through yesterday. We are on it, Ms. Dylan," she said.

"Oh. Hazel's fine. Thanks. I'm glad to hear it."

"Call me Jenna. Have you remembered anything else?" Griffen asked.

"I haven't." I turned to look at her more straight on. "Are you from Black Vulture?"

"No, ma'am. My wife just got a job at the place the locals call The Institute. I was an officer in Oregon when Allie got the offer. She couldn't pass it up. I was glad to find that the chief here was looking for some help."

"I'm glad to have an experienced officer," Verro added.

"Welcome to Black Vulture," I said. "Both of you."

"Thanks," she said. Quickly, she added, "You saw the skeleton yesterday?"

"I did."

"Initial thoughts?"

"The victim's limbs were disarticulated from the body before the bones were defleshed. Probably male, probably about middle age or so, but none of that is confirmed, and it's not much to go on. The teeth might help with identification." I paused. "I'm sure you two will be fully informed soon enough."

Jenna nodded. "When I got the job, I read up about Black Vulture. Your father was mentioned. The chief and I speculated that maybe your father's old job and disappearance might have something to do with a skeleton sculpture."

I nodded. "I think Calloway thinks the same thing, but, as I told him, a bone sculpture isn't taxidermy. In fact, for the most part, bones aren't used in the craft."

"He was an interesting man."

"I don't understand. My father disappeared a long time ago. How was he mentioned?"

Jenna nodded. "Your father's job and disappearance are fodder for lots of speculation."

A wave of disquiet ran through me. I was used to my father's story; it was almost as much mine as his. It wasn't often that locals mentioned or asked me about him anymore. Even visitors to the museum didn't bring him up much. The place was more about the mounts than the man who'd created them. But certainly, I knew there was speculation. Except I had more important things to do than indulge it because I lived it.

Jenna continued, "Did you listen to the podcast?"

I was sure she was referring to Minnie Chavez's true-crime podcast, the one Calloway had asked me about. "Minnie's?"

Jenna nodded. "It's good."

"People listen to it?" My tone was proof I still hadn't had any caffeine. I should have apologized for the snark, but I just cleared my throat.

"Lots of people. Minnie's podcast has a big audience."

Minnie lived on the outskirts of Black Vulture. Last I heard, she hadn't become an amateur investigator or podcast detective or whatever they called themselves, but she had put together podcasts that told the stories of all kinds of Arizona mysteries and crimes.

I knew Minnie, and I'd heard she'd done a series on Wilmot about three years ago, but I hadn't given it any attention. She'd tried to interview me, but I'd told her I wasn't interested.

Jenna lifted one eyebrow. "Something's happening in Black Vulture, and, considering yesterday's events—you and the bones being found—you might want to take a closer look at your own home."

She *was* no-nonsense and direct. I've heard the same said about me.

"Well, I'm on the state's payroll, but I haven't been made official to this case yet," I volleyed back.

"Whatever you say."

"I think your coffee's been poured," Verro said as he nodded toward the counter.

I was being dismissed, but I wasn't sure if it was because of me or because of something Jenna had said to me.

I didn't need to be nudged twice. I stood, and we all told each other that we'd talk again later. Before I could walk away, though, Jenna said, "You never get the whole story from the internet. I'm sure the podcast has some holes to fill."

Not sure what she was getting at, I just nodded, and then turned to make my way, having to prove to Dixie that my cut was still well bandaged.

I hiked up into the seat.

"How'd it go?" Sonny asked out of the side of his mouth.

"Fine," I said, mimicking his fake furtive expression.

"Do they know anything about the guy who attacked you?"

"Nothing yet." I sipped some coffee. "Her wife just started working at The Institute. Do you know who that might be? Allie something?"

"Not offhand, but I'll look at the new folks. I just got there myself."

"Yeah?"

Sonny nodded. "I've only been in town for two weeks."

"Welcome to Black Vulture," I told him, just like I'd said to Verro and Griffen.

"Thank you. So far, it's been . . . interesting."

My phone buzzed.

I gathered it from my pocket, seeing it was Calloway calling. "Hey, Sheriff."

"We've got another one, Hazel. I'm dropping a pin. Get out here. Now, please."

The sheriff ended the call before I could. I stood from the stool. I left a five on the counter as I looked back to where the police had been sitting, but that booth was now empty.

"What's up?" Sonny asked.

"I have to go."

"Where?"

"Work."

"Got it. Can I see you later? Are you free for dinner? I'd like to—"

"Sonny . . ."

He held his hand up. "Sorry. Maybe another time. Go. Work. It would be impossible not to see you around town. We'll run into each other."

I took a deep breath and nodded. "Right, gotta go."

As I hurried toward the door, Trisha called, "Let me know if you hear anything about Joey."

I waved and then hurried to my Jeep.

CHAPTER

8

SWEAT BEADED ON my upper lip as I contemplated which path I needed to choose so I could meet up with Calloway, who was crouched down in the distance with a man I didn't recognize. I hadn't taken time to gather my hat or the gun, and I really missed the shade the hat would have offered.

The two men were deep in a patch of cactus and tumbleweeds about fifty yards away from where I'd stopped the Jeep.

The sun was already halfway up, and there wasn't a cloud in sight. I used my hand to shade my eyes but still couldn't figure out how to get to where they were.

I hopped out and put two fingers in my mouth, blowing a loud whistle and garnering Calloway's attention.

I called, "Which way?"

Calloway put his hands up to his mouth. "Doesn't matter. Just get here. Walk from there."

"Copy that," I muttered quietly.

But in the next instant, I froze in place. A distinct warning rattle reached my ears. I suddenly missed the gun more than the hat.

"Damn it." I tried to locate where the snake was coiled or if it was coming my way.

At least I had my boots on.

I listened and inspected the landscape around me, knowing that I could be looking right at the rattler as it camouflaged into its surroundings.

I'd seen hundreds of snakes, but no matter that I'd popped my snakebite cherry back when I was eighteen, rattlesnakes always scared me. My body hadn't gone into anaphylactic shock, but there was nothing fun or painfree about the experience. Antivenom wasn't a great time either. There was no way around it, snakebites hurt and debilitated. I didn't want to ever be bitten again.

Wilmot had had an uncanny sense about snakes, knowing from where one might slither or attack. More than once, he'd directed me off a route just before I heard a rattle. He'd saved the day a time or two.

The rattle was a warning. *Hey, I'm here and I don't want any trouble. Don't piss me off, and we'll be just fine.*

I just needed to figure out in which direction he wanted me to make my retreat. I wouldn't go against his wishes if he made them clear.

A diamond head showed itself, leading the rest of a huge body out from behind a rock. Snakes could move much faster than Mother Nature should have allowed, but this one was taking his time today, smelling the fear coming from the human who'd disrupted his day and enjoying the power he held.

I was about to lift one boot-clad foot and step backward toward the Jeep when the boom and ring of a gunshot shattered my concentration.

I wasn't one to panic at snakes or jump at gunshots, so I must have been losing my edge . . . or on edge.

"Missed," a voice said.

I looked up to see Calloway about ten feet away, his gun aimed downward. I glanced back at the ground, confirming the snake had hurried along its way, which was not toward either me or the sheriff.

"Why didn't you shoot it?" he asked.

"I didn't bring my gun."

Calloway holstered his. "I want you to carry your gun with you at all times until further notice."

"Okay." I hesitated. "Sounds serious."

"Believe me, I wouldn't order it if I thought you were anything but smart with a weapon, but I want you on guard."

"Okay," I said again.

"Come with me." Calloway turned and trudged back to where I'd spotted him out in a genuinely wild part of The Wild.

We were silent as I followed, both of us watching the scrub and cacti covered ground for another threat. There were plenty, but we both knew how to keep our ankles safe from cactus needles. We didn't hear another rattle, but the hum of the hot wind seemed to get louder as we approached the thing I'd been called out to see.

Though I'd already seen the work of the mystery bone artist's first desert sculpture, this one still pulled my eyes wide, my throat tight. I'd seen lots of gruesome and bothersome things over the years. These sculptures weren't necessarily gruesome—no blood or bloated bodies—but it was impossible to look at any sort of potential crime scene and not immediately wonder: why? Whoever had done these sculptures wanted to make some sort of shocking statement, that much was obvious. What suddenly became a more concerning unknown was whether this was just someone finding and making things with bones—or was this murder?

These were not recently defleshed and cleaned bones, making me wonder about my immediate assessment of the first set.

I stopped next to Calloway and went into a crouch, letting my eyes wander. The same materials had been used. I couldn't imagine the hours put into the artifacts.

Someone had sculpted, again obviously using wire and pieces of wood, the form of a scorpion. The subject matter was immediately recognizable. The arm bones had been stuck out and up, the hands making pinchers, the leg bones were bent to look like a set of the creature's legs. A scorpion had six legs, but four that were made of extra shards of wood were convincing enough.

"Is that a barbeque fork?" I asked after my eyes had finished their first once-over.

"Yep," Calloway said.

Stuck up from the tailbone was a barbeque fork, something you could buy in a supermarket or discount store. No matter the strange choice, there was no question that the fork was put there to represent the scorpion's stinger.

"Wow," I said as I stood. "How did . . ."

When I didn't finish my question, Calloway said, "A teenager headed out to hunt found this one. Hazel, I want you to meet Graham Kucera. He's here from the University of Colorado in Boulder."

Graham extended his hand but didn't smile as his eyes squinted at me. "I specialize in artistic forensics."

We shook. "That is a specialized profession."

"When you think you're going to study art but find out you like science too, things like my job can become a thing." His voice was deep but almost hesitant, like he wondered if I might judge him for his profession. I was the last person to judge anyone for much of anything, most particularly how they got their jobs.

"Good to meet you." I nodded toward the sculpture. "This feels right in your skill set."

"Possibly."

"Where are the Tucson people?" I asked Calloway.

"On their way here again."

I nodded and gave Kucera a quick and hopefully furtive inspection. On the far side of middle-aged with a dirty old blue Mobil Motor Oil cap on his head, he wore faded jeans and a T-shirt emblazoned with the stuck-out tongue associated with the Rolling Stones. His ratty running shoes bothered me, and I thought maybe Calloway should have at least offered the man some boots. I hoped the gunshot had scared away all the local lethal creatures, or Graham's ankles might be tempting targets.

I turned my attention back to the sculpture. Though I was sure it had been created by the same person who'd made the first one, these bones were very different than the first set. These were older bones, discolored, not chipped at the joints as if the limbs had been cut from the body. I spotted a few smudges of dirt here and there, but no organic tissue. These were older bones and had been buried, I thought, but the lab would confirm.

"What do you make of this?" I asked Graham.

He nodded. "My quick conclusion is that whoever created this is very patient and talented."

"I thought the same thing. I now also wonder if what we're seeing will lead back to murder or just someone finding bones and wanting to make things with them. Anything from Tucson that might give us more details about the first set? Did they say when they thought they were defleshed?" I looked at Calloway.

"Not yet."

It had only been one day.

Graham said, "The perp or creator, whichever, knows art, they have patience. They know animals, but," he paused dramatically, "they don't know bones."

"What makes you say that?" I asked.

Graham pulled a laser pen from his back pocket and aimed the red dot at the forearms, the representations of the pinchers. "The radius and ulna are reversed, on both arms."

It might be an easy miss for someone who didn't know bones. I hadn't noticed it yet, but I should have. "Good catch."

Graham nodded and turned off the pointer.

I'd already concluded, to myself at least, that the earlier bones couldn't belong to Joey. And these were potentially buried bones from some time ago—they weren't pristine white. I couldn't help but wonder about the empty state of the Smoots' trailer. Where were Joey and his grandfather? I added that to the list of things I wanted to talk to Calloway about when no one else was around.

"What can you tell me?" Calloway asked me.

"Not much more than we've discussed. I'd love to take a close look at each . . ." Suddenly, I remembered, and my eyes went to the pincher hands. "Oh."

Silently, I berated myself for missing the one very obvious thing I should have seen immediately. Stuck between two fingers of a pincher was another extra phalanx.

"Yeah, it's another one," Calloway said. "Can you two determine from which finger this one came?"

In tandem, Graham and I both stepped even closer to the sculpture. The bone was there, but somewhat hidden under another finger phalanx. It was almost impossible to see.

"Not with any certainty."

"Agreed," Graham added.

"It's cleaner than the other bones, whiter. I need a better look." I sniffed, confirming that there was no smell of bleach with this set of bones.

"After the Tucson folks," Calloway said.

We stepped back and I looked at Calloway. "These really could just be found skeletons, Sheriff. This is stained with time and dirt. It was probably buried. There are laws about digging up remains, but the penalties aren't that of murder."

"It doesn't change the fact that we need to find whoever is doing this. No matter what, they might be dangerous."

"Yeah," I said.

Graham made a noise of agreement. He considered me for a moment. "I know about your father."

That seemed to be the theme of the day, though I couldn't understand why. "Okay."

"I told him about Wilmot before you got here," Calloway said.

"Again, okay. This isn't taxidermy." I nodded at the bone sculpture. I wondered how many times I was going to have to repeat it.

"No." Graham shook his head. "It isn't." He looked at Calloway.

"What's going on?" I asked.

"It's why I got him here," Calloway said.

"What is?"

Graham frowned. "Have you heard of something called rogue taxidermy?"

"I don't think so."

Graham gave me a long look as a distant bird's caw added to the bizarre scene's soundtrack. He was weathered in a way that I wouldn't have associated with a university professor. His face was tan, but his neck was white. I wondered if he had long hair but had tucked it up under the cap.

"Are you going to explain?" I asked.

"There's not a lot to know, but I'm familiar with it."

"Share," Calloway said, though I knew he'd already heard whatever Graham was about to say. This round was for my benefit.

"It's been a thing for over twenty years. The big kickoff, when the world was exposed to this new artform, was a show that took place back then. The seeds of rogue taxidermy were planted in Minneapolis. The first art was mixed and multimedia, animal skins or hides combined together with other items." He looked at the barbeque fork stinger on the sculpture and back at me. "Nothing is off limits. The key is that it's a no catch, no kill artform. If animals are used, they must have been found dead. Maybe roadkill or other non-human-involved deaths. Imagine a fish mixed with a squirrel with a clock stuck in the gut. Rogue taxidermy changed the entire world's view of what your father used to do. If animals aren't killed for the purpose of creating a trophy, the act of 'recycling' them via rogue taxidermy even appeals to PETA."

"I didn't know any of that."

"You haven't paid attention, that's all," Calloway said.

I thought about the timing. Was it coincidence that my father had disappeared in November twenty years ago, a month after the show that Graham had mentioned? Maybe. Now it seemed I was becoming inclined to tie these strange goings-on to my father.

However, though I hadn't paid attention to rogue taxidermy, Wilmot would have. Anything about taxidermy would have garnered his attention.

So what, though?

"These are human bones." I returned to the case in hand. "Maybe the results of murder."

"Or maybe it's all some sick person's interpretation," Calloway said. "Another step, beyond even rogue taxidermy."

He'd definitely put his teeth into the idea that Wilmot was somehow involved. I didn't know how to fight that other than with proof, and I could see how keeping an open mind about the possibility was the right thing to do anyway.

Graham said, "Look, I couldn't resist coming here. You're right, this doesn't seem to be any sort of taxidermy, but there's something about it that gives off the same vibes. The artist's need to push themself to create something that speaks to their creative process using dead creatures."

I looked at Graham. "Do you have any sort of sense of who did this? Do you know of someone?"

"No."

Calloway's cell phone rang. He answered quickly.

"Yeah? Okay, that's good news. I'm listening. No . . . fucking . . . way . . ."

Calloway looked at me with big eyes as he listened to the last few seconds of the call before disconnecting it.

"What?" I demanded.

"We've got some news, Hazel."

"There's no chair around here, Sheriff. If you're waiting for me to sit down, it's not going to happen. I can take it, whatever it is."

Calloway shook his head. "I'm so sorry to tell you this . . ."

"Damn it, Calloway, spit it out."

"The first skeleton has been identified. He was a homeless man up in Tucson. There are dental records because of visits by local dentists to some shelters." He paused but not for long. "The records connected directly to a man named Wilmot Dylan."

"Well. Damn." My chest hollowed some, but I didn't get wobbly at the knees. I looked out toward the sun, planning to blame its rays for the tears that would surely come.

They didn't. I didn't shed even one.

CHAPTER

9

THERE WERE QUESTIONS and inconsistencies. The age of the skeleton at death did not match Wilmot's timeline. My father had been over six feet. The coyote sculpture, put upright, probably wasn't that tall. Time might account for shrinkage in height, but the bones would have shown that, and they didn't immediately. It was early days yet.

I didn't fall apart with the news, at least not visibly. I knew my focus had been compromised, but it didn't matter at that point. The Tucson people arrived and took over the scene as I pulled Calloway aside and told him about my visit to the Smoots. He was curious about what I'd done, though he hadn't seen anything to make him think that Jerry or Joey was involved with what was going on. He was glad to have the information, though, and would follow up, maybe stop by the Smoots' place himself.

Dismissed by the Tucson folks and our trip up to the city delayed for now, Graham and I walked to the Jeep, and I gave him a ride back to town.

He was sticking around, apparently, even if a more official investigative team was going to work on the case or cases. He wasn't sure how he could help, but Calloway asked for a few more days and he didn't have anything pressing back at the university in Boulder, where he was a professor. New classes started in two weeks.

We made that sort of small talk on the way back into Black Vulture, though he ended up telling me more about himself than I told him about me. I sensed that he was embarrassed by mentioning Wilmot, and he kept up a stream of details like the specific classes he taught, the recent death of his dog, and the online order he was going to place this evening to get more appropriate clothing.

"We have boots here in town," I said as he directed me toward his truck and camper, which he'd parked in the small parking lot of the old grocery store that I nodded toward. "Right there. Believe it or not, the best boots are in there. There's some old story about a salesman coming through town fifty years ago. The previous owner, Norma, bought out all the guy's boots and they just keep getting resupplied."

"I like that story," he said.

"It's probably not true. That's how we roll around here. Legends, stories. It happens when real life is pretty boring."

Graham gave me a long look and seemed to almost laugh. "Thanks."

I noticed the trailer and said, "I have a lab of sorts. If you need it."

"Thanks. I've got something small in the trailer, but I'll let you know. I'm . . . sorry about the news. That had to be pretty awful. And, of course, it might not be your father."

But my father *was* somehow involved, that seemed clear. Wilmot Dylan's name was somehow attached to the first set of bones, the man who attacked me, and probably the second set too. It was feeling like Calloway's instincts about that part had been correct.

"Right. We'll see," I said.

Graham nodded. "Let me know if you need anything. I'm a good listener."

"Who told you that?" I asked trying to add some levity to the moment. It was a weak attempt.

He sent me lifted eyebrows before realizing I was kidding. "No one, but I would do my best to listen if you needed to bend an ear."

"Thanks, I'm good."

"Thanks for the ride."

I nodded and watched him make his way toward the grocery store door, which was locked.

"Sorry about that. Sometimes the store closes early, but it opens every morning at seven."

"Thanks." Graham waved and made his way to his truck. Another day and time, I'd be curious about the trailer's insides.

Now, after I'd driven the short way home and made my way to my lab, I tried again to focus on the past, see if there were any answers lurking there, waiting for me to remember them and solve the present-day mysteries.

This lab was the place where I spoke to Wilmot, though I didn't do that very often. This was the room where my love for bones had been born. That mountain lion's femur. It had all been so fascinating. It still was.

I took a deep breath and invited in whatever old images might like to come to me.

My father's disappearance when I was so young had been a shock and his abandonment had tormented me, but it was also something that had fit with his personality.

Before he left for good, there were mornings when I'd awakened to find him gone, out for a hike to his beloved Vulture Caves, or a drive over the terrain that was so much a part of him that he wouldn't ever consider a move to a more civilized place like Tucson, let alone somewhere outside of Arizona.

This room was where he did his job. He'd worked day and night, tirelessly on a project, until it was finished. Once the final touches were in place, he'd need time to himself. It never occurred to him that leaving me alone for a day or so was the wrong thing to do to a kid. I'd figured it out. We'd figured it out.

"I left a note," he'd say when he came back home, and I asked where he'd been.

I'd go with him on hikes sometimes, my legs always working double-time to keep up.

"Aw, little bit, I'm sorry," he'd say. "I'll slow down. Here, you go ahead and set the pace."

I would slow him and his exuberance down every time, but he never complained. He'd point out tracks and scat, knowing exactly which creature had left them. He'd see animals that I didn't immediately.

One day, we came upon a fox caught in trap.

"Oh, God damn it," Wilmot had said. He'd hated traps.

"Do we put it out of its misery?" my ten-year-old self had asked.

Wilmot studied the fox and sighed heavily. "Nope. I'm going to free it."

"You told me that it's unsafe to free an animal from a trap, and the fox might suffer."

"It is unsafe, but look at how it's caught. No blood. It's like its leg is just stuck in between the teeth."

"Papa?"

"I'll be fine."

"I'll help."

"You will watch, so you can do it when you're a grown-up like me. You might need to know this someday."

My eyes wide, I nodded. When it came to animals, I never questioned my father. I never questioned him about much of anything.

Wilmot had taken off his jacket and put on some gloves. In quick, sure moves, he threw the jacket over the fox's head and then grabbed onto the frantic animal. He managed to pull its foot from the trap with one quick tug.

"It's not broken, Hazel," he said as he took a look and felt the leg. He let go and retrieved the jacket just before the fox jetted away, not limping a bit.

"You did it!" I said gleefully.

"Yep. Trapping is illegal out here. Remind me to call Calloway when we get home."

"Okay."

And then he'd muttered quietly even though I'd heard, "Evil fuckers."

I smiled to myself now. I had never once come upon a creature, fox or otherwise, that I needed to free from a trap. Still, I was ready. Sort of.

A blank spot that wouldn't fill in was made of my mother, a blurry image from the one photograph I had sometimes crossed my mind, both how she looked and who she was. She'd died giving birth to me, and Wilmot never talked about her. Even when I'd asked him to tell me something, he'd say that none of that mattered. It was me and him against the world and looking backward never did anyone any good. He'd only let me keep one picture, which was probably cruel, but I didn't give it much thought.

Just keep going forward, one foot in front of the other, little bit.

He'd made it seem like yesterday wasn't important and, for the most part, I'd bought into that.

In fact, though ethereal thoughts made of her image ran through my mind every now and then, I couldn't understand why my mother, Catalina, was appearing there now. I kept shaking thoughts of her away.

I couldn't have told you if I had any birthday parties, if Wilmot even wished me a happy one on those days. I remembered his kindness, but no parties, no cakes.

Until I'd been about eight, around the time Wilmot had thought it was okay to leave me alone, I'd been a welcome interloper into his studio. I'd observed and even assisted in the tasks that came along with being a taxidermist. Those were the days that laid the groundwork for what I'd become, why my world was made of bones. I wouldn't have traded them for anything.

But not too long before he left, Wilmot changed, and he became more secretive, more private about what he was doing. He'd lock the studio door.

"Dad?" I'd said as I knocked. "Let me in."

"A minute, little one."

After a series of shuffling sounds and indistinguishable thumps, he opened the door.

"Why was it locked?" I'd asked.

Wilmot shrugged. "Safety."

Though he'd never turned me away when I came calling, he did keep locking the door. What had he been up to? I looked around now. I'd cleaned out the space completely when I turned it into my lab, brought in bones to search for the answers they could give. I hadn't found anything that had made me question my father, wonder what he'd been up to. Though I'd been an adult by then, it was still about a decade ago. Nothing was the same as it had been when my father had been there.

I had cleaned up the room with the hopes of finding something, uncovering something that would help me understand what Wilmot might have been up to that would lead me to where he'd gone.

I'd grieved his disappearance—in private. Even as a kid, and now, I put on a stoic face for the public, but I'd missed my strange father. I didn't understand it back then, but our lives weren't necessarily conventional. Not many people in Black Vulture lived any sort of polished television or movie family existence.

Wilmot was no odder than anyone else in Black Vulture, frankly.

But what had he done that might have led to whatever was going on now?

That day. The last day. I still didn't remember it beyond the moments I'd come into the house, finding it cleaner than usual and Wilmot not there. I didn't remember calling Calloway, but he said that's what I'd done. I didn't remember the searches, the confusion.

The days right after that were still a blur of questions without answers. Calloway and Dixie were always there helping or feeding me. Others trying to figure out what to do with me, social workers, judges, and then . . . life just went on, and those old days fell away to "life before." I'd had to figure out all the after.

I still missed my father, grieved him, but not with devastation or gut-wrenching immobility.

My phone buzzed in my pocket. Glad to have something else to focus on, I answered, "Hazel Dylan."

"Ms. Dylan, this is Police Chief Verro. I need you to meet me in front of the post office."

"I'm on my way."

I gathered both my hat and the knife and cut through the middle curve of the S, next to the diner, coming out on the other side. Verro stood across the street and in front of the post office.

He nodded. "Thanks for being so quick about it."

"What's up?"

"This is the direction you saw the man who attacked you run?"

"Well. Kind of." I pointed behind me. "From in front of the diner, he disappeared around the end of that building. I hurried to follow him but didn't see him anywhere. I thought he could have run through the spaces in between the buildings here, but I didn't even see any stirred-up dust out there." I moved to point out toward the open desert. "I didn't see anyone."

"But he could have come this way and gone through behind the post office."

The longer I thought about it . . . "It's possible."

"Follow me," Verro said.

We made our way around the post office to an area that I knew about but hadn't thought about. It wasn't an alley, but it was used like one. It was dark, a closed-off old patio area where garbage cans and other random things were kept. It didn't smell and it wasn't filthy, but it wasn't a comfortable place.

Jenna stood at the far end of the space, next to another opening and some old garbage bins that appeared not to have been used for some time. I didn't know the business that used to be on the other side of the wall, but I knew the small spot next to the post office had been empty for a while.

The closer we got to the bin, the better I could tell that it wasn't a garbage bin but an old barrel.

Verro put his hand up to stop our hurried pace. "I want you to look inside the barrel and tell me what you see."

Jenna grabbed her phone, illuminated the light, and aimed it inside the barrel.

"Got it," I said.

Verro lowered his hand, and I took the remaining few steps so I could peer inside too.

Along with old, dirty debris, there were two items inside the barrel. One was an old boot that appeared to be stuck to the bottom by a crusty film that spread side to side.

The other item wasn't as dirty. It was a red scarf, just like the one around the first bone sculpture's neck.

"Oh." Some mental gymnastics set off in my mind. Was the man who'd accosted me the same one who'd built the sculptures? Why had someone left a scarf here? Was this all just random?

"We heard about the scarf on the first sculpture," Verro said.

I nodded at him. "The one in the barrel looks like a match."

"Do you think the man who attacked you was the one to put the scarf in here?" Jenna asked.

"That he might be the one who created the sculptures?" I asked.

"Yes," Verro said.

"I suppose it's possible . . ."

"You sure?"

I glanced into the barrel again. "Well, no, I'm not sure about anything, but at least I think the scarf is a match. Calloway and the Tucson folks will want to know."

"Yeah. They will." Verro grabbed his phone and made his way around Jenna and then back out into the daylight.

"Did you find this?" I asked Jenna when he was gone.

"No, Verro did. I didn't know this space was back here, though I might have found it eventually. Verro's been spending a lot of time walking around."

I nodded. "Did you guys find anything else?"

"No, nothing," Jenna said. Even in the shadowed space, I could tell there was more she wanted to say but seemed to be hesitating.

"What's on your mind?" I asked her.

"I . . . nothing."

"Okay."

The air between us became fraught with a sort of electricity. We didn't even know each other, but I knew she didn't like me. I hadn't formed an opinion, but I wondered what I'd done.

"Jenna . . . Officer Griffen, what's going on?" I asked.

She sighed. "Verro thinks I might have come on a little too strong this morning."

I rewound my mind back to the time in the diner. "I don't remember."

She frowned at me. "Hazel, you need to learn things about your father. At least . . . look at what's out there. There are things—"

"He was my father. I lived it."

"But you were a kid. You didn't know him fully. Others might have. Take a closer look. See if anything helps you put together some answers."

"Is there anything you want to tell me? An abridged version maybe?"

"No, Hazel. You need to take a deeper dive yourself."

I nodded once, but I didn't answer. The stubborn part of me still wanted to argue, but if I knew anything, it was that whenever I wanted to dispute, taking a step back first was always the wiser path to take. Not that it was always the one I took.

Verro returned a moment later but didn't offer a summary regarding the call he'd made. I was dismissed as Verro told Jenna to gather and bag the scarf.

I didn't think I was here because of my position as a consultant. The lines between the things happening in Black Vulture and my job were blurring. I was a witness as well as someone who could potentially provide answers to some of the mysteries—both professionally and personally. I needed to be careful, though I wasn't even quite sure what that meant.

I left, but what I didn't tell them was that I would make my way back to that patio as soon as I could. The local police were focused on the scarf. The boot meant nothing to them.

But it might mean something to me.

The twenty years since Wilmot disappeared had both trudged along and flown by. The desert demolished everything. The sun was a hungry and cruel beast. But this barrel had been shaded by some old wooden slats for a long time. It could have been around for just a few years, but it could have been longer—a lot longer.

That boot, though covered with grime, looked familiar. Sure, lots of people wore the grocery store boots, but when he'd disappeared, so had Wilmont's boots—everyone assumed he'd been wearing them, along with the jeans and sweatshirt that I'd witnessed him wearing the morning of his disappearance.

I was going to fish out that boot and give it a good once-over.

I had to wait until the police were gone first, though.

CHAPTER

10

My thoughts about my later return to the barrel were interrupted by Sonny, who was sitting on the bench outside the diner, watching my door as I came back out the space I'd gone through earlier.

"Hey." He stood and smiled.

"Hey, Sonny."

"Have you had dinner?"

I put my hands on my hips and looked at him. "I think you and I are going to need to have a talk."

"So soon? We just met." He smiled again, not oblivious to my unspoken message, but certainly trying to make me reconsider.

I opened my mouth to say something like "I'm not interested," but he put his hand up and stopped me.

"Hang on," he said. "It's just dinner. I promise."

"I . . . Why?"

He put his hands in his pockets and shrugged. "I'm not sure, except that I would like to get to know you better."

"Dinner and that's it."

He huffed a laugh.

"Dutch."

He smiled as if he'd won a prize and I fantasized about punching him in the nose and hopefully breaking his glasses—for just a second. Then I suddenly felt like I needed to fight off a smile of my own. He was undeniably a nerd, but cute, and had an attitude that was a bit too infectious. The opposite of mine.

"I actually have an idea for another location. Would you come with me?"

"I don't want to go to Tucson."

Sonny feigned shock. "Not on the first date!"

"Date?"

"I mean—you know what I mean."

I did. I knew exactly what was going on here. I'd offered up rejection a time or two over the years. Not that I was immune from it myself, but I just hadn't been able to find much interest in dating anyone. My life had been made of me figuring out how to take care of myself and immersing myself in my passions, things that included human remains—what was left of dead people. It simply didn't occur to me to look for any sort of partnership.

I could have done the same with Sonny. I could have been blunt, and I would have if I really wanted to. There was suddenly . . . something about him. I didn't want to hurt his feelings. Not yet.

"Yes, I accept—"

"Good—"

I lifted a hand. "Hang on though. I need to do something. Want to come with me?"

"Sure."

"It involves getting dirty."

"I sit behind a computer all the time. I'd love the chance to get a little dirty." The double entendre was punctuated with lifted eyebrows.

I tried not to smile. "Wait here. I need to get some things."

As Sonny waited out front, I gathered a box of gloves as well as a shovel. If anyone saw us, there would be questions, but I would think of answers if I had to.

I handed Sonny the shovel and said, "Follow me. Try not to be too obvious."

He considered the shovel as if wondering how he could possibly hide it.

"Just act natural," I added as I set off back toward the space at the end of the diner. Sonny followed behind.

If anyone inside the diner was looking out the front window, they'd notice us, but as I led the way, I veered away from a direct line of sight and kept my gaze downward so as not to make eye contact.

As I figured they'd move quickly, the police were gone. It was even darker under the old patio covering now, so I flipped on my phone's light. I'd decided that the only person who might catch us back here would be Pearly, the postmistress, who I needed to talk to anyway. I was waiting on a box from Missouri. Had it arrived?

I thought about Jenna and her words, her quick read of me. "Have you heard anything about the new employee named Allie?" I asked Sonny.

"I did some reconnaissance."

"Oh. Well, thank you. What did you learn?"

"She's a new computer engineer. Apparently, brilliant. She and her wife moved here from Oregon. Sound about right?"

"Yep. Anything else?"

"No real impressions yet. Want me to get to know her?"

"I don't know. Can I get back to you on that?"

"Absolutely."

"Put on some gloves," I instructed. "Aim the light into the barrel. Hand me the shovel."

"What is that? A boot?" he said as he peered inside.

"Yes."

"From the last century?"

"Maybe, but I don't think it's quite that old."

"Want me to get it out?"

"I'll do it."

I put the shovel into the barrel and dug away at the debris. When motes floated upwards, I said, "Do you want a mask?"

"No, I'm okay. How did you even see this in here?"

"Long story."

The boot didn't completely fall apart. My methods of retrieval weren't as careful as they would be if I was sure that this was evidence of some recent crime. If anything, it was too old to offer any real answers, to anyone except for maybe me, but as I scooped up the boot when it was released from all the grime, doubt ran through me. Should I have told the police to retrieve the contents of the barrel? I still could if I thought it was important. I was too curious to stop now.

Once the boot was out of the barrel, I set it and the shovel on the ground. Sonny and I crouched.

"What are we doing?" Sonny asked.

I looked at him, back at the boot, at him. "My father disappeared twenty years ago. This might be his boot."

"What?" Sonny paused. "How—"

"I need to get this back to my place," I said.

"Want me to carry the shovel or the boot?"

"Either. We might get caught."

Sonny shrugged. "For getting rid of some garbage. We'll say we're helping the environment. Or something. We got this."

The short trip back to my lab was uneventful. Once the boot was on the lab table, looking old and barely held together, Sonny said, "I'm sorry about your dad, Hazel. Do you really think this could be his?"

"I don't know. But there's a way I could know for sure. Here, put on this mask and the goggles." I handed them to him.

Once our airways and eyes were protected, I re-gloved.

It was an old leather work boot, similar to the boots I always wore, identical to the boots Wilmot wore. The same one that lots of people around Black Vulture wore. Definitely a grocery store boot.

"My dad wrote his name inside the back flap of his boots. He would camp with friends and names in boots were helpful."

The leather was worn and cracked, stiff and flakey. I stuck my hands into the top part of the boot and spread the opening enough to see inside and the top of the back upper. The tag that displayed the size was still there, almost pristine since it had been tucked away.

"The size is correct," I said.

"Really?"

I pulled the opening wider and aimed the overhead light fixture into the boot.

"Do you see anything?" Sonny asked.

"Well, yes."

"Cool."

"And no."

I grabbed a magnifying glass and looked again. I glanced at Sonny. "There are remnants of Sharpie writing in here, but nothing legible."

"May I look?"

I handed him the glass, and he got close to the boot. "Yeah, I can see it, but . . . shoot, it could be anything."

"Exactly," I said. "And lots of people write their name in their boots."

"What other tests could you do? DNA?"

"I doubt it. It's been too long."

"I'm sorry, Hazel," Sonny said sympathetically. "That was fun, though."

"Gathering an old boot from a barrel?"

"Yeah. Thanks for inviting me."

I knew the boot was a long shot. I'd roped Sonny into something that the police may question me about at some point, but probably not.

"You're welcome. And this still could be his. I won't give up."

What would it mean if it belonged to a man who disappeared twenty years ago? What were the odds I was on to something? Almost nil.

"Good."

"Hey, weren't you going to buy me dinner?"

Sonny pulled the mask down and smiled. "Let's go."

CHAPTER 11

I BAGGED THE BOOT for later contemplation and left the gun and hat at home. We hopped into Sonny's work truck, The Institute's logo, a shooting star aimed toward other stars, emblazoned on the driver's door, and made our way down poorly paved roads toward the mountains.

"I'm taking you to where I work," Sonny said.

"Uh, I don't think so. Your work is on the other side of the freeway."

"Nope, mine isn't."

I thought for a moment. "Am I going to see something top secret?"

Sonny laughed. "No, we keep all the secret stuff locked in an underground vault. However, we don't advertise what I'm going to show you, and we don't allow visitors, unless they are very special."

When he continued up the mountain and then took a dirt road off it, I sent him some raised eyebrows, but he only smiled.

"You'll see," he said.

"Where did you come from?" I asked.

"University of Arizona. I worked on the Webb Telescope project."

"That's cool."

"It was. I gave up tenure to come here."

"That's a big deal."

"It is, but it was an easy decision."

"Why?"

"I love what's going on out here. I'd love to be a part of a giant discovery, but this is also a fun adventure. It's only forty-five minutes from Tucson, but a world away."

I nodded. "The money must be really good."

He laughed. "They pay me well."

I nodded.

Sonny steered the truck around a short curve, and we came upon a security shack.

"I can't believe I didn't know this was out here."

"Not many people do."

There was a tourist spot not far from Black Vulture that claimed to display an alien's body, but I hadn't bought into the idea, and I didn't know any locals who'd toured the place. I wondered if we were about to see something similar, something billboard worthy.

Sonny came to a stop at the guard shack as light glimmered off the heavy-duty chain-link fence and gate in front of us.

"Hey, Bruce," Sonny said as a guard stepped out from the building.

"Sonny." He bent over and shined a light in my direction. "This your girl?"

"This is Hazel Dylan, my guest." He looked at me with fake horror in his eyes behind the glasses.

I'd never seen Bruce around town. I waved. "Hello."

"Hi there. Neither of you have any firearms, do you?"

"No," we both said. I assumed we were both being honest.

Bruce went back inside the shack and pushed buttons to open the heavy gate.

"So, is this going to freak me out?" I asked once we were through.

"Maybe. However, I'm not taking you to see an alien, but that would be very cool."

"I'm not disappointed, and I'm very curious."

"Excellent!"

Sonny steered the truck around two more curves before we came upon a valley.

"Oh my God," I said.

"Right?" Sonny stopped the truck.

We leaned forward and looked out to the expanse in front of us.

The cup of the valley held a field of giant satellite dishes, illuminated by lights like I'd seen in outdoor stadiums and baseball fields. There were four rows of five satellites, each of them aimed the same northwesterly direction.

"That's a lot of bars."

Sonny laughed. "It does have a good reach."

"Who are you guys talking to?"

"Anyone who will listen."

"Has anyone replied?"

Sonny looked at me, glare from one of the giant spotlights brightening his playful smirk.

"No," I said. "I don't believe it."

"It's not what you think, but I want to show you something else." He nodded forward. "See that small building. That's where I spend most of my time. It won't take long."

I nodded, eager to see what was next.

We were a world away from Black Vulture, with millions of worlds above us. It was a nice break from my real life, and any hesitation I'd felt dissipated, giving way to something that felt like fun and intrigue.

The aluminum-walled shed that seemed small from the outside was, indeed, a tight space inside. Computer screens covered a wall in front of a desk set up with a laptop and a mouse. There was room for the two of us, but it was tight.

I nodded. "This is where you work?"

"It is. I'm a computer scientist. These computers, data, spreadsheets, all my jam." He paused and then reached toward the keyboard. He typed for moment and then cradled the laptop in one arm as he pointed.

Five wide graphs filled the screen. The lines inside them reminded me of EKG readouts.

"This one," he put his finger on the second graph, "look at the slight upward blip."

"I see it. Is that someone talking?"

"At this point, it's only a possibility. We need more information, but this is the kind of stuff I look for. And we need a pattern before we can decide anyway. Here." He set the laptop back on the desk. A move of the mouse brought the wall of screens to life. Sonny nodded at one of them with a cluster of white dots over the otherwise black screen. "The blip came from here. This galaxy four thousand light years away."

"If it's not communication, what else could it be?"

"Pulsars, magnetars, collisions . . . the list does go on. But this one is curious because of . . . well, things we look for, so I'm on alert for more, that pattern."

"That's where I get a little lost with this stuff. I mean, it's fascinating, but so . . . unreal to me. Thousands, millions of light years away just seems way too far to be important in my life."

"I get it." He nodded and then smiled like he knew something I didn't.

"What?" I asked. "If you know the secrets of the universe, I'd like to hear them."

Sonny shook his head and then sat on the corner of the desk. He crossed his arms in front of himself. "Nope. It's not a secret."

"I'm listening."

"We, you and I, are both into the same things."

"Explain."

"Bones, Hazel. You know this, but you might have forgotten. Bones are made of all of this stuff up there. Bones came from stars."

I felt my breath hitch a little. Of course, I knew what he was talking about. Essentially, we are stardust. Bones are forged from the calcium that lived and died in space long before we were born.

I chuckled once, finding that elusive thing—fun—again. "I do know that. We are stardust. But everything is."

"Sure, but I was thinking mostly about bones. You and I study the same things, but just from different directions."

"I suppose I can't argue about that."

"Don't make me quote the old Joni Mitchell song."

"We should always listen to the hippies."

"I don't disagree. See how much we have in common?"

"Okay, I get it." And I didn't even want to add anything like "but I'm not interested." Was I, though?

I stared at him for a long moment, wondering at what point the shift had come. This really was a date. This guy had my attention. I wasn't quite sure what to say or do next.

"Hungry?" Sonny asked, seeming to key in on my strange but delightful confusion.

"Absolutely."

"Glad to hear it." He stood and then reached under the desk, retrieving a giant picnic basket. "Want to eat under the stars?"

"Yes, I do."

"Awesome."

I laughed, but it was good to get out of that small building and breathe in some fresh air. My head needed a little clearing.

Sonny led the way down a short, paved walkway which ended in a patio with two picnic tables.

"This seems convenient."

"Right? It's good to have a place to go when the walls start closing in inside that closet. It can happen."

"Yep. I get it."

"Have a seat."

Sonny placed the basket on a table and then moved to a giant lever attached to a thick steel pole. With his other hand he pushed a button and spoke into a speaker. "I'm going lights out, Bruce."

"Copy."

Sonny looked at me. "Okay, don't panic. It's going to get dark, but your eyes will adjust quickly. The stars will take over in just a few minutes."

I'd seen lots of starry skies, but I was very curious about "lights out."

In dramatic fashion, Sonny flipped the switch.

And it got really dark.

A zip of surprise ran through me, though it wasn't quite panic. I said something like "Oh."

In the time it took for Sonny to make his way back to the table, my eyes adjusted enough to see the outline of his body. He sat next to me.

"You good?" he asked.

"Yep."

"Okay, look up."

There was not a drop of sky pollution out here. The blanket of stars was unlike any I'd ever seen before.

"That's amazing," I said.

"I agree."

"There are so many. It's overwhelming. It's intimidating. It makes me feel small."

"It does the opposite for me. I get to be a part of this gigantic organism. How lucky is that?"

I looked at Sonny. He'd taken off his glasses as he peered upward. He didn't look much different than he did with them on, but I found something charming about his farsightedness.

Okay, that was weird. I checked myself and then forced my eyes back up to the sky.

"Look at all those bones," Sonny said.

I laughed and a smile stayed behind.

It was late enough now. He could stay in the shadows as he made his way to Hazel's lab, the room that had once been a studio, the place where it had all gone wrong.

He needed to see it. He needed to know if he would recognize it—when Hazel wasn't inside it, which was the only way the old ghosts would show themselves.

There was no moon tonight, and Black Vulture had been a dark-sky community for as far back as he could remember. If no one came outside, no one would notice him. The cap hid his face well if he kept his face down. His clothes were nondescript, casual like everyone else around.

He took the path through the old closed-off space behind the post office. He'd scoped it out a while ago as a shortcut through town.

A back door flung open, stopping him in his tracks, still in the shadows, about ten feet away from the interloper.

It was the post office's back door, and an older woman stepped out. What was her name? He should remember, but he couldn't.

She was humming something to herself as she exited the space, closed the door, and then locked it. He held his breath as she tested the doorknob. Barely five feet, her old hands struggled with the key, but she got it done.

Why in the world did she leave through this door instead of the front?

He reached into his pocket. He carried only a folding knife, one that was so familiar to him, to most people around Black Vulture, probably. His real tools were well hidden away from any curious eyes. No one would ever guess what he kept hidden, and what those things had done.

He was good with tools. He was good with any knife. If this old lady turned his direction, he'd stab her so quickly she wouldn't know what had sliced into her. By the time she put the pieces together, she might have only half a breath left.

No one would catch him. There were no cameras back here—that's why he liked it so much. Black Vulture wasn't wired up for security, which, it turns out, can be mighty convenient.

He gripped the knife, his thumb on the button that would snap it open and ready to use.

"She'll be comin' 'round the mountain when she comes," the woman sang as she turned the other direction and began to toddle away.

He loosened his grip on the knife but didn't let go. At the same time, he let out the breath he'd been holding, sending an airy whistle through the darkness.

The old woman stopped in her tracks as he reflexively gripped the knife again.

She might have been in her eighties, old enough that she'd seen quite a few things over the years. She'd probably seen him all those years ago, but she wouldn't recognize him now. No one would.

Was she smart enough not to turn around, not to look back? Sometimes just a glance can change everything.

A second after seeming to consider her options, she continued in the direction she'd been going. She moved quickly now.

For a moment, he considered whether he should give chase, but she hadn't seen him. She hadn't seen a thing, which meant that if he did kill her, it would be someone who hadn't done anything to deserve their demise.

No, he'd let her go for now.

He still had a goal in mind, and he didn't want to miss the opportunity to explore Hazel's back room, that space that had set in motion the person he'd become.

The place that had made him what he was.

CHAPTER

12

SOMEONE HAD BEEN in my place. I couldn't pinpoint any specific disruption, but I knew something was off.

It was past the middle of the night, close to four AM, that witching hour when further sleep would probably only make me more tired.

Some mystery thing had awakened me and told me to look around. More kids with rocks? My attacker? It had been a while since someone had sprayed graffiti on the front of the building, but anything was possible.

I'd gotten home at ten, fresh from dinner with Sonny. The non-date. It sure felt like a date. I'd probably smiled to myself a little until I fell asleep.

I hadn't then, but now I flipped the museum light on and looked around.

I was so used to the mounts that their shadows, their realistic eyes that alternately fascinated and repelled so many people, didn't register with me. I tried to shift my perspective so I might catch any disruption. It wasn't a stretch for my imagination to take flight with the owl's feathers and hear the sounds the creatures had made when alive. The hoot and screech, the call of the eagle, the howls of the coyotes, the growls and screams of the mountain lions. The sounds were the backdrop of my life, my childhood, the lifeblood of Black Vulture. I'd know the sights and sounds even if Wilmot hadn't been a taxidermist.

A small old brass chandelier hung in the middle of the ceiling, and I knew which way the shadows were supposed to aim.

I examined everything.

My eyes ultimately landed on a desert box turtle. It hadn't been hunted but had been found dead on the side of the road—perhaps like the subjects of the artists who did rogue taxidermy. I was only ten or so, but remembered the day an old woman had brought it in, tears streaming down her face.

"Can you do anything?" she'd cried.

"Do you want me to take care of it for you?" Wilmot had asked. He'd taken her hands in his as she'd cried. "It's dead, my dear. Perhaps I could give it an appropriate burial."

"No. Can you," she'd peered over his shoulder as he stood in the museum's doorway, "just do what you do?"

"Taxidermy. That's what I do."

Wilmot had been proud of his work. He hadn't shied away from any of the haters, and he'd never apologized.

"Okay. Yes. I don't care how much it costs. I'll come pick it up from you."

"All right."

Wilmot usually took a fifty percent down payment on his work, but he let this woman go without asking for money. Though until that very moment, when I'd been rifling through the past for something off, I hadn't thought about the woman and her real tears for a long time, at this moment I remembered it well. Wilmot had closed the door when she left and turned to see me watching.

"Hey, Haze," he'd said.

"You didn't charge her."

"I couldn't bring myself to ask the poor woman for money. I'll do the job and then I'll ask for payment when she picks it up."

But, of course, she never came back, so into the museum the turtle went.

Why did that turtle garner my attention now? There *was* something off. I made my way to it and squinted. It was displayed so I couldn't see its front right foot unless I moved it away from the wall a bit.

I peered in between the wall and the mount, and knew I'd come upon something that wasn't right. I couldn't be sure that this was the thing my subconscious had keyed in on, but I knew something had changed from the last time I'd looked at the turtle.

I grabbed my phone and flashed the light, spotting something that shouldn't have been there.

"Oh. Damn," I said as I looked at the bone—possibly another phalanx, a finger bone. "Damn."

I didn't know who to call—Calloway or Verro. I called both.

Verro was the first to arrive, but Calloway wasn't far behind. For a moment or two as they questioned me, I wished I'd gathered the bone first and looked at it closely, but a sense of responsibility won over and now it was bagged evidence, beyond my grasp. I hadn't even really gotten a close look at it. It hadn't been very visible, tucked under a foot—why hadn't I looked closer?

In a strange scene, the turtle was also bagged—in a very big evidence bag—and taken out of the museum. I had no idea when the bone had been left there, but I told the officers that I felt like something was off when I woke up at four.

We went through the sequence of events that led me to discover the strange display. Neither Verro nor Calloway scoffed at my "instincts telling me something was off."

Calloway nodded. "Did you look around the rest of the place?"

"I did. I touched the front door's knobs, but no others. I didn't touch the windows either, just looked. No one broke anything to get inside."

"The door was locked?"

I sighed. "I think so."

"Do you typically lock it?" Verro asked.

"I do."

"What would make you think you might not have this evening?"

I was not going to tell the police that I was floating a little from my time under the stars, but that was the truth. I shrugged. "I got home late. I just don't track those minutes in my memory. I don't know when the intruder came in either. Though I didn't sense anything was off until early this morning, maybe it happened another time and my intuition just took some time to realize it." I paused. "However, I always lock the door. And, the lock on that door—unlike a deadbolt—could be opened with the slide of a credit card. Maybe I've been fooling myself regarding my own security."

"That's true. Let's get a deadbolt on there."

"I'll do it tomorrow."

Calloway said, "Good. Were you here, working in your lab today?"

"No. I spent some time with Chief Verro looking in the barrel."

"That is true." Verro nodded.

"I heard," Calloway said. "The scarf is up in Tucson, and it has been confirmed to be identical to the one around the sculpture's neck, but we still don't have any further answers."

"Okay."

"You said you got home late. What time?"

"About ten."

"And you're not sure if something was out of place then?"

"I don't know. I came in, but then made my way upstairs. I didn't look around."

Calloway sighed. I knew that he was silently debating whether he should process the whole place. It would mean bringing someone down from Tucson again, which was his prerogative, but, to me, it didn't seem necessary.

"Lots of people touch the front door, Sheriff. I really didn't sense anything else was disturbed."

"How'd someone get in and leave a bone under a turtle's foot?"

"Either I left the door unlocked, which wouldn't be like me, or someone slid a card in the opening and broke in," I said. "Oh, hang on!" I fumbled with my phone. "I put up a camera."

"You did?" Calloway said as he looked over my shoulder. Verro joined us and did the same.

"I put it out front." I looked up at Calloway. "I aimed it across the street, toward the space next to the diner. I did that because of the scarf and boot. It might not catch someone at the door."

"Let's look anyway," Calloway said.

I opened the app and scrolled to the views. The camera only recorded when some sort of motion set it off. I'd only put it up the night before but any movement by the diner should turn it on.

"There are only three things," I said. "That can't be right."

"Let's look at them." Calloway took the phone from my hands. Normally, I would argue, but I just let him have it.

"It looks like the recordings are from this morning. Trisha going into work. Pearly leaving the diner and heading up toward the post office. And a dog. That's it."

I took the phone back and looked at the bottom of the screen. The battery indicator showed that it was dead. "Well, that didn't work. It's an old camera. It didn't hold a charge for long. I'm sorry."

Calloway shook his head. "It's okay. It was a good idea. We need more cameras around town."

"I'll pull prints off the door," Verro offered. "We've got a kit in the office. We might find something we can use."

Calloway nodded at the chief. "Thanks."

"I'll be right back," Verro took quick steps out the front door.

It was only four-thirty in the morning, still dark. Once Verro left the room, I turned to Calloway. "Are you including him on things?"

"Sure. His call to me regarding the scarf helped."

I gave the sheriff a half smile. "He has to prove himself?"

Calloway shrugged.

The distant sound of an owl's hoot came from the back patio.

"Hang on." I stepped around Calloway and made my way to the sliding glass door.

"Stop!" Calloway commanded as I reached for the handle.

"We looked at this door," I said.

"But not from this angle. Look at the handprint."

I didn't see a handprint from where I stood. I moved back by Calloway.

"I know that door was locked, and it's not an easy slide to open," I said. "Whoever was in here didn't come in through that door."

"Maybe not, but they still might have touched the glass. That print does not belong to you."

He was right. The hand that had touched the glass was significantly bigger than mine, with thicker fingers and a wider palm. Could it have been Sonny's? I didn't want to say that out loud. Time would tell.

Something else bubbled in my thoughts. Had I made sure the door closed after the rock had been thrown? I had a distinct memory of wanting to make sure the doors were locked, but had I just made the typical motion of closing the door without making sure of it, because I was more concerned about the front door?

I was second-guessing myself. I wasn't flakey. Of course I made sure it closed. Right?

I looked at Calloway. "I hope Verro brings enough powder."

"Me too."

CHAPTER 13

"ARE YOU KIDDING me?" I opened my eyes as a knock sounded from downstairs and woke me up again.

I reached for my phone, surprised to see it was almost ten. I'd gone back to bed after the police left, thinking I'd try to grab another hour or so. I'd been tired, but ten was ridiculous. I needed to get out of bed.

I hauled myself up and out and made my way downstairs. I did and didn't want it to be Sonny on the other side. I wasn't presentable, but I wouldn't mind seeing him again.

"Who is it?" I asked.

"Graham Kucero. We met yesterday."

I opened the door a crack and squinted out. "Is there another sculpture?"

"No. Well, not that I'm aware of."

I pulled the door wider. "What's up?"

"I have some details to share about the skeletons." He held his hands behind his back and looked uncomfortable. This was not an assignment he relished. He looked almost the exact same as he had the day before, but his brown T-shirt was unemblazoned. He wore the same cap.

"Graham, could I meet you at the diner in twenty minutes or so? Will that mess up your schedule too much?"

"No. Sure. That works."

I closed the door and hurried back up to the shower, washing away the night—the bad stuff and the good stuff. I needed full focus.

"It's not your father," Graham said as he held on to a coffee mug's handle. He'd removed his cap. His salt and pepper hair was short, though it didn't appear to be from a professional cut. It was like he'd chopped at it with regular, plain scissors. I wondered briefly if that's why he wore the cap. "It's confirmed."

I'd already taken a couple of gulps from the cup Trisha had delivered. Relief spread through me, even though there had been quite a few doubts. "That's good to know. Thanks."

"You were pretty sure it wasn't him?"

"Wilmot was tall. One look at that femur and I thought the skeleton was under six feet. My father was just over. Of course, that couldn't have been conclusive from my distant examination, so it's nice to hear. Can you tell me more?"

"Well, the Tucson lab already had some of your dad's DNA, back from when he disappeared—"

"I remember giving it to them, from his hairbrush."

"Right. Anyway, that's how they determined that it's not a match."

I took a deep breath and then another gulp of coffee. "It is good news, though I'm surprised it's not Calloway who's telling me."

"He's busy this morning, asked me to come tell you. He thought it deserved an in-person visit, not a phone call. I'm now a contact for Tucson too." He swallowed hard, again as if he wasn't fond of the position he'd been put in.

I'd helped with being the contact before, the go-between. A brief flame of jealousy lit inside me, but then I remembered that my father might somehow be involved. The investigators needed to keep me at a slight distance, even as I helped when asked. Besides, Calloway needed whatever assistance he could get.

I said, "Can you tell me more? The first set of bones haven't been clean for long, have they?"

"They have not. In fact, the bones are pristine. No sign of ligament attachments or anything. No ID, but the dental records still might help. The police are investigating, even looking at some homeless shelters and visiting dentists. Nothing was immediately pinged."

I nodded. "Any ID on the second one?"

"Not yet, but . . . Sheriff Calloway wanted me to ask you if you've listened to a local podcaster and if you know her. Minnie—"

"Chavez. I know her. Not well. I don't listen to her podcasts, including the one about my father."

"You need to listen to it."

"Why do people keep telling me that? I mean, if someone would just relay to me what they want me to know from it, that would help."

"I don't know, but I think the sheriff wants your input."

"What do you know about it?" I said sourly. I raised a hand. "Sorry. I guess I need more coffee."

"Calloway mentioned that you don't remember everything from back then. He thought the podcast might help fill in some blank spots."

That wasn't totally unfair, but I wished Calloway had told me his thoughts instead of sharing them with this man that we'd all just met. "Graham, my father disappeared just over twenty years ago. I was thirteen. I didn't know all that my father was up to. Why would I have cared? I was a teenager. It was a long time ago. I was in shock, and it's not like I don't remember . . . everything. I just didn't digest some details from those nearby days. And now, I've lived more life without my father than I had with him."

Graham nodded. "Right, but things went on, according to Chavez—"

"What does she say?"

"Well, she was one of his students."

I blinked at him. The surprise couldn't have been more genuine. "What? My dad didn't have students."

Graham's expression turned a bit sheepish, tinged with a tiny bit of I-told-you-so. I suspected he wished Calloway were telling me these things too. "Well, Minnie Chavez claimed he did, and that's the direction Sheriff Calloway is looking now, at his students. He wants the students' names."

"Can't he get those from Minnie?"

"She's not giving them up. They all made some sort of vow not to tell."

"Why?"

"There was . . . an incident. Look, I just listened last night. I don't think you want me summarizing."

I did, but I could tell he was uncomfortable. "My father taught taxidermy?"

"I guess."

"You guess?"

"Ms. Dylan . . ."

I shook my head. "Don't do that. You know my name. Tell me something."

Graham took a deep breath and let it out. He'd abandoned the coffee. "Ms. Chavez, Minnie, claims that your father taught six people. They were young, teenagers at the time. She claims that your father never got their parents' permission and that was wrong, that things happened in those classes that were . . ."

"What?" I screeched this time, garnering Dixie's attention. She beelined in our direction.

"What's up?" she asked me. "Who are you?" she asked Graham.

"Sorry, Dixie. He's okay. His name is Graham Kucero. He's helping Calloway. He told me some surprising news."

"Okay?"

"Nothing important," I said.

Dixie didn't believe me. She angled her eyes at Graham. She didn't need to say anything to get a nod from him that he'd behave.

When she walked away, I lowered my voice and leaned forward, "What happened in those classes?"

"Please, Hazel. Listen to the podcasts and then talk to Minnie if you know her. She won't tell Calloway the names, and he was hoping you could help. He thinks the killer might have killed because of those days with your father."

Anger simmered through me. It wasn't valid anger, but it wasn't frivolous either. I didn't appreciate Graham as the messenger. I didn't understand why I had to listen to a whole podcast, like some school assignment, about the man who'd raised me until he was gone.

I looked around the diner, suddenly wondering how many people here had listened to it. Had Dixie? Doug? Did everyone in town know about classes that . . . I didn't remember?

Was it a lost memory or something else?

What was going on, and why hadn't someone mentioned the classes to me before now? Also, why were they suddenly important?

Once again, I wanted to storm out of the diner. I didn't want to be that person, so I tried to keep it low key as I grabbed my wallet from my back pocket and left a ten-dollar bill on the table.

"Hazel, wait . . . I don't think I handled this right."

"It's okay." I worked hard to control my tone. "It's not your fault. Thank you for all the information."

I stood and made my way to the door. In the background, I thought I heard Dixie say something like "Let me know if you need anything."

I debated calling Calloway on my way out to Minnie's trailer, but I thought better of it. He might be a friend, but he was also the sheriff, and he was working. I wasn't sure yet if I had the right to be angry or of all the things I had the right to be angry about.

Or if I was just plain old ornery.

Though there were some days I wasn't thrilled about the lack of paved roads around town, today they gave me something else to focus on. They also helped to calm me down.

I was sure that if my father had taught anyone but me any sort of taxidermy, I hadn't witnessed it. Why wouldn't he have shared his skills, though? He was very good at what he did.

I'd been rattled by what I'd heard because I'd felt left out. But maybe that was my own fault. And if I really thought about it, maybe no one had mentioned the classes to me because everyone in Black Vulture had been assigned to take care of me, which probably included not upsetting me.

I thought about Calloway's nudge for me to listen to Minnie's podcast, Jenne Griffen and now Graham piling on. I snorted a laugh. What exactly was I so upset about? That Wilmot might have shared his skills or that I didn't remember him doing so? Or that I'd ignored the podcast for some reason that ultimately led to what—self-preservation? Did I know something that I didn't realize I knew or was I just being stubborn?

I still didn't want to listen to the podcast, but I would.

Wilmot was my father. Mine. I didn't want anyone to take away the good things I remembered. I didn't want to have to explain to anyone the happiness he'd left me with. I'd missed him and, only learned little by little after he'd gone, how he might not have been as perfect as I'd made him in my mind. He was human, and we don't see that in our parents until we grow up a little too.

I'd stopped bringing him up in conversation a long time ago. I didn't want to listen to anyone's stories about him. I just wanted the memories I had about him to stay right where they were. I didn't need more good stuff, and I certainly didn't want anything bad.

Now there were horrific things happening in Black Vulture that he might have been a part of. Or was still a part of.

That tenuous sense of my life with my father, the past that should stay in the past, was beyond wobbly now. It was falling apart. I was a grown-up and I should be able to handle it, but I wasn't sure I could. I certainly wasn't doing so great at the moment.

I needed to talk to Minnie Chavez.

The Jeep took bumps and divots like a pro, but as I came to a stop outside Minnie's trailer, I wondered why she hadn't moved closer to town.

Lots of people with trailers out in the middle of nowhere were content with their life choices. I didn't really get it. I wasn't much of a people person myself, but I still didn't understand why this sort of life was ideal for anyone. I enjoyed my own company, but the moment I needed someone else to talk to, I could just walk to the diner or the bar or even the post office. The thought made me remember that box of bones on the way. I still hadn't heard from Pearly, but I needed to check my mail.

"Minnie Chavez, it's Hazel Dylan. I'm going to knock on your door."

The trailer was a single-wide that had been painted yellow and orange at some point. All the paint was peeling now. A firepit sat in front of the trailer, its border done in big rocks probably gathered from a nearby riverbed—dry except when it flooded. The ash inside the circle was black. I reached a toe into the pit, but it was cold, with no sign of a recent fire. Even if it had been doused the night before, water might not be visible.

"Minnie?" I called.

From what sounded like a distance farther than inside the trailer, I heard, "Come in!"

I climbed the two rickety steps that led to the door and turned the wimpy handle. I took my hat off and held it as I stuck my head inside. "Hazel Dylan."

"So you said. Come in."

I stepped inside, taking in the sights as my eyes scanned for Minnie.

The trailer was cute, decorated with Mexican décor, in bright colors and Dia de los Muertos masks on many of the walls.

The small kitchen was clean, with a coffee machine, a half-full pot sitting on the curve of the fake wood counter. The living room sat to my right. Minnie was there, behind a desk. She peered around a computer screen as headphones sat off to the side.

"Have a seat." She nodded at the couch; it and one end table were the only other furniture in the living space. There wasn't a television, but the computer screen was huge.

"How in the world do you have a signal out here?" I asked Minnie.

"You missed the satellite out there?" She rolled her chair back and then stood.

Minnie Chavez wasn't "cute" like some thought she might be, considering her name. She wasn't adorable or precious. She was stunning; tall with wide shoulders, long black hair, and dark eyes that told you immediately she didn't suffer fools. She wore a lot of turquoise, which was something I'd forgotten about her. It had been months since I'd seen her in town.

"I did not notice the satellite."

"It's on the roof. I can reach Pluto, I think." She smiled, but her eyes remained fierce.

I'd run the logistics by Sonny at some point.

"How's the podcast going?" I asked when I set my hat on the kitchen counter.

"Are you going to sit down?" Minnie inspected me.

"Yeah. Sure."

"Wait," she said. "Before you do, if you want a coffee, you're closer to the machine. Mugs are in the cupboard right above it."

"I'm good, but can I top off your cup?"

"Nope. Let's just sit and talk. I suspect I know why you're here."

As we sat, I considered where to begin.

"I'm guessing you have questions about the podcast about your father?" she prompted.

"I do, but I haven't listened to it."

Minnie's fierce eyes cut at me. "What? Then how do you even know the questions to ask? And why in the name of all those damn bones you like haven't you listened? I spoke some truths you might want to know."

I shrugged. "Maybe I didn't want to know. My truth is what it is. Maybe I didn't want someone else's to interfere with that."

"Well, I could go along with that if you were still a child. You've been a grown-up for a while now."

"Right, but also until now, no one had mentioned my father's name in the same breath with what might be some horrific crimes."

Minnie huffed a laugh. "Then you haven't been paying attention."

I cocked my head. "Maybe I have some holes in my memory around my father's disappearance, but I . . . I know I don't remember him teaching classes."

"If you listen to the podcast, you might be able to fill some of those holes." She paused. "But you might not want to?"

"That's not what I'm saying. Look, any chance you could summarize for me? I've got lots going on."

Minnie smirked. "Why don't we know each other better? Neither of us is great at mincing words."

"We're probably too much alike."

"Yeah." Minnie's eyes went to the window on the opposite wall. The blinds over it were closed. She took a breath, let it out, bit her bottom lip, and turned back to me. "All right. I can give you some of the highlights."

"You can skip over anything that doesn't have anything to do with the classes my father allegedly taught."

"You don't remember them?"

"No, and I just heard about them today."

Minnie nodded. "Okay." She sighed. "Well, you weren't around, and there was always a sense of secrecy with them. Wilmot might not have told you."

I was pretty sure he hadn't, but it was good to hear that Minnie might have thought that too. "You don't want to give the sheriff the names of my father's students, even if it means maybe finding a killer."

She nodded. "I might have listened to a message from the sheriff come in, but I haven't returned the call. He should come out and talk to me, but I made promises."

"You'd tell him in person?"

"More than I would over the phone."

"He's busy, so I'm here."

Minnie smirked. "You represent him?"

"Not in an official capacity, but I'll tell him everything."

I knew how precious crime fighting and solving resources were in Black Vulture and the county, but I was surprised that someone hadn't knocked on Minnie's door before now if the list of names was that important. I kept my expression neutral. Minnie didn't need to know my doubts.

"That's fine. I talk about the classes in the podcast, but I don't mention the students' names because I value their privacy. I've heard about some strange things going on around here and, though I can't fully understand why your father is being mentioned, he is. Mark my words, though, Hazel, I will investigate all this too. I don't think any law enforcement does anything well enough."

I chuckled. "Another thing we agree on. I respect Calloway, and he's a friend, but I always like to take my own look at evidence."

Minnie nodded. "Exactly. Okay, well, I was one of your father's students."

"Why were you interested in taxidermy?"

"I'm interested in everything, and there wasn't much to do around here back in the day. I was a teenager and there were boys. In fact, it was during the few classes that I had the realization that I was more interested in the girls than the boys anyway."

"Stinky boys," I said as she looked at me as if I might be surprised by her words.

Did anyone care about that stuff anymore? In Black Vulture, the answer probably was yes, but I didn't spend much time hanging out with that group either.

"I was bored, or that's what I'll chalk it up to. Your dad was good to young people around town, do you remember that?"

"Sure."

"Right. There are so many poor people in town. If he saw someone, particularly a teenager, who might need a meal or something, he'd buy them dinner."

I nodded.

She continued, "Wilmot was approached by one person, but he didn't want to have to get his parents' permission, so he asked your father to keep it on the down-low. I bet that meant even from you, I'm afraid. You're just a couple years younger than me and the other students."

The locked doors, the change in Wilmot welcoming me into the lab. I didn't remember seeing any students anywhere. I didn't remember him not opening the door, but there might have been a time when he hadn't.

But, knowing what I knew about Wilmot, his teaching willing students even if he should have run the idea by some parents didn't surprise me. He was proud of what he did, and he looked at it as a service. It was his job, but he saw something spiritual in the mounts. If someone wanted to learn the skills, he probably would have jumped on the opportunity. And if they didn't want to ask their parents for permission, then he was just arrogant enough to think that he could handle that appropriately too. I didn't know laws or rules about parents needing to know about taxidermy lessons, but common sense told me it would have at least been polite to talk to the parents.

"What happened in the classes?"

She bit her bottom lip for a moment. Notification pings sounded from the computer, like she was receiving a slew of emails. She ignored the noise better than I did.

"So, I didn't have the intestinal fortitude to be a great student to your father. I mean, your dad didn't do anything really, but he showed us pictures first to give us an idea what it was all about. There were only seven classes. I was going to stop after the eighth class, but during the seventh . . . oh, Jesus." She wiped her hand over her face as her skin paled.

"What?" I demanded.

"Okay. When I arrived that day, I made my way directly to the workshop and . . . there was something inside, but there were no people yet."

"Jesus, Minnie, spit it out."

"Someone had brought in something. It was a bird, but only in the front. A fish in the back, and it had . . . feet. I didn't know what animal they came from."

For the first time in days, it felt like some information suddenly became organized. Now I thought I understood why Calloway and Graham had brought up rogue taxidermy to me, and why Calloway had asked Graham for help. "Minnie, rogue taxidermy became a thing back then. It's art."

Minnie nodded. "I know what rogue taxidermy is, Hazel. It's really quite interesting. But while that might be what someone was using as an excuse to create a horror, that's not what this was. This wasn't made from the skin of the animals, it was made by parts of the bloody corpses."

"Oh my God," I said. "My father probably lost his mind."

"I ran out of there so fast, I don't know the details. I never looked back. A few days later, your father tried to talk to me, but I was a kid, and he knew better than to try to force any conversations with me."

"Minnie, who did that? My father never would have . . ."

I was listening to her words, but somewhere in the back of my mind, something else was spinning. Did her podcast somehow accuse my father of . . . whatever this was? Why hadn't I listened?

"I never found out. The other kids came to me later, telling me the classes were over, that it got even worse, but no one would tell me more. We made a pact, a vow of silence, but the others know even more than I did. None of them have told me anything else."

"You're not a kid anymore either. That shit doesn't matter, and it appears people are being killed, their bones posed like desert creatures. If Calloway heard this on your podcast, it's no wonder Wilmot's name is coming to mind." I sighed. "I'm going to need the other names, Minnie. Calloway is going to need them."

She shook her head. "Well, I didn't know about the sculptures until very recently." She paused. "We made vows."

"Do you understand what's going on here?"

"Yes, and I hear you, but I do think that looking at your long-gone father is a stretch or an easy look or something. Posed skeletons aren't taxidermy."

Before she'd given me this new information, I would have said, "Exactly!" But things were different now, and, frankly, I was surprised she didn't see it.

I didn't want to tell her about the finger bones, that, no pun intended, seemed to point at Wilmot's potential involvement. I didn't know what the sheriff wanted to keep under wraps—maybe I wasn't even supposed to talk about the sculptures, but I would have been surprised if the news hadn't hit social media somewhere. I could only hope that I was allowed to share the details.

"Minnie, the first skeleton had a red scarf tied around its neck, representing blood. It made it seem like something . . . different. If Calloway heard your podcast, I can see why his thoughts went where they went."

Minnie's eyes widened as I'd told her about the scarf. She suddenly looked rattled, which was probably something that she rarely was. "Hazel . . ."

I waited for as long as my impatience at her incomplete sentence would allow, which wasn't long. "Damn it, Minnie, what?"

"I've never told anyone about this part, but on that . . . thing that I saw, there was a red scarf—well, a scarf, I think it was soaked in blood—around its neck."

"Oh boy."

She nodded. "Yeah."

"This is going to sound absolutely ridiculous, but was there, by chance, also a barbeque fork?"

She gasped and tears filled her eyes as her hand covered her mouth, and she nodded. "A tail," she managed to whisper the words.

She was beginning to freak out, and none of us needed that. "Okay, okay, let's step back a moment. We're here and we're fine, and these are all helpful clues. Okay?"

She pulled her hand away and seemed to listen to reason. "Yes, I agree."

I leaned forward, my hand on my knees. "We're going to need those names, Minnie. Right away."

CHAPTER

14

MINNIE GAVE ME the names.

I was itching to get the list to Calloway, as well as do some of my own investigating regarding what the former students remembered and might be up to now, but Minnie convinced me to stay for a few more minutes.

"Rogue taxidermy," she said.

"Okay?"

"That day, I know that whatever that thing was in your father's studio, it was an abomination, a disrespect of an artform that had only begun to see the light of day. Back then, it was all just something . . . wrong. It was a misinterpretation, meant to shock."

"Sounds like it."

"I didn't think your father created it back then. Even when I first saw it, I knew it wasn't him."

"I assure you, he didn't. Not because of the ideas behind the art, but because of the blood and gore you saw. He would never have allowed such a thing."

"Are you sure?"

"One thousand percent." I paused. "But you don't know who did?"

"It could be any of the five others on the list." She bit her bottom lip again. "It's not unusual out here, but we all came from instability. We were all also artistic." She hesitated again. "And so you know, Thalia and I did date, later when we were in our early twenties, but it just didn't work out. She never told me what happened after I left that day. They all kept quiet. Vows and secrets all around. The podcast ends with your father's disappearance shortly after the abomination was brought to class." She paused. "I did the podcast to see if I could get answers regarding where Wilmot went or why he left, but no one was talking, including Thalia to me."

"You were grown-ups when you dated?"

Minnie shook her head. "Yes, but it didn't matter. None of us were going to talk about it."

"Until you did the podcast."

"I didn't name names."

"Did you think one of the students hurt my father?"

"I just didn't know. Anything was possible, and I hated myself for running away."

I wondered about the light she'd put my father in, but it seemed only fair at this point that I listen to her podcast. I would, and then I'd probably want to discuss more with her.

"Do you know where Thalia works?" I asked.

"No, but last I knew Danielle worked at the butcher shop."

"That's a bit on the nose," I said, thinking about the sculptures.

"I don't know."

"The butcher shop. Okay, what about Silas Reynolds, Jeff Ranke, and Johnny Clark?"

"Jeff Ranke is still in town. I have no idea what happened to Silas Reynolds or Johnny Clark. I never saw them or their fathers ever again. I think Silas's mother died when he was a baby, and Johnny's just didn't stick around."

"Did you try to find them?"

"Yes, but I couldn't. When I did the podcast series, I talked to Thalia. She made it crystal clear that I still shouldn't mention names." Minnie's eyes widened briefly. "Hazel, she was still concerned for her safety if their deeper secret got out. I swear to you, she wouldn't tell me what it was."

I didn't have all the pieces of the puzzle, but if the abomination was as awful as it seemed, fear for their safety might make sense.

"No social media contact with any of them?"

"No. I have professional pages for my business, and I've checked my followers' list, but none of their names have come up. Even Thalia doesn't follow me. Of course, lots of people have fake accounts just because they can, so I guess there's a chance they're still watching what I'm doing. When the podcast first aired, which was years ago, I received an anonymous email, telling me I was 'putting my toe in waters that might get them bitten off.' I forgot all about that until this minute. I suspected that it was one of the students and knowing I wasn't going to mention their names so it wouldn't go anywhere anyway. Maybe Calloway could trace the IP address."

"You still have the email?"

"I'm sure I do. I save everything."

"Could I see it? See the address it came from."

"I suppose. Hang on, let me find it on the computer and then I'll let you read it."

Minnie made her way back to the other side of the desk and sat in her chair. I couldn't see her face for a moment, which gave me a chance to let mine relax from the shock and awe she'd mainlined into me.

A bloody artifact in Wilmot's studio? Abomination? Oaths and pacts? This was little old Black Vulture, but I supposed things like that could happen anywhere.

"Okay, come on over," Minnie said.

Behind the desk, the space was tight. I hadn't noticed the microphone or the stack of files from the other side. Based upon the size of the mic, a satellite along with the nice computer, Minnie had the right equipment to create a good podcast.

I crouched next to her and looked at the screen.

Minnie said, "It's from AZBOY2435, which, of course, doesn't have to mean a thing about where they lived, their gender, or whatever that number was supposed to tell us."

It read:

Minnie. You have to stop. You are dipping your toes into alligator infested waters. You know what alligators do when that happens. They bite things off. They take the bones.

Minnie looked at me. "It's even weirder than I remembered."

"Yeah," I said. "It doesn't mention your Wilmot podcast. Are you sure that's what this is about?"

"No, but it arrived three days after the podcast became live. I do a series each month. Like I said, I forgot all about it until right now. It might not have anything to do with your father or those classes."

But I knew it did. So did she, I could tell.

I stood. "Are you calling Calloway or am I?"

"I'll email him, then call. Call him if you want, but your coverage will be spotty on the way back to town."

"I'll call when I get a good signal."

"I'll email."

I put my hat back on my head and hurried out to the Jeep.

He'd been watching Hazel Dylan long enough to know that she didn't spend all day every day in her lab. Other than the one time inside, he'd peeked through one of the building's narrow windows. He'd watched from a distance as she emerged for food or fresh air.

She often had a look on her face that wasn't welcoming. For the most part, he didn't think she noticed the world around her. Her mind was always working, even as she sipped coffee at the diner.

He didn't think she'd ever noticed anyone watching her. He didn't think anyone had really noticed him. He'd disguised himself at first. No one would have recognized him then, and he didn't think anyone had now. He was a stranger to most, new to town to others.

That old Smoot guy sure got curious, though. He'd taken care of that. At least Jerry Smoot wouldn't be telling anyone anything about what was going on in the desert.

After Hazel took off in her Jeep again today, he'd tried to peek in the window again. It had been covered.

Adrenaline had zipped through him. Someone had covered it. If that had happened, someone suspected that someone was looking inside.

Was it the police or Hazel?

He'd been so careful inside there. The lock on the front door was easy to pick. He'd gone in, looked around quietly, hadn't gone upstairs. He'd worn gloves when he took put the bone under the turtle's foot.

How had she found it so quickly? He thought he'd turned the turtle enough that she might miss it or it would take some time for her to catch on.

It didn't much matter. No one suspected anything. They couldn't. It would all be chalked up to something Hazel did, maybe accidentally.

It was all good, and would ultimately be done as he wanted it to be done. One step at a time.

He did, however, contemplate checking the door to the museum part of the building while she was away. She was very good at keeping the door locked, but was there any chance?

He decided against it. Maybe he'd just stop by the post office, see how that old woman responded to him. If she looked at him funny, he might have to take care of her too.

He was good at catching suspicion. No one was good at hiding their initial reactions to anything. Sure, there were good actors out there, but that first instant someone's eyes landed on him, he could read their thoughts.

As casually as possible, he made his way back around the buildings and sauntered toward the post office.

He'd remembered her name. Pearly. It was time to see if something needed to be done about Pearly.

CHAPTER

15

I DIDN'T TAKE THE trip back to town as slowly as my back or my Jeep's shocks might have liked. I'd never been gentle with vehicles, hats, or boots.

I'd gotten off the main path, thinking I could make it back to town more quickly if I tried a straighter line—as the vulture flies, so to speak.

It had been a bad decision.

I'd taken shortcuts through The Wild lots of times, but I'd never attempted this one, and I should have known better. The straight line I'd hoped to take was more like switchbacks down the side of a mountain though on fairly flat ground. I'd get back to a familiar road and then town eventually, but I was most anxious about not having a cell signal and I kept checking my phone. And it was too hot to stop. I had to keep going. I counted on Minnie getting ahold of Calloway.

I realized that all I would need to do to check on the Smoots' place was to drive around a mound of boulders that had probably been there since the dinosaurs roamed. Cacti and other things grew out from in between the rocks' cracks; more proof that if life can take hold somewhere, it will, even in brutal landscapes.

I hoped there'd be a clear way to the Smoot trailer once I made my way around the rocks. As long as I was out, I might as well check on them.

The Jeep (bless its heart) continued to take the terrain like a champ, though I had no choice but to slow down. I wished for a tall tree with shading branches, but there were none.

I had three bottles of water rolling around on the back seat floorboard, but none were cold. It didn't matter.

I brought the Jeep to a mostly level stop and made sure my hat shaded my head well enough. I reached around for the water and grabbed two.

The forced moment of stillness gave me pause. What was I doing all in an uproar anyway?

"Damn it, Wilmot," I said after I swallowed a big swig and then wiped my chin with the back of my hand.

I read bones better than most, sometimes even better than the so-called experts. It was why I was brought in to offer my opinion so often. I loved my work.

When I thought about my father, the pain of his disappearance would sometimes become real, a sharp knife in my gut. Some thoughts didn't bring pain but a fog of confusion instead, something that my subconscious didn't want to clear away. Whatever it knew, it didn't want me to face it.

At this moment, I wasn't sure if I was ready to learn anything more about him. As I looked out over the landscape toward town, I tried to remember something else. I tried to think about those days before he took off. Did I know about the classes? Had there been any hint at all?

Try as I might, still nothing came back to me.

Except for a hint of blood in the back of my mind, bold and red. I didn't feel much danger with the fuzzy vision, but I thought I should. My mind's eye couldn't see much of anything clearly.

"Aargh!" I slammed my hands on the steering wheel.

I knew or had heard of all the students. They were all a few years older than me. I'd known Minnie as far back as I could remember. I didn't remember her hanging around or running away screaming from Wilmot's lab.

Minnie didn't have much of a reputation beyond her podcast. I'd only heard about her friendliness. She loved researching true crime or just real-life mysteries maybe. Not only had I never listened to her podcast about Wilmot, I hadn't listened to any of her podcasts. I knew I'd probably missed out, but when I wasn't working, I was . . . well, it was more like I was always working. Even if I wasn't on assignment, I was doing something regarding my job, my passion. I had people throughout the state I'd visit, see if I could offer any sort of assistance. They were usually happy to see me and would have at least a question or two.

I had my own explorations too. As I looked out over the landscape again, I realized that though I might not have pushed the Jeep over all the terrain, I'd hiked most of what I could see.

I'd been looking for my father ever since he left, even if I didn't think about him every day.

I had a faint picture in my mind of Danielle Harold. One memory was made of her freaking out in the post office, yelling at Pearly, the postmistress even back then. I'd walked into Pearly's firm expression as she told the teenager to calm down.

I didn't think I remembered Danielle's exact words, but I thought she began her next diatribe with "Look, bitch."

But then Danielle had turned to see that I had entered the post office. She'd sent me a fiery look and then fell silent, grabbing a stack of mail from the counter and storming out.

Pearly and I hadn't discussed it, and I hadn't run into Danielle in years, though I knew she kept some horses on the outskirts of town.

Silas Reynolds had been one of those kids who were bullied throughout high school. A smaller guy with greasy hair, acne, and glasses, even the scant population at Black Vulture High School (total enrollment last time I heard was little more than a couple hundred) wasn't immune to bullying. Though he was a couple years older than me, I remembered him well enough, at least until I didn't. If I ever knew what happened to him and his father, I didn't remember the circumstances.

Jeff Ranke was still around, still changing oil and fixing cars in his garage, and all probably without any sort of proper business license. I didn't know him well, but, of course, I knew of him. He'd worked on the Jeep once. We'd probably been in the diner at the same time or passed each other on the streets but he hadn't given me one indication that he had taken some sort of taxidermy class from Wilmot. He didn't behave like he knew anything about me.

I remembered Johnny Clark. He was on the opposite end of the popularity spectrum than Silas. Johnny wore a leather jacket, had a pierced lip, smoked Camels and was, if not too cool for school, way too cool for my thirteen-year-old self. If I'd seen him in Wilmot's studio, I would have probably tripped over my words and stuttered, like all the girls did back then.

Surely, I would remember him there if I'd seen him. But I didn't, and I had no idea what might have happened to him or his father.

Taking a few moments to wrangle the memories and thoughts I had about Wilmot's purported students had given my anxiety the break it needed. Usually I was a cool cucumber, not rattled by much of anything. But my adrenaline had been spiked for hours now.

It was time to get going again, check on the Smoots. Take my time and be smart about a route. I knew these parts better than most people.

But before I could put the car into gear, I heard the buzz and rumble of another engine. It wasn't coming from something big. I looked up to the sky for a passing small plane, but that wasn't it. I glanced out to the desert, my eyes spotting movement, a plume of dust forming behind it.

Someone was on an ATV and coming this way.

"Shit. Someone thinks I'm in trouble."

I turned the Jeep off and waited.

When the rider was about ten feet away, I finally recognized him.

It was Graham Kucero.

He brought the ATV to a stop and hopped off. "Oh. Hey, Hazel, are you okay? I'm so sorry about earlier."

I watched him approach. He had on some new boots that I recognized as being from the local grocery store.

"It's fine. Why are you on an ATV? Is something happening?"

"Oh. No. I tow one inside my mobile lab. Calloway didn't need me for the time being and we're just waiting for more lab results. I thought I'd get a lay of the land." He looked around. "I keep wondering if we're missing something. There's a lot of open but oddly hidden space out here. I haven't found anything, though my leg got stabbed by something." He looked down at his denim-covered thigh. Blood had soaked through a little.

"You need to get that taken care of," I said.

"I will. I was headed back to my lab when I spotted you. Is there a problem?"

"No. I was just taking a break."

"In this heat?" Graham's face was sweaty underneath his cap's bill.

"Before the break, I was heading back to town. I didn't choose the best route."

"Okay. Uh . . . You want me to follow you?"

I looked at him. "Is your lab far away?"

"No, I just parked it up there by some caves, on an elevated ridge. I was trying for a valley-wide view. I'd like to catch someone in the act, you know."

"The Vulture Caves?"

"I have no idea what they're called. There aren't signs."

"Any chance I could have a tour of your lab?"

"Sure. Follow me." He hesitated. "I mean, if I can see yours too someday."

"You show me yours and I'll show you mine."

"Deal. Let's go."

My plans kept getting diverted. Maybe I'd check on the Smoots tomorrow. I liked labs, even small ones.

I started the Jeep and followed the ATV.

CHAPTER

16

THE CUSTOM LAB inside the recreational trailer was compact. Graham had made interesting use of space. Set up over the couch was a long table that, today, held a pair of goggles, a microscope, and an unused sketch pad. It was clearly a temporary setup, not something he used every day.

"You're based in Colorado? You have a lab there too?" I asked.

"Yes, at the university in Boulder. I also teach facial reconstruction and age progression, though most of that is computer generated now. I'm pretty good at it. It's not why the sheriff asked me to come. He's more interested in the rogue taxidermy possibility. When I told him I knew about it, he invited me."

"This isn't rogue taxidermy, but a twisted idea of it might have led to all this. You heard the podcast?"

"Yes, the abomination. I agree, but I don't think we know enough yet to determine anything."

"Will you stick around a while?"

"Not much longer if I'm not needed. I'm making myself as useful as possible. I'm trying to be a good go-between for

Calloway and the investigators in Tucson. Your local resources are scant, and I've never been asked to be so involved . . ."

I nodded. "You travel with an ATV?"

"I do." Graham shrugged.

I hadn't seen any signage on the outside of the trailer, and it wasn't set up like some sort of bigger entity had put it together for him. This was his stuff.

"My lab is homemade too," I said.

"I know. Sheriff Calloway and I talked about it. You've done a lot of good work."

"Thanks. I credit my mentor, a professor up in Tucson. Dr. Fulgi. She's amazing and has taught me so much."

"But you didn't go to the university?"

"I didn't. I doubt I ever will."

"If you want an in at the University of Colorado, I'll make sure you get accepted."

"I'll keep that in mind. Thanks."

There wasn't anything else to really see and the space was crowded, so we stepped back outside.

Graham had set up camp near the opening to the Vulture Caves. He'd been right about having a great view of the valley from his spot. He could see all the way to town. I took a moment to look out over the desert, quickly realizing how close I'd been to a better route. If I'd just taken a left when I took the first right.

A table was set up outside the trailer and held both a small telescope and two different binoculars. He'd been surveying the valley from here as well as driving the four-wheeler around.

"I want to find who's doing this," he said when he noticed my curious and impressed expression.

His search efforts were on him. Calloway hadn't asked him to do this.

"I've got something," he continued.

"What?"

Graham gathered his phone and scrolled to some pictures.

"I know this isn't much, but I looked around the sculptures and found something at both of them." He held the phone toward me. "Matching heel prints, from a boot." He lifted his own foot. "Unfortunately, it's just like the one you told me that everyone buys. I got some too, but . . . maybe this will lead to something at some point."

"It might. Show Calloway."

"Right, I did. It isn't much anyway. Even all the experts who came out to gather the sculptures didn't look around much."

"Really?"

"IDing the bones is Calloway's priority. That's what they were there for."

"Sure."

"What about the extra finger bones?"

I shrugged. "I haven't been given a chance to look at them."

"Damn. No one from Tucson has said a word. I'll ask if they know anything more when I talk to them again."

We both scanned the desert. A dust devil swirled up in the middle distance."

"Hazel, you really haven't heard from your father in all these years?" Graham asked.

"Not a word."

"Do you think he's still alive?"

Sometimes people who investigate crime or gruesome scenes weren't careful with their words. It wasn't that we were intentionally careless, we just knew we needed to get answers as quickly as possible. The question didn't bother me, but it surprised me a little.

"I have no sense of it at all. I don't 'feel' him, dead or alive. I wish I did."

"What about your mother?"

That question surprised me even more. "She died in childbirth."

"Oh. I'm sorry." Graham blinked as if maybe he was trying to go back in time and not ask that question. "Loss of a loved one can ruin you."

I didn't explain my complicated feelings about my mother. I'd never met her, so the loss of her wasn't what he was talking about, but it was real, nonetheless. "Don't worry about it."

"Right. All right. You're from here, and this place is . . ."

"Different?"

"It is that, but every place has its quirks." He paused. "This place has something running through it that is . . . I wouldn't say evil, but certainly unwelcoming. I feel like there should be a sign saying, "Go Away" or some such deterrent. A real black vulture eyed me as I entered."

My first thought was that I hadn't noticed what he was talking about. I wanted to defend my hometown because people liked to defend where they lived. But he wasn't completely wrong.

"It's brutal out here," he continued. "Even with the modern amenities, it seems like it would be easy to get away with murder. There's so much open space."

He had another good point. I nodded. "Do you have any idea if the authorities have found a kill site? Where at least the first set of bones became defleshed? Maybe a place where the sculptures were created?"

Graham shook his head. "Calloway says they have no idea."

"The bones didn't just put themselves there, but I can see how someone could work unbothered, unnoticed for a few days. My impression is that someone worked somewhere else and then put the sculptures out there, put together."

"I agree, but I'll keep looking around. I've run into plenty of wildlife. Snakes, scorpions, javelinas—they stink. Bats." He nodded toward the caves.

"You've been busy."

"I'm trying to help in any way I can."

"You've been inside the caves?"

Graham's eyebrows furrowed and he shook his head. "What? Absolutely not. That sounds terrifying."

"You saw the bats fly out at night?"

"I thought I might die."

I laughed. "It can be quite the experience."

"I'd say."

I didn't mention it, but the bats' nightly exodus was one of the things that Wilmot loved so much. Briefly, the thought warmed my heart. But then it transformed into something else: the flash of something that might have been a memory or an old dream. I'd gone out to look for my father one day. I found him by the caves, and he had blood on his cheek. But as I thought back to that memory, I knew it wasn't real. It was just a way for the image of blood that kept coming to me to show itself.

What was trying to come to me?

"Hazel?"

I blinked back to the moment. "Sorry. What was that?"

"It's small but mighty enough."

I tried to figure out what he was talking about.

"My lab."

"Oh. Of course. Yes, I see why you travel with it." I didn't really, but if I could take a lab with me, I would take it everywhere, probably.

We watched the dust devil as it dissipated and came to a stop.

I said, "Thanks, Graham. Stop by my place any time and I'm happy to show you my lab. Bonus, it used to be the place my father did his work in case you're interested."

Graham smiled. "I heard, and I can't wait to see it."

I thought about taking a quick look inside the caves since I was there, but I didn't have the appropriate lighting or jacket. It was dark and damp in there, sometimes downright cold. I hiked to the caves a couple times a year, not because I wanted to explore or see the bats, but because if my father left of his own accord, he might have gone there. I had never found any sign of him.

I'd found the bones of a bat once, splayed at the opening as if they were some sort of gift or invitation made just for me. The specimen had been pristine, stripped clean of tissue by the hot sun, all the bones intact.

The bat's radar must have been off, and it smashed itself into the side of the cliff, falling to its demise and then decomposing quickly. I realized that the bones would have made a perfect contribution to rogue taxidermy or Jerry Smoot's piles.

I'd found the skeleton beautiful. Wouldn't others? And what a shame for others not to see it.

Sometimes I had to remind myself that the passion of my life might be unique. Not everyone liked bones.

Even if I thought they should.

CHAPTER

17

THE SUN WAS low on the horizon by the time I left Graham's setup. On the way home, I listened to the first episode of Minnie's podcast about Wilmot. He was my father, but he'd left my life a long time ago. Some stuff I knew, but some I didn't. Mostly, I found Minnie's reporting compelling. She was very good at her job.

The first episode was about Wilmot's beginning. He had been born near Black Vulture. His parents had died before I'd been born. He'd talked about them a little, but he wasn't big on reminiscing. I knew they'd lived in the mountains, off the land, in a cabin Wilmot's father had built himself. I hadn't known that my grandfather had been killed in a mining accident when Wilmot was five, sending him and his mother into town so she might get a job.

Before the diner had become a stronghold, other restaurants fed locals, and my grandmother had worked in one until she died when Wilmot was seventeen. Their neighbor had been a taxidermist, and Wilmot had needed to do something to help pay the bills, so he'd become a willing and, apparently, naturally talented apprentice.

Wilmot explaining his childhood to me had consisted of "It was rough. We were poor. We figured it out." But I hadn't researched my father.

Once I was home, I called Calloway to give him an update, but he said he already had the names from Minnie. He asked me to meet him the next morning. I said I would.

"You know, you could have just told me about the classes," I said. "I didn't know a thing about them."

"I wasn't sure, Hazel, and . . . I don't know, taking care of you and your well-being is still important to me."

"Whatever is going on in Black Vulture is more important."

"You are right. Thank you."

I would never bring up his delicate treatment of me again. I'd made my point, and I appreciated his words too.

We ended the call, and then I listened to two more episodes before I fell into a deep sleep, exhausted from the full day. I even missed a call and some texts from Sonny, to whom I apologized the next morning and said I'd get in touch later. I was surprised when the next day didn't start with a knock on the door like the few before had. I got ready quickly and headed to the sheriff's office. I resumed listening to the podcast on the way but didn't make it much further into the episodes.

Inside the sheriff's trailer were Calloway and one of his deputies, Chris Marker. Calloway was standing behind a desk and looking at some things set atop it. Chris stood next to a whiteboard.

"Thanks for coming in," Calloway said.

"Sure."

I nodded at Chris who returned the gesture.

I wasn't popular with much of the local law enforcement. As for Chris, offhand I couldn't quite remember why he didn't like me. I had hopes for the new Black Vulture police force. Maybe we could all get along.

Chris resumed writing on the board, listing the members of the class. He ignored me as I approached and inspected his handiwork. Calloway headed back to his office for a moment.

Suddenly, I recalled why Chris didn't like me. I'd once told Calloway that Chris was a waste of a badge. I do feel like that might have been harsh, but the week before he'd dug a human skull out of a dried-out wash and then had been unable to guide us back to the spot to see if there was more to the skeleton. It had never been recovered, and he should have better marked the spot.

But I had been able to identify the skull as belonging to a young girl who'd been kidnapped from Mexico, being taken to who knows where. I'd traveled to Mexico to work with authorities there. Calloway hadn't been happy about that decision, but, ultimately, he was glad we'd been able to give the girl's family some answers.

I watched Chris, silently reading the names again and pondering if I knew more about them than I previously thought I did.

"The only person I could reach right off was Thalia. I wanted to confirm she was still around before going to talk to her. I'll find out more," Calloway said as he came back out of his office.

"I just started listening to the podcast," I said, "What should everyone remember? Minnie calls the sculpture an abomination, right?"

"Yes, and she says it was scary but that's about it."

"Okay. So, what happened then?"

"Then the classes ended."

"That's it?"

"That's what she says in the podcast."

"And that's compelling?"

"She's good with the buildup and the remaining mystery."

"And Wilmot disappeared shortly after it?"

"Yep."

I looked at the names. "Something bad, worse than a bloody artifact, happened back then. I don't know if it's tied to the current problems, but . . ."

"I feel like it is."

"Me too."

"Minnie was a kid. They all were, but I wish I would have known about this back then. I've been the sheriff for a long time." Calloway rubbed at the back of his neck.

"My father could have told you."

Calloway nodded, and I could tell that was the part that might bother him the most; Wilmot hadn't come to him after something bad had happened. Wilmot could have trusted Calloway with anything, or that's what I thought. Probably Calloway thought so too.

I said, "Minnie said that Danielle works at the butcher shop."

Calloway shook his head. "Not anymore she doesn't, and her number is disconnected. I'm going to head out to her place too."

"Jeff Ranke is still fixing cars in his garage."

"Yep. I'm going to swing by there."

"Want some company?"

"Yeah, I want you to come along. That's why I called you."

Even if I couldn't have seen it in the corner of my vision, I could feel Chris bristle.

It had been long enough that I wasn't quite as angry at him as I'd once been, but still, I sure would have liked to have more of Maria Galvez to return to her family.

"I do. Thanks," I said.

We left my Jeep, now embarrassingly covered in grime, out front. I was going to have to clean it at some point soon.

We headed toward Calloway's old but air-conditioned Tahoe. I hopped in and buckled up.

"First stop, Jeff. He's not far," Calloway said.

As we made our way, I told him about my visit with Graham by the caves.

"I thought I'd have more for him to do, but the investigators from Tucson took everything and did not invite him along. I'll send him home soon."

"He's trying to catch someone in the act of setting up another sculpture."

"He told me. I'll take the help."

"Would the new police chief help? Jenna?"

Calloway didn't answer immediately.

"Sheriff?" I asked.

"I'm sure they'll be fine."

"What's going on?" Quiet music had been coming through the speakers. I turned the radio off as I asked the question.

"Nothing. I just don't know them yet."

"You seemed to get along a couple nights ago." I thought back. "They were gathering fingerprints when I went to bed. Did something go wrong?"

"No, they didn't find any helpful prints, including on the handprint, but nothing went wrong. They have a good computer rendition of the handprint too, so I'm hopeful we'll find something."

"What is it, then?"

Calloway shouldn't have said the words he said next, but we knew each other well enough to know we could trust each other.

"I don't think Verro is from where he said he is."

"Virgie could verify. She hired him."

"I'm aware of that."

"Wait, what is making you suspicious?"

"I can't find record of him in Prescott."

"That's not good."

"No, but maybe not accurate. Things get lost in . . . translation."

"What does Virgie say?"

"She gave me his references to call myself. I haven't had time yet."

I was speechless.

"Hey," Calloway said. "Don't read too much into this right now. I'm being extra careful. That's all. I'm sure it will all be fine."

I nodded. Had I said anything to Verro or Jenna that might compromise something important? I didn't think I had, but Verro had been the one to gather the prints. I'd been way too tired to supervise, so I hoped he'd done a good job.

"Seriously, Hazel, put it out of your mind for now. We've got plenty to do."

I nodded again.

To get to Jeff's place, we had to travel through town. As Calloway slowed the vehicle because we were in the town limits, Pearly stepped out of the post office and waved us down.

The sheriff came to a stop and rolled down his window. "You okay?"

"Fine, Sheriff, just fine. Hello there, Hazel. How are you?"

"I'm good. You?"

"Fine," she said again, but the frown on her face belied the continual repeat of the word. She glanced back toward the post office.

"What's going on, Pearly?" the sheriff asked. "Do you need me to check something?"

"I . . . no, I just . . . I'm old, Sheriff."

"Okay."

"If I've learned anything at all, it's to listen to my intuition, and my intuition was telling me something two nights ago. I leave out the back door. I park my car on the side, so's the customers can have all the places out front if they need 'em," she nodded in that direction, "and it's easier for me to get to my car. Anyway, two nights ago I was sure there was someone back there."

The sheriff and I were listening intently. I'd been back there recently enough to wonder if maybe she'd heard me. "Did you *see* anyone?"

"Did you look around?" Calloway finally asked.

"No, no. I did not, because . . . well, it was my intuition. It told me not to look back. It told me I might see someone who didn't want to be seen."

I nodded, glad she'd listened to her gut but wishing she'd called Calloway back then. Or even me.

"It was late. My knees were giving me fits all day, so I had to take a break in the afternoon. I might have napped a bit. I ended up staying late to get my work done."

"That's good to know, Pearly." Calloway paused. "I'll take a look back there this afternoon. Keep the back door locked for now. And, hey, how about you go out the front door for a while? Park out front. Customers will figure it out."

"Okay. If you think so."

"I do. Thank you for letting me know, and do me a favor, call me if you sense or see anything at all. Anything." He handed her a card even though she probably already had his number.

"You're welcome." She fell into thought for a moment, and then her eyes lit as she looked up at me. "I have a box for you, Hazel. From Missouri. Want me to go get it?"

I shook my head. "No, I'll come back later. Thanks."

We sat there for as long as it took Pearly to turn and make her way back into the post office.

"Did you charge that camera again?" Calloway asked.

"I didn't see the point. I ordered a new one, though. The box from Missouri isn't it."

"Go ahead and charge the old one. Put it back up. Could I have access to that app too?"

"Sure. I'll text you the details and the password."

"Thanks, Hazel."

As he put the car back into drive, Calloway grabbed his radio and called for Chris, who answered at once. Calloway ordered him to take a look at the space behind the post office. Chris said he'd get right on it.

I hadn't told Calloway about gathering the boot. I should have, but I didn't have confirmation that it had belonged to Wilmot, and I felt kind of foolish for fishing it out anyway.

"The scarf?" I asked when the call to Chris was finished. Graham had told me about it, but I wanted to confirm.

"It's identical to the one around the skeleton's neck, but there's no helpful DNA on it."

"That was Verro's job too, getting the scarf to the investigators?"

"Hazel, I'm on everything. I shouldn't have told you my suspicions, but I did. Let's put it on the back burner for now."

"Copy that," I said.

Jeff's garage door was open. His property spread over about one acre, most of it covered in gravel that he'd thrown down. A stray weed or two popped up through the rocks in the spots where he didn't park the vehicles he worked on.

His home wasn't zoned to conduct business, but he had no nearby neighbors, and no one complained. He did good work, and charged fair prices.

Most of the home businesses around town prepared food. It had only been recently that an Arizona law was passed allowing home kitchens to cook food for sale, but I knew there'd been nothing to keep Jeff's business safe from enforcement, except, of course, the citizens of Black Vulture who would cause a big stink if anyone tried to shut him down.

He worked alone, but I'd witnessed his wife, Claire, sitting on a stool next to the lift, drinking beer from a bottle and talking to him about Jesus. Jeff claimed he still wasn't a believer, but for a reason no one seemed to understand, he and Claire had a watertight marriage, even though she spent most of her time proselytizing.

Jeff sent us a suspicious frown as Calloway and I got out of the Tahoe.

"Sheriff. Hazel. What's up? You all find some bones you need to ask me about?"

"In a roundabout way, maybe," Calloway said.

"I wondered."

"You did? Why?"

Jeff shrugged. "Don't know. It just . . . those . . . sculptures I've heard talk about. There's something about 'em. That's all."

He'd confirmed my suspicions regarding the spread of news regarding the sculptures. It was out there.

"Hm." Calloway watched as Jeff put a wrench back into a toolbox.

"Come on in. We'll have Claire pour some lemonade."

Jeff led us inside his 1980s home. It was clean and neat inside, but the furniture hadn't changed for decades. Mine hadn't either, and mine was even older. Against the backdrop of Black Vulture, most things were just old and tired.

"Sheriff?" Claire came around a wooden pillar that separated the kitchen space from the front room. "What's wrong?" She gave me a cursory once-over but didn't say hello.

"I just have some questions, Claire. We won't be long."

"How about some lemonade, honey?"

"Uh. Sure." Claire retreated to the kitchen and opened the refrigerator door.

"Have a seat," Jeff said.

Calloway and I sat on the couch. Jeff relaxed in the recliner I was sure he probably always sat in when he was in this room. I eyed a colorful ceramic Jesus sculpture on the end table next to me. It looked very fragile.

"Okay, what's going on?" Jeff asked.

"I wonder if you remember something from back in the day," Calloway began.

"I have a good memory. What day?"

"Wilmot Dylan's classes."

Jeff's eyes widened for a brief moment. "How did you figure out I was a student? Minnie's podcast didn't mention our names."

"She said you all swore yourselves to secrecy," Calloway said.

"Which means she's the one who spilled the beans, amirite?"

"Couldn't be helped, Jeff. Things have happened to make it important for us to know."

"Yeah. Like I said, I wondered. Those 'sculptures.' They're like taxidermy, right."

"They aren't taxidermy," I said.

"I know, but—"

"I get it, Jeff," Calloway said. "The same thing occurred to me. We don't have a direct tie, but Wilmot Dylan's name has come into the conversation."

He looked at me quickly. "Your dad's bones?"

"We aren't sure," Calloway said. "We're investigating. So, you do remember the classes?"

"Sure. Of course." He looked at me. "It got crazy back then, right?"

Calloway nodded at me, prompting me to reply. "Jeff, I don't remember one thing about those classes. Should I?"

He sat forward on the chair and rubbed the stubble on his chin as he fell into thought for a moment. "I can't . . . Hang on . . . No, I guess I don't remember you being around much during that time, specifically. I mean, you were always a part of Wilmot's life, so it was rare for anyone to think of one without the other, but I can't bring up any scene with you there." He paused again. "But I don't remember your dad telling us to keep anything from you." Jeff smiled. "He adored you."

I swallowed the surprise wave of emotion his words had prompted.

"Jeff, I need to ask you about the dynamics of the class. Something happened to scare Minnie away, then end the classes. Are you aware of that incident and do you remember what happened?"

Jeff took a breath and blew it out through puffed cheeks. Claire brought in a tray with glasses of lemonade and set it on the coffee table. As she stood to leave again, she sent Jeff a look that I interpreted as "don't talk," but he didn't seem to notice as he reached for one of the drinks.

Calloway and I each took one as well, but neither of us sipped.

"Okay, okay," Jeff said. "Let me start from the beginning. So, I had taken in a buck for Wilmot to mount. I was seventeen and it was my first buck." Jeff shrugged. "I was proud."

Though I didn't hunt and I knew that Calloway didn't either, there was no one in or around Black Vulture who would criticize any sort of legal kill. Hunting was a way of life for lots of people out here, as well as a genuine way to feed their family.

"We get it," Calloway said.

"Sure. I told Wilmot that I would love to learn how he did what he did." He held his hands out, palms up. "I work with my hands, and it just seemed an extension of that, as well as something creative. Wilmot told me that he would teach a class if I could round up four or five more students. He said he'd do it free of charge." He paused and shifted in his seat.

I noticed the move and said, "What, Jeff?"

"I need to add something here, but this isn't really the right spot. Those of us who took the classes never told our parents. There weren't many classes anyway. From this vantage point, I know we should have told them. I don't know the laws, but maybe us doing such a thing without our parents' permission was a big deal, but that day we all talked about it, we just said we didn't think it was. I gotta admit, though, from that moment, it felt like we were all part of a bigger secret, and then . . . well, when it happened, we knew we had to keep everything to ourselves."

Calloway set his lemonade back on the tray. "I think we're getting ahead of ourselves, Jeff. Tell me about the first few classes. What did you all do? Who were the students and how did they behave?"

"Okay. Right."

For the next five minutes, Jeff confirmed the names of the students in the class and shared unimportant details. Wilmot had gone over the basics for taxidermy, not working with anything but finished mounts. He shared the supplies used and made sure everyone was aware of what really happened—the reality of the skin or hide of an animal that had once been alive being placed over a form to give it a lifelike look. He shared tools and materials. He talked about the ethics of the business, the range of opinions, the downright hatred that he'd felt from some people.

Jeff remembered Wilmot seemed to work hard not to insult those who'd insulted him, but he hadn't been great at it. I knew that if I hadn't been in his life, there was a good chance that Wilmot would have been one of the many locals who planted a trailer out in the middle of nowhere, welcoming visitors and customers as he aimed a gun in their direction. With me around, he tempered any paranoia.

Hearing from Jeff about Wilmot's efforts to be balanced left me slightly doubtful, but Jeff didn't seem to be anything but straightforward.

"Shoot, I'm the one who got everyone together for the class. I didn't look at it like this back then, but we were all outsiders in one way or another. You know. Minnie was unconventional but not intimidating, except she was the only one of us who didn't come from some sort of abusive situation. My parents were, still are, assholes. Thalia's grandmother burned her back with cigarettes. Danielle's mother was always drunk—and a nasty drunk. Silas and Johnny were beaten daily."

"That's horrible, Jeff. I'm sorry to hear that," I said.

"Me too, Jeff. I . . . well, we're not always made aware of those situations, but we do try to do something about them," Calloway added.

Jeff shook his head. "Nah, Sheriff, I know. That's not why . . . I guess I just want you to understand why we thought it was such a cool thing to have Wilmot teach us, of all things, taxidermy. It gave us a place to go that wasn't home." He looked at me. "Your father wasn't cruel. Most of us were used to some cruelty in our days."

My throat tightened again, but I wouldn't allow myself to cry here, no matter how hard I had to dig my fingernails into my palms.

"Go on," Calloway prompted.

Pain or stress pinched the corners of Jeff's eyes. "Something got ugly and way out of hand."

"That's what we're here for, Jeff. Tell us. Look, if you were involved in something that you're afraid of being in trouble for, let me assure you that spilling the beans to us will go a long way to helping you through."

"Don't believe them, Jeff," Claire called from the kitchen. "The police don't ever take care of people like us."

A shadow passed over Calloway's eyes. He simply looked at Jeff and gave him a confident nod.

"I didn't do nothing," he said. "But someone did."

"We're listening."

"It was only about the sixth or maybe seventh class or so. I was running late, literally running to get downtown from the bus stop in front of my house. Anyway, I missed everything that happened to lead to all the yelling that I heard when I went through the museum's door. I could hear everyone screaming and yelling from back in the studio. I remember I hesitated but ultimately couldn't stop myself from seeing what was going on. I pushed through the door to the studio and opened it wide." He shook his head. "There was a lot of blood, everywhere. My eyes went from person to person. I wanted to know who was hurt. Wilmot was trying to calm everybody down, but even he was covered in blood. Minnie wasn't there, but everyone else was, and so was . . . a thing on the table."

"Blood? What thing?"

Jeff described the thing almost exactly like Minnie had, but she hadn't said that everyone was covered in blood. I gulped away the chilling fear that Jeff's words instilled in me. I needed to focus.

After he gathered himself for another moment, Jeff looked at Calloway. "I never saw him do it, but I figured it was Silas who brought the thing in. It was Silas who brought in the blood too, I'm sure, a bucket of it."

"Bucket?" Calloway said.

This was news to both of us.

Jeff sighed and nodded. "Yeah. Let me back up just a little again. Silas heard about rogue taxidermy and told us all about it at the previous class. We all thought it was cool, artistic, but Silas . . . I don't know, I guess he twisted it or something. He created the thing for us to see, but somehow along the way, his dad heard about the class and was pissed. You know, Silas's father, Bud, he actually hired Wilmot to create some mounts over the years. I don't know, Sheriff, I think Bud was just always looking at a reason to be angry with his son. Silas got beaten, and then, again this is only hindsight, he took it out on us by bringing that thing in."

"He brought the thing and a bucket of blood?" Calloway asked.

Jeff nodded.

"Where did the blood come from?"

"Dunno." Jeff eyed the sheriff. "But I got the heck out of there, scared. I know that none of us saw Silas or Bud ever again. Heard they left town that day."

"You got out of there?" Calloway said.

Jeff nodded. "I ran like a scared little kid."

"At what point?"

"Right after I saw everything. Wilmot yelled at me to stop, but I didn't. I ran."

"When did you all come together to make a vow of secrecy?" I asked.

Jeff shook his head. "We never came together. Thalia just told me about it. I said I wouldn't say a word. Shoot, I was too scared for anyone to know anyway. I wasn't gonna tell a soul. We just talked about it as we ran into each other, I guess."

"So Silas couldn't be in on keeping it all a secret?" I asked. "He was gone."

"Thalia told me that Wilmot was taking care of talking to Silas and Johnny."

"Johnny Clark?" I asked.

"Yep."

"Why didn't you talk to Johnny?" I didn't believe that my father would have asked kids to keep a vow of secrecy. Calloway and I exchanged a glance that told me he thought the same.

"I never saw Johnny again either. But I'd never seen much of him before. He barely went to school. After some time passed, I just kind of forgot about him."

Calloway looked at Jeff again. "Have you heard from Silas or Johnny over the years?"

"No, sir, but . . ."

Claire came around the wall. "Jeff . . . Don't . . ."

"It's okay, baby. They need to know."

"What?" Calloway asked.

"Claire and I were in Tucson a few years back. We came upon a homeless man who walked up to us and said he was Wilmot Dylan." Jeff's eyes darted to me. "He wasn't, but he looked like Silas might look like as an adult, sort of like his dad, but still Silas. I tried to talk to him, but he ran off, muttering something like 'sins of the father' or some such nonsense."

"It isn't nonsense," Claire said. "It's biblical. Exodus 20:5 and Numbers 14:18. But, later, Ezekiel 18:20 clarifies that the child shall not suffer for the father's sin. Still, though, lots of people hold on to the earlier testaments regarding children somehow paying for the sins of their father."

"Whose father?"

Jeff shrugged. "Never got any clarification."

Calloway nodded at Claire. "Thank you." He looked at me. He knew what my attacker had said to me. I just frowned.

Jeff said, "I wondered if he was talking about Hazel, but she was here, and I really didn't think he was Wilmot. I thought maybe, but only maybe, it was Silas and that he wasn't well. We kind of forgot about it not long afterward. Time goes on, you know. Things keep happening to get your attention."

"It was disturbing at the time, though," Claire said.

"I get it." Calloway bit his bottom lip. "Can you tell us more about the blood?"

Jeff sighed. "Claire, sweetie. You don't want to hear this part. Okay, hon?"

A range of emotions pulled at Claire's features, but ultimately she seemed to agree. "I'll be in the bedroom, praying for all of you."

"Thank you, baby," Jeff said.

We watched Claire disappear down the hallway.

Jeff scratched his neck before giving Calloway his full attention. "I made a vow not to talk about this."

"What if your safety, or Claire's, is in jeopardy?"

"I can take care of us."

"I don't disagree, but this is serious, Jeff," Calloway said.

Jeff frowned. "All right. When I walked into the room, Silas was standing in a corner. He was covered in blood and holding a bucket with even more. Everybody had blood on them." Jeff put his hand on his stomach. "God, the smell alone was horrific. Everyone was freaking out, trying to get him to put down the bucket. Thalia was trying to get out of the room, but Wilmot kept stopping her. He was trying to get everyone to calm down. When I came in, he looked at me and told me to shut the door. I did, behind me as I ran. I heard that Wilmot took care of getting everyone cleaned up and home. Let them take showers and everything. Washed their clothes. I found some blood on my shoes later. Threw them away and wore my pop's old sneakers until I could buy something else for me."

Calloway looked at me. I could see the question in his eyes. Did I remember any of this strange behavior? A group of teenagers taking showers, bloody clothes, the bloody lab?

I shook my head. "I don't remember any of it."

"Susan helped, I heard," Jeff said.

I blinked at the news, the name. "Who?"

"Susan," Jeff said.

"Who the hell is that?" I asked.

"Your aunt, I guess." Jeff shrugged.

My world spun, tipped on its axis. I didn't have an aunt—no, that wasn't it. I didn't have an aunt in Black Vulture.

Wilmot had been an only child, but my mother had grown up with a sister. I kind of remembered meeting her as she traveled through town when I was a little girl, but that was all I knew of her.

"Susan Shaw. She's your mom's sister."

I squinted as I looked at Jeff. "No."

"What do you mean, no?"

"What are you talking about?" I demanded.

"Do you know Susan Shaw?" Jeff asked Calloway.

"Not at all."

"She lives somewhere around here, in the county, I think," Jeff said.

"I don't know all the residents of the county, Jeff," Calloway said.

Jeff looked at me again. "I saw her not long ago. She's still around. Wilmot introduced her as his sister-in-law. She was around during the classes. She was . . . mostly quiet. If I look back on it now, I wonder if Wilmot thought it would be better to have another adult around, so she was there. I don't know, though."

How big was this black hole in my memory? I didn't remember Aunt Susan other than faintly that one time. Had she been hanging around our place when I wasn't there? Where had she been after Wilmot disappeared?

Where had I been during all this time, which was sounding more like a slice from some horror movie than real life?

Had it all been so traumatic that my brain had suppressed it?

"Jeff, I don't remember any of this," I said.

"I guess that checks out because I really don't remember seeing you around, but I don't know how your dad managed to keep it all hidden from you."

I didn't either. "Does Minnie talk about Susan in the podcast?"

"No. She doesn't mention any names other than Wilmot's."

I looked at Calloway. "She didn't mention her to me."

Calloway nodded at me and then put us on track, cleared his throat. "What happened after that?"

"Nothing. It was done. Over. Never to be spoken about again, until now, I guess." He dragged his hand over the stubble again. "Look, I don't know anything about mental health stuff, and I really didn't know anything back then. We were kids. But knowing the little that I do know now, I would probably say that Silas had some sort of mental break. He was inconsolable, wild."

"Can you remember anything he specifically said?" Calloway asked.

Jeff considered the question and then nodded. "Yeah. Silas said something like he hated us all and would kill us before we could kill him. I got out of there. Seeing something like that, with vicious eyes and all that blood. The best word I have for it is 'scary.' It was plain old scary. We were all eager to put it behind us, make that vow to never talk about it. It made it less real, and I was all for that."

"Any chance you know what specifically prompted it, Jeff? You mentioned his father's anger, but do you know what happened to Silas?"

Jeff sat up straighter. "Nope."

Calloway looked at me and then back at Jeff. "Do you think Susan would know more?"

"She was the only other adult around, but, shoot, I have no idea. Maybe she made some vow too."

I listened as Calloway asked more questions that Jeff didn't have answers for, but not with the gusto I'd originally had.

How had my father kept all of this from me?

And what else was I going to learn about his long-ago secrets?

CHAPTER

18

Susan Shaw did, indeed, live in the county, not in a trailer out in the middle of nowhere, but in a house about five miles south of Black Vulture.

Calloway and I received this information through his radio a few minutes after he called Chris and asked him to look her up.

She'd lived there for six years, but he couldn't pinpoint where she'd come from or if she used to live somewhere else nearby.

"She never came around after Wilmot left?" Calloway asked after the information came through.

"No. I'm sure of it."

The radio buzzed again. "Sheriff?"

"Go ahead, Chris."

"We just got some information from the lab."

"I'm listening."

"They got a confident ID on the first set of bones."

"Okay. Who?"

"Is anyone with you?"

"Affirmative, but it's okay." Calloway looked at me as if to ask if it really was okay. I nodded, prepared to hear that my father's bones had, indeed, been found, even though I'd already been told they weren't his. The hits might just keep on coming.

"The bones are confirmed as belonging to a man named Silas Reynolds, a homeless guy who lived around Tucson."

The news landed with the heft of a silent weight in the truck. It was a lot to process, particularly since we'd just heard Silas's name from Jeff.

"Sheriff?" Chris's voice came through again. "You there?"

"Yeah. Listen, I need you to try to track Mr. Reynolds's movements over the past twenty to twenty-five years, if you can. Copy?"

A long pause later, Chris responded, "Copy."

"Wait. Any word on the second set?" Calloway asked.

"No, sir."

Calloway placed the handset back on its hook and looked at me again.

"It feels like we're on to something, but as we learn more, the details get more confusing." I huffed out a nervous breath. "What in the world happened back then?"

"It must have been terrifying."

I lifted my finger and looked at the simple bandage I'd used this morning. There would be little to no scar. It felt like ages ago that the man from the street had attacked me. I could still conjure the stink of his body and breath. But he hadn't been Silas.

"The guy who knocked you down wasn't Silas," Calloway spoke my thoughts.

I'd been certain that it hadn't been Wilmot either. I would know my own father, wouldn't I? Considering all that he'd kept from me, maybe not.

I shook it off . . . for now.

"Where to?" I asked, hoping we were going to talk to Susan but knowing I needed to dig deep for some sort of foreign strength if we were going to see her.

"Let's talk to Thalia, if you're up for it."

I would be up for it. I just needed to put everything else out of my mind for now. It was a lot. "Of course." Similar to Chris, my tone was infused with forced confidence. If Calloway noticed, he didn't comment.

* * *

Thalia Deem lived in one of the old miner's houses, built to give shelter but not much more than that. She'd married Freddy Deem, a good guy who worked all kinds of construction. I didn't know them well, but when he was employed on a big project or maybe some building in Tucson, he'd stop by the diner at that same time I was there early in the morning for a large coffee and a cinnamon roll to go. Leaving cash on the counter, with a smile and a friendly salute, he'd thank whoever had packed up the items before he took off for work.

Today, Thalia was wrangling two toddlers as we stopped on the street in front of the house. She seemed to be in a bad mood, a frown pulling at her mouth. When she spotted us, it only got deeper.

The two kids did not appear to be listening to her, but when they spotted us, they moved right next to their mom, one grabbing a hand, the other wrapping her arms around Thalia's leg.

"What's up?" Thalia asked as we got out of the car. "Freddy?"

"We aren't here regarding Freddy," Calloway said. "As far as we know, he's fine."

Relief relaxed the deep discontent of her features, but she still didn't look happy. "Why are you here?"

"Can we come in?" Calloway asked.

Thalia's eyes darted back and forth between Calloway and me, her eyes landing on me. "Again, why are you here?"

"Have you heard about the . . ." Calloway lowered his voice probably because of the kids. "skeletons?" he asked her finally.

"I have, but I thought maybe it was made up. Sounds made up."

"It's real. Hazel is a forensic consultant. She's helping."

"The bone woman. Yeah. You're here because of the skeletons?" Thalia didn't hesitate to speak in her normal voice and volume.

"Thalia, could we come in for a minute?"

"Shit, Sheriff. Sure, I suppose."

"Mom, you said a bad word," the little boy said.

I worked to keep from smiling, but Thalia wasn't amused.

"For good reason, buddy." She turned toward the house but looked back over her shoulder. "Folks think they can just interrupt schedules and all."

Calloway and I followed everyone else inside.

The window air conditioner cooled the small front room well. The house was decorated in almost a modern flair, even though there were toys everywhere. I wondered how she managed to keep the light-colored furniture from getting dirty. Only one of the couch's cushions was off kilter.

"Give me a second," she said to us as she led the kids into the kitchen.

Though there was a half wall between the front room and the kitchen, from the couch Calloway and I could watch as she set the kids up with juice boxes and snacks. She didn't offer us anything but came back to the front room and put her hands on her hips.

"Be quick," she said.

"Thalia, do you remember the taxidermy classes that Wilmot Dylan conducted back when you were sixteen or seventeen?" Calloway asked.

I'd never witnessed the color actually drain from someone's face until that moment. That's what happened as her eyes got wide.

"No." She stepped closer to us and lowered her voice. "We can't talk about that in front of the kids."

Calloway nodded. "That might be, but we have a few questions. Is there someone who could watch them for a few minutes."

"No, there's just me." She glanced back at their peaceful enjoyment of the snacks and back at us. "Step out front for a minute. I can watch them through the screen door, but you'll have to keep your voices down."

So much for the comfortable couch and air-conditioning.

We did as she asked. She stood at the door, making sure she could see the kids through the glass. She kept her hand on the knob.

"I made a vow not to talk about this shit," she said. "I know we were kids, but who spilled the beans?"

"It doesn't matter," Calloway said. "We just need to know what happened."

"Jesus, it was a fucking nightmare." She glanced inside at the curse but then turned back to us. "Blood, a terrifying animal thing. That crazy bastard, Silas, and his 'creativity.' His behavior messed with all of us. I'm sure we could have all used therapy because of just that day, but who has the money for that crap?"

Calloway had more questions than she was going to take time to answer, I was sure, but he cut to the chase.

"So, Silas brought in the . . . thing?"

"Well, I didn't see him do it, but I was there when he threw the blood on all of us. He was freaking out, but I don't know what happened much before that. I wasn't there yet."

"Do you know what happened to him after that?"

"I think he and his father left Black Vulture, but I don't know. I never saw him, them, again. I thought maybe Wilmot told them to leave." She looked at me. "Your father kept it together during something that few people could."

"But he didn't call the authorities?" I asked.

Thalia gave a gruff laugh. "No, he didn't." She paused. "He separated us, though."

"What does that mean?" Calloway asked.

"He put me and Danielle on the back patio and took Silas and Johnny to the kitchen." She paused. "My God. It was awful." She brought her gaze back up. "And I don't like thinking about it."

"Then what happened?" I asked.

Thalia sighed. "Some woman came out to the patio. I can't remember her name, but she'd been there a couple times before. She calmed down me and Danielle, told us we were going to be okay." She paused. "She brought us some sodas and told us she'd get us cleaned up in a few minutes. She went inside." Tears filled her eyes as she stared at Calloway.

"Thalia. What?" he said.

Thalia sniffed away the tears, wiped her nose with the back of her hand. "Then she screamed."

"Inside the museum?" I asked.

"Yeah, she screamed, and . . . we couldn't run." The last word came out choked. "That God damn door was locked, and we didn't want to jump over the wall and run through The Wild."

I felt her fear. It had to be terrifying. I reached to touch her arm, but she pulled it back. "Don't."

I nodded.

"We freaked for maybe only a couple of minutes, but it felt like forever. The woman came out and got us and took us upstairs. She got us cleaned up. Washed our clothes. Fed us. She calmed us down before she took us home."

"Where did Silas, Johnny, and Wilmot go?"

Thalia shrugged. "I never did know. I never saw any of them again. I swore my ass off that I would never tell anything. I didn't ever want to talk about it again. I'm a mom now, you don't get to blame me for anything." She glared at Calloway.

"I'm not, Thalia. I just need the truth."

"And that's what I've told you. Here's another truth, I'm going to punch Minnie in the face when I see her again."

"That would be assault."

"Yeah, we'll see. Bitch wasn't even there but made us live it all again for her friggin' podcast. She promised she wouldn't tell, so she broke the promise first."

"I'm sorry, Thalia," I said.

She looked at me. "Yeah, whatever. I heard about those skeletons, and I thought there was no way they could be real, but then I thought that if they were, I bet Wilmot Dylan was involved."

"Why did you think that?" Calloway asked before I could.

She shook her head slowly. "I don't know, but I just did. And I don't like it. You better keep us all safe, Sheriff."

"Yes, ma'am."

"Mom!" a voice called from inside.

"I gotta get in there."

Calloway extended a business card to Thalia. She looked at it like she was going to throw it away, but at least she could rummage around her garbage can for it if something important came to her.

Without a goodbye, she disappeared inside and closed the door.

Calloway and I shared a look. More layers, maybe answers, but who knew if they were helpful.

"Next?" I asked.

Calloway nodded and we made our way to the Tahoe.

Okay. Enough. He was supposed to be done by now. It wasn't supposed to take this long, but . . . well, the best laid plans and all.

He unfurled the felt pack and inspected the knives. Shiny steel sparkled in the light, the edges so sharp they even looked *sharp. He kept them that way always.*

His work had been labor intensive. The kill had been the easy part. It was everything that had come before and after that that had been difficult. He'd had to track everyone down, figure out a plan that would put him in the middle of all of them—hiding in plain sight.

Cleaning the bones, then digging up the other ones. It was all so much work.

His main target of course had been Hazel Dylan. And he still hadn't killed her. He could have, but he'd been too curious to get to know her, hoped for more answers before he finished all he needed to do. Got rid of her once and for all. Forever.

He didn't think anyone had figured out that he was here for her. Even she didn't know that her bones would be his masterpiece.

No one had suspected him. There was time. So far, so good.

He needed to get to Hazel, at the right time and in the perfect place, of course. It would happen, soon enough. But now he liked her. He didn't want to like her, but he did. He respected her. He wanted to watch her work. His mouth watered at the mere thought of watching her brain as she inspected bones, deduced what might have happened to the person who they used to belong to.

She was smart.

And, sexy as hell, frankly.

"Stop it," he told himself.

Well, maybe he could think about her for just for a minute or two. It couldn't hurt.

He could see the two of them together. Both were products of broken homes, strange circumstances. Black Vulture. Coming from the town was almost enough in itself to create a commonality that was tough to crack, something that created a forcefield around you to keep you hidden from the regular world, the one that was normal. The one that wasn't Black Vulture.

He could see them standing next to each other, holding hands, embracing, and then . . .

It was like fireworks silently exploded in his mind's eye. White static, flashes of uncomfortable light. Pain in his temples.

He fell to his knees, the palms of his hands at his temples. It would calm down. He just had to stop thinking . . . of those things.

The things he hadn't been able to think about for years, all because of what happened in Black Vulture.

All because of Wilmot and Hazel Dylan.

No, he didn't want to hold Hazel Dylan's hand, pull her close. He wanted to rid the world of her, get rid of the last sign of Wilmot Dylan.

Changing his thoughts helped. The pain eased, and the lights and flashes calmed to manageable. He opened his eyes a crack, testing the light. He'd be okay in a few minutes.

Now he just had to remember to put his thoughts about Hazel Dylan where they were supposed to go.

He couldn't wait to cut away her body's excess and expose and then touch her bones. He couldn't wait to touch her femur.

His life would be complete then. He would be free from the past, and he could finally live the life he was meant to have.

He couldn't keep putting it off.

CHAPTER 19

I WASN'T INVITED TO talk to Susan. I made it clear to Calloway that if he didn't take me, I would go on my own, soon enough. I had questions. He made it clear to me that back when my father disappeared, the authorities did reach out to her, but she didn't respond. This left me unsettled and angry, which was a good reason for me not to go with Calloway right now.

What the hell, Aunt Susan?

He pulled the Tahoe next to my Jeep. "I'll call you later. Take a break, Hazel. This is . . . all so weird. I didn't mean to pull you into something that seems to be turning quite this personal. Is there anything else you can work on? Go get that box from Pearly."

"Yeah. Okay."

"Good. Put your thoughts there. I'll let you know what I hear. You need some time, and I can't talk to Susan with you there. You know that?"

I didn't move. "This is all coming from some sick take on art and a bucket of blood?"

"I don't know. I'll figure it out, but I want you to be on your toes."

I patted the knife in my pocket. "I'm good."

"There's always someone better. Carry the gun."

"I'll be careful."

"Get home."

I shut the passenger door and watched him drive toward Susan Shaw's house. I couldn't help but think that there was some mistake, that my biological aunt did not live in the same county as I did, without so much as saying hello to me after Wilmot disappeared.

There was no better take on this: I'd been abandoned by my father. Was he dead or alive, and did that make it better or worse?

It was like the old adage—is there other life out there? Either answer is terrifying. The thought made me think of Sonny.

I grabbed my phone and texted him: *Dinner? I know a great pizza place.*

He answered quickly. *How about I cook tonight? I make an amazing pizza pie.*

He'd already prepared a picnic for us. We could go out. It would be fun. But the idea of a quiet house and pizza with a guy who challenged my typical sour mood and expression wasn't unappealing.

An address came through. It was attached to a home in Tumacácori, the community right next door to Black Vulture.

Okay then. I texted. *Let me get cleaned up.*

See you in an hour or so?

I'll be there.

I hopped into the filthy Jeep and steered back to the post office. I picked up the box from Pearly, who mentioned that "that nice boy Chris looked back behind the building and didn't find anything." Maybe she was imagining it all, she said. I told her that it was good that she'd mentioned it to the sheriff and she should stay on her toes.

I set the box inside my lab before I hopped in the shower and searched my closet for something that wasn't a T-shirt and jeans. The one dress I owned was for work meetings, so clean jeans and a blouse with some fringe it was. The shirt made me look like I was headed to a rodeo, but it would have to do.

As I was in the closet, my eyes angled toward the back corner. I needed to get going, but I spotted three boxes that had been tucked back there a long time ago. I hadn't forgotten about them, but I hadn't really remembered them either.

I set the clothes on the bed and then dug through shoes and smaller boxes, making my way to the three that I was pretty sure had been packed and tucked away by Wilmot.

They were all about two feet by two feet cubed. They'd been sealed shut, the edges of the tape browned from time.

Once they were out of the closet, I put my hands on my hips and glanced down at them. Were there things inside that might help solve crimes, answer mysteries? I wasn't interested in looking into the past for any other reason. I was going to talk to Susan, but I wasn't going to search the boxes for who she was or had been.

I took a deep breath and let it out. I grabbed my knife and sliced open the first box.

Inside were books. That was it. They looked like interesting enough books, but I could not understand why they might have been boxed up and saved. Even if they'd been my mother's, why had Wilmot wanted to keep them?

I grabbed the first couple on the top. I was a reader, and I knew enough about popular fiction to understand how these books were a time capsule of sorts. If they were, indeed, my mother's, she'd liked romance back in the day. I'd heard of a few of the authors, but my tastes went mostly to thrillers and mysteries. I set the books back into the box.

The second box knocked me off my axis for a moment. Clothes had been packed tightly inside it. Feminine clothes. Pastel colors and pretty flowers.

Tears choked my throat.

I had never met my mother. Wilmot hadn't spoken about her. There weren't pictures of her everywhere. He hadn't disrespected her existence, but he hadn't celebrated it either.

Those around Black Vulture who'd known her said she was "lovely and kind," but I would never know. Unless Aunt Susan wanted to tell me more about her.

Now at least I knew that she liked to dress in a much more feminine way than I did.

I swallowed the surprise tears and grabbed the item on top of the box. It was a pretty dress with tiny blue flowers.

"This seems suspiciously fortuitous," I muttered to myself as I held up the dress in front of me and looked in the dresser mirror.

I wasn't sure if the entire image was pretty or not, but the dress was, if maybe dated. However, Black Vulture was never considered fashion forward.

I sniffed the thin fabric. It didn't smell like anything at all. I slipped it over my head and watched in the mirror as it flowed down, the hem stopping at the top of my knees.

It fit fine, maybe a little tight in the shoulders, but the cinched waist didn't make me feel like I needed to suck in my gut.

I'd washed and dried my hair with the plan of pulling it up into some sort of tail or twist to keep it out of my eyes, but the dress seemed to call for me to keep it down. It touched my shoulders and would probably drive me crazy in a matter of minutes.

"Yeah. No." I grabbed the brush and a giant clip from the dresser. A twist and clip later and my hair was piled into a messy bun. I freed a couple of strands on each side of my face. I looked downright girly or at least more feminine than usual.

Without notice, an old memory flashed in my mind. It was bright and vivid and stopped me in my tracks.

Wilmot and I were in the kitchen. He'd opened a small package on the table and pulled out a dress. I was probably six or seven and the dress was clearly made for a little girl. Inside the memory, the print was small blue flowers.

"Who sent that?" I'd asked.

"I'm not sure, but I bet it's for you."

"It's a dress."

"That's correct."

"I don't wear dresses."

"You can wear whatever you want, but it's a pretty dress. Maybe you could wear it to the Easter egg hunt this Sunday."

"But I have to hunt hard for eggs."

Wilmot laughed. "You can do that in a dress."

"No, I can't! No one can run in a dress."

"I see."

Wilmot set the dress on top of the box, and we finished our breakfast. I had no idea who sent it or what happened to it, but I never wore it. Wilmot never pushed me to do much of anything.

My father hadn't been a great parent. He hadn't had a lot of time to give to me that didn't include him working on a project.

We didn't read books together. We didn't just hang out and watch television. We didn't even go to the Easter egg hunt together. If I remembered correctly, he'd given me a paper bag to hold the eggs and then sent me on my way by myself.

But he wasn't a bad father either. He wasn't cruel or mean. I knew he did the best he could. He just didn't know what to do with me. And he had work to do.

Now I wondered what happened to that dress.

I sighed and smiled sadly at the memories. Most days I just went on with my business. I'd been on my own for a long time. I hadn't spent many moments thinking about what could have been.

Searching for my father's remains, along with what he'd done for a living, was probably why I'd turned myself into a bone expert. I didn't need a professional psychologist to diagnose that one.

I smoothed the dress and glanced at the time. Then I took it off and put the jeans back on. The dress just wasn't me.

I needed to get going. The last box was going to have to wait until after dinner. I didn't want to be too late.

And I needed a little recovery time.

I made sure I had the gun in my pack, locked the doors (I still needed to get that deadbolt), and then climbed into the dirty Jeep. My jeans and the fringed shirt would be dirty by the time I got to dinner, but it was going to have to be good enough.

* * *

The house that Sonny rented sat at the end of a paved road, right at the edge of a dirt road and next to a small farm that kept a few horses in a dusty pasture, though it appeared the owners watered a large patch to keep some grass growing. I parked the Jeep on the road and was greeted immediately by the curious horses, who trotted forward to welcome me.

I didn't know who lived there, but I had known the old guy who owned the house that Sonny had rented. At ninety, he'd moved to Tucson to be closer to his doctors. Old Lou had been a friendly companion around town, and I hoped he was doing well.

After petting the horses' noses, I grabbed the bottle of wine I'd found in the back of my fridge from the Jeep's passenger seat and made my way to the door.

I'd been on dates over the years, but nothing had grown into a long relationship. I wasn't sure where this was going with Sonny, but it was the first time I'd thought about putting on a dress for a long time, and that seemed like something. Even if I hadn't kept it on.

"Hey," Sonny called from the open doorway. "Give me a minute. I've got carrots and apples."

"Sounds good." I waved.

A few moments later, Sonny hurried toward me carrying produce-filled bags.

"They are not even slightly shy," he said as he handed me the carrots. "I told them I was a stranger, that they shouldn't be so easy, but they didn't care. Now that I bring them treats, I don't think they'll ever leave me alone." He smiled at the horse that nudged at his hand.

"I can see you don't like it at all." I smiled too as I worked double-time to pay attention to the other two as well.

"I've never been around horses. I admit, they are fascinating."

"Yes, they are."

"I also find them playful and majestic when they are running around the corral. Do you ride?"

"I don't. I've driven the Jeep forever, which gets me into parts unattainable by non-offroad vehicles. I had an assignment up at the Grand Canyon a few years back, and we had to ride burros down thin switchbacks. I was terrified and sore afterwards."

"May I ask what the assignment involved?"

"Sure. Someone found a tooth underneath what was thought to be First Peoples' bones. Indians, Native Americans, have the right to take back the bones of their ancestors so they may bury them in the proper ways of their traditions. The tribe didn't trust the government guy they brought in, so they called me. After the arduous journey into the canyon, I could quickly determine that the bone belonged to someone who'd lived in the 1980s and were definitely not Navajo or any other tribe."

"How did you make the determination?"

"Well, the skull mostly." I tapped my brow and then my temples. "Shapes and measurements."

"Interesting."

"I love my job, but that trip into the canyon was . . ." I paused. "Who am I kidding. I'd do it again in a heartbeat."

"You mentioned a tooth."

"Yes, the tooth was under the skeleton, but they couldn't get at it without disturbing the skeleton. Once I determined that the skeleton wasn't First Peoples, we could remove it carefully and then get at the tooth. It belonged to a saber-toothed tiger."

"A real one?"

"Well, yes, but from a long time ago, of course." I offered a couple more carrots. "Once we got the skeleton out, I could further determine that the man had died by a gunshot wound to the head. We tracked down that he'd come from Chicago and were able to reach his family who'd thought maybe he'd just run off about ten years earlier. With the information we put together, the killer was found. Sadly, the killer had died a few years earlier so he couldn't pay the price for his crime. But the family of the victim got his remains and some answers. Not knowing is the worst."

"That's amazing, Hazel."

I smiled again. "Any alien response yet?"

He laughed. "Not yet, but I have faith. I mean, if there really were saber-toothed tigers, then anything is possible."

"I do *not* disagree."

"You, uh, look pretty. Is that okay for me to say?"

"Thank you. Yes, it's okay. And you look great." He did. He was cute. I wanted to smile every time I looked at him. This man might be a real threat to my sour constitution. I wondered what he'd have thought if I'd worn the dress. Maybe the next date.

"I'll take that." Sonny swiped his hands together, as if wiping off some dust. "I hope you're hungry."

"Starving. Literally. I might waste away if I don't eat soon."

"Can't have that. Come on in."

Lou had left the house in good old cowboy shape. The brown leather living room furniture matched. Lamps sat on two end tables, the bases made of wrought iron bucking broncos.

Paintings of cows and horses filled the walls. The space was masculine and smelled like tomatoes and oregano. My fringed shirt fit right in, and my stomach growled.

Sonny made his way behind the peninsula that sat in between the kitchen and living room. Its burnt-orange top matched the old appliances and the other counter space. The small house was tidy, though, so the old accoutrements only seemed sort of retro hip now.

"I wasn't sure what toppings you like so I made a few with different combinations of meat and veggies. I'm not good enough to make all the edges a perfect circle, but I think you'll like the sauce. Everyone does."

I sat on a stool on this side of the peninsula as he opened the bottle of wine. "Can I pour you a glass?"

"Sure."

Once the wine was poured, I watched as Sonny wiped black olives off the counter. I couldn't help but notice the small smile that played on his lips. He was moving easily and comfortably, which calmed me too. He was an easy kind of guy.

"How's the skeleton stuff going?" Sonny asked as he deposited the olive remains into the sink.

"Just keeps getting stranger."

He gave me a long look. "Isn't everything that you do kind of unusual? I mean, saber-toothed tigers and all."

"I also have a box of random bones from Missouri now sitting in my lab waiting for me to determine what happened to the people they were once inside of."

"A box? Tell me more."

The assignment wasn't confidential.

"I met a guy, Chuck Workman, in Flagstaff a few years back—we were both there to hear Douglas Owsley, an anthropologist who is famous in our world and the curator of physical anthropology at the Smithsonian. Owsley spoke to a full house at the University of Northern Arizona. I spent dinner with Chuck and his colleagues. Chuck is a journalism professor at the University of Missouri and found a strange box in the basement of the journalism building. He'd approached the anthropology department with the box, but they were bound by university rules that didn't allow them to take a closer look at what Chuck found because it didn't go through their proper channels. He asked if I'd take a look."

"They found it in the basement?" Sonny said

"Bones are everywhere."

"Well, sure, but . . ." Sonny squinted at me. "You have an idea of what it's about, don't you?"

"No. Well, not really. It's important to go into these things with an open mind, but I'm pretty good at reading bones. I bet I figure it out quickly."

"Why the journalism building?"

"I might not be able to solve that part, but who knows? Maybe someone gathered the bones from the anthropology department at some point and was going to write a story. Things get derailed."

"That's true." The timer on the oven beeped. "Ah, dinner is ready."

"Best news of the night."

I placed one slice of each flavor on my plate. It was crowded, but I couldn't resist. I took a bite.

"Oh, my God," I said as I chewed. "What do you put in that sauce?"

"It's a secret."

I swallowed. "It's so good."

"I know. Right?"

We ate and somehow found things to talk about that didn't have anything to do with our jobs. I asked Sonny about growing up in northern Wisconsin in mostly winter weather and how that worked with his opinion of the desert he'd moved to ten years earlier when he'd taken the job in Tucson.

"I always look forward to the Arizona winter. This summer has been hot."

"It always is."

"I like the people, though."

"Well, I doubt you've met everyone."

"I've met the important ones."

I nodded and dug into the next slice of pizza on my plate.

Once dinner was finished, I had an onset of claustrophobia. I didn't understand it, because I liked this guy, but I needed some space, some air.

I asked if we could go for a walk, and Sonny seemed glad to do so.

We didn't venture farther than the street that would lead us back to town if we walked long enough. I didn't need a few miles under my belt, but the night air smelled pleasantly of sage and a distant campfire, so we moved slowly. I also caught waves of a bitter smell that didn't stick around long enough for me to identify, but it kept me on olfactory alert. Smells could be warnings out here.

The night was clear and the air warm. Not surprisingly, Sonny was a star expert and could point out everything in the sky above with authority.

He pointed toward the horizon. "There's Scorpius."

"It looks like a scorpion."

"It does. It's my favorite."

"Why?"

"It's distinctive. Some are a little more difficult to see until you get used to looking for them. Scorpius never appears with Orion because myth has it that Gaia sent a scorpion to kill Orion. I guess I like the story behind it."

"It's a good story."

With the dark-sky rules, the light pollution was low, and it was easy to spot the stars above, but it was also so dark along the road that we walked that it was difficult to see much going on in the houses as we passed by. The only pattern to any of the streets in Black Vulture and Tumacácori was that there really wasn't much of a pattern. Small houses on small plots were located next to bigger places almost willy-nilly. Like the horse property next to Sonny's small place, the rest of the streets were laid out the same.

Fences and trees—mostly mesquite and palo verde—dotted the front yards. There wasn't much grass, but desert plants and succulents added layers and charm even if sometimes you had to change your perspective to appreciate the rest of the stark terrain.

There were plenty of places to hide, observe from a dark spot. Roaming around in the local landscape in the dark wasn't wise, even if you were a seasoned desert dweller.

As we walked and talked about the sky and I drank in the night air, that bitter smell became more constant.

I stopped walking. "What *is* that?" I sniffed.

Sonny's eyebrows came together as he sniffed too. "I don't know. I'm not smelling anything distinct."

I turned toward the smell and walked to the side of the road. I peered into the darkness of the sage and tumbleweed filled landscape at a spot that didn't have a house or a trailer. I took a big pull of air through my nose and then bored my eyes into the darkness.

"I smell that man. The one who knocked me over."

"You do?" Sonny stepped even closer to me. "Out there?"

"The scent has been with us the whole time. I thought it might be the horses, but it's not, and it just got stronger."

Something rustled in the sagebrush about twenty feet ahead.

"There." I pointed.

"Hazel, let's step back." Sonny put his hand on my arm, and we took some steps away. He stepped in front of me and looked out toward the movement. "Who's there?"

No one answered, but the rustling and the smell advanced.

In the span of just a few seconds, I realized that something was coming at us, but if it was human, they were low to the ground so probably moving on all fours, which didn't seem reasonable. Still though, we stepped back. We didn't run. I suspected Sonny was probably coming to the same conclusions I was. Something strange was happening, but not from someone walking upright.

As those split seconds ticked by, it wasn't too long before the worst of it came into view.

I put my hand on Sonny's arm. "We need to run."

He didn't argue but kept stride with me as we took off. I ran backward, so he did too.

Another brief moment later, the predator showed itself by bursting out of the brush and onto the street.

"It's a javelina," I said. Wild, piglike creatures with even bigger teeth, they were not attractive, but they could be cute.

It didn't appear to want to come after us, so we quit running.

"I've seen and smelled a few walking by the house at night," Sonny commented. "But never one that big. I didn't see any in Tucson. Would it really hurt us?"

"Usually not, but they have big teeth and it's not worth the risk. They eat cactus, needles and all. They aren't fond of dogs and if they're protecting their young—"

I was interrupted by the appearance of three smaller javelinas who joined their mother.

Sonny laughed. "Now, they're adorable."

"They are, but, yeah, it's probably good to keep a distance from mama. She was coming out of the brush hot."

Though we were a good thirty feet away from them, their scent was strong. We must have been downwind. We watched as the mother piglike wild creature led her babies down the street and away from us.

Sonny looked at me. "That wouldn't happen in Wisconsin. Maybe in Tucson, but not where I was."

"No javelinas in Wisconsin, huh?"

"Nor scorpions, in case you wondered."

I nodded but didn't respond right away.

"What's on your mind?" Sonny asked.

"That man who attacked me. He smelled like that, as well as other things."

"You think he's living next to a family of javelinas?"

"I don't know, but that along with the other smells tells me he's outside most of the time."

"Okay. Do the police need to know?"

"Maybe, but not at the moment. I told Calloway and the new police chief what the guy smelled like, but not specifically like that. I just said he stunk, like body odor. But it was more than that, I realize, and it wouldn't hurt for them to know."

"Want to give them a call?"

I shook my head. "I know what I'd like to do, though."

"Tell me."

"Let's go back to your place." I paused. "Do not waste any time wondering if that's a pickup line. It is." I started walking back toward Sonny's house.

We didn't clean up the pizza and the walk had been short, but it was enough. I'd had plenty of air—fresh or otherwise.

Maybe it was the evening or the stars. Maybe the jolt of adrenaline-infused fear, but I felt a lot better. I'd been considering the idea all night, and I just couldn't come up with any reason why not. It had been a while, which wasn't a good reason—by itself. But there were plenty of green flags to go along with my interest.

It was time for some inside activities.

CHAPTER 20

"Hazel Dylan, are you doing the walk of shame?" Trisha asked as I parked the Jeep and slid off the driver's seat.

She'd been sitting on the ground, her back up to the wall, next to my front door. It appeared that she'd been waiting for me.

"Not working this morning?" I asked.

"Nope." She stood and wiped off her behind. "I need your help."

"Okay."

"Will you come out with me to Joey's place?"

"Why?"

"Because something strange is going on and I want you to see it. No one has time for me or Joey."

She probably wasn't wrong. "Tell me more."

"On the way." Her eyes moved up and down me. "Who's the lucky guy?"

"Let me change before we run out there."

I was just as curious as she was regarding the whereabouts of the Smoots. I wondered about Joey, but my concern was mostly for Jerry. Why hadn't he gotten in touch?

"Can I wait inside?" she asked.

"Sure."

I unlocked the door and let us both in. Immediately I took a silent inventory. Nothing felt off this time, but I scanned the rooms as I went through, looking for something out of place. There was nothing.

The boxes I'd taken out of the closet were exactly as I'd left them.

I would have enjoyed the time with Sonny even if I'd worn the dress, but I was glad I saved it for another date. The sense of stepping out of my normal skin and into someone else's had made me feel like a phony. It had given me a new perspective, one I didn't want to have all the time but might take on a little.

I put on fresh jeans and a T-shirt. And my boots had molded to my feet far better than the sneakers I'd put on last night.

I hurried back down to join Trisha, who was looking closely at the skunk mount. "You know this is Joey's grandpa's, don't you?"

"The skunk is Jerry's?"

"That's what Joey told me."

"I didn't know that. I wonder why he didn't take it with him."

"Joey thought it was because the trailer was just too small, and all he was interested in were the bones."

"I guess I know the feeling. Let's go."

We climbed in the Jeep, and Trisha held her phone toward me as I steered us toward the Smoots'. "Look here."

"I'm driving. What is it?"

"A text from Joey. I got it yesterday."

"And you didn't tell me before we hit the road?"

"You might not have driven me out here and I needed you to."

A part of me admired her manipulation "What's it say?

"I'm in Nogales, babe. Had to get out of town for a bit."

"So, Joey was in some sort of trouble?" This was not a surprise to me.

"Maybe."

"Trisha. Talk to me. Why are we driving out to the trailer?"

Trisha didn't answer immediately. "Because he never calls me 'babe.'"

I stopped the Jeep. Dust flew up around the open-air vehicle. "Trisha, this doesn't make sense. Even with him calling you that, you don't trust that he's in Mexico?"

"I don't."

"Why?"

"Look, I know people don't like Joey, and everyone tells me that I'd be better off without him. I hear everyone's comments. I know."

"Okay?"

"Joey made me put a location thing on my phone, so he could know where I am all the time."

"And you agreed?"

She looked at me. "I've got enough balls to tell him that he had to put one on too so I could track him."

"That's great, Trisha. You've known where he was this whole time? And it's not Mexico?"

She shook her head. "His phone was off for most of the time, so I didn't know anything, but when I got the text, I hurried to see where he was. It said he was at his trailer."

"So, he was lying to you?"

"No, Hazel, that can't be it. He knows I'm not a fool. He knows I would see where he was or wasn't."

I nodded. "Where does it say he is now?"

"The phone is off again."

I considered her powers of deduction and thought she might be on to something being wonky. I just didn't know why I was involved. "Did you tell the police?"

"Yep. That new police chief said I need to give him more time. He and his officer, what was her name—what an asshole—talked to me like I was five, telling me that 'sometimes boyfriends wander.'"

"Talking down to you wasn't professional, but they aren't wrong."

"They're wrong about Joey." She looked at me. "You have a gun. I don't. You work with the law, and you don't talk to me like I'm a fool. Please, Hazel, let's just check."

I frowned at her.

"Joey's allergic," she said.

"Um. What does that have to do with anything?"

"He's allergic to scorpion venom. He's been stung a few times, but the first time he almost died. Jerry got him into town quick that day, and the doctor happened to be there, so he stuck him with one of those EpiPens. It was almost too late. He's supposed to carry the shot with him all the time now."

"Supposed to?"

Trisha nodded, and a tear fell down her cheek. "He forgets sometimes. I hope he has one, but what if he doesn't and he got stung?"

Then he's probably dead, I thought. My heart went out to her, and I put the Jeep back into gear.

As we approached the trailer, my eyes scanned for something different from my last visit. The door had been open last time I'd been there. I'd closed it, and that was how it currently was. It might be nearly impossible to notice if the piles of bones had been disturbed, but they didn't appear any different to me.

I parked the Jeep and put my hand out to stop Trisha from moving too quickly.

"Jerry? Joey? Anyone here?" I called.

The silence that followed left me feeling mostly confident that there was no one around.

"Hang on one second, Trisha. Let me check the place first."

"Well. Hurry."

I nodded, but I wouldn't move too quickly. I was worried about the Smoots' whereabouts, but it wasn't uncommon for folks to take off and not report in for a few days. What was strange was the door having been open the last time I was there and Trisha's noting of the location of Joey's phone.

On their own, none of those things might be too unsettling, but combined with everything else going on, something was most definitely off.

I glanced at the ground as I made my way to the trailer's door. Footprints would have been a wonderful gift, but the dirt hadn't seen a speck of water for months. The wind constantly blew. There wasn't a hint of a print anywhere.

I continued to call out, even as I turned the flimsy handle on the door. Inside, I found the exact same scene. At first glance, it seemed that nothing had changed at all since my last visit. But on second glance . . .

I pushed open the door and signaled to Trisha. "Come in."

She hurried to join me.

"Joey?" she said as she moved through the trailer, looking in rooms and closets. It took less than a minute for her to join me back in the small kitchen. "He's not here. Neither is Jerry. No EpiPens either."

"Last time I was here, this drawer wasn't open at all. I'm pretty sure, at least."

Together we zoned in on one of the kitchen's small drawers set under the old counter. It wasn't open enough to see inside, but it wasn't closed all the way either.

"Okay?" she said.

"Let's just look." Since I didn't bring gloves, I used my knuckle to pull on the drawer's handle.

Inside was the sort of stuff that was ubiquitous to junk drawers, but atop the rolls of tape and collection of rubber bands and small screwdrivers was a cell phone.

Trisha gasped as she reached. "That's his phone! I'd know it anywhere."

I grabbed her hand before she could touch it and shook my head at her. "Nope. It's time to get the police out here."

"They won't come!"

"Yes, they will. Don't touch a thing. Let's get back outside. I'll make the calls."

Trisha's eyes filled with tears. It was just a cell phone in a drawer, but no one left their cell phone behind on purpose. I wasn't sure exactly what might be going on, but something wasn't right.

"I can turn it on," she said. "I know his passwords."

"Save it for the police."

I got her out of there and called Verro.

Jenna answered the phone. She didn't know where Verro was. I could sense hesitation when I told her where she needed to meet us, but she didn't argue. I dropped a pin on her cell phone, and she said she'd be on her way.

I asked Trisha to sit in the Jeep as I looked around again. I didn't see anything helpful.

"Shit," I muttered.

As I made my way back around to the front of the trailer, I wondered, where in the world were Jerry and Joey? Why would they both be missing?

A couple of days of no communication here and there wasn't too unexpected, but this, mostly because of the appearance of Joey's phone, was cause for real concern.

A red sedan kicked up dust as it came toward us from the main road. I watched it approach and then met Jenna as she stepped out of the vehicle.

"This car's not the best out here," I told her.

"I'm aware of that, but no one has offered me a new vehicle so I'm going to have to figure it out. I'm here, though."

"Yeah. Okay. Right."

Trisha slid out of the Jeep and joined us, though she kept quiet as I explained what had brought us out to the Smoots' trailer.

"Let me see the text from Joey." Jenna extended her hand to Trisha, who opened her phone and got to it quickly. After Jenna read it, she said, "You searched for his whereabouts because you didn't believe him?"

"I didn't." Trisha's eyes filled with tears. "He and I went to Nogales last year. He forgot he had a knife in his back pocket, and we were detained on our way back into Arizona."

"A knife, not a gun?" I interjected, knowing what a bad idea it was for anyone to try to cross the border with a firearm. They could be detained in Mexico for a long time.

"Just a knife."

"That's not illegal," Jenna offered.

"I know, but we got scared." A tear rolled down her cheek. "Joey and I got together about two years ago, but he'd been a hell-raiser before that. I told him I would only date him if he shaped up. He did! I mean, he really did." Trisha wiped off the tear and then a few more. "I freaked when we got detained. I was worried they were questioning us for something else Joey had done, but he kept saying he was on the straight and narrow, and I just didn't see any sign of anything else. I mean, he is kind of lazy, but we were working on that too. He's a diamond in the rough—really, he is."

Jenna and I nodded at her to continue.

She did. "This text is too casual, if that makes any sense. Plus, I think he'd be scared to tell me if he was in trouble. It didn't fit, so I opened the location app right away after the text and realized the phone was at the trailer. I was hoping Joey was too, but I gotta tell you, I didn't think he would be." She held out the phone. "This is all so not Joey, you know?"

Jenna looked at me. I could see she was searching for my reaction. I thought about it for a moment and then nodded. I didn't think Trisha was overreacting.

"Okay, then. Let me look around." Jenna said.

"Wait, do you want me to turn on Joey's phone?" Trisha asked. "Hazel wouldn't let me touch it because of prints and stuff."

"Good call. Yes, let me get you some gloves and then we'll see what we can see. I'll look around."

"Good." Trisha nodded and sniffed.

I could tell she was relieved that Jenna was listening to her. I was too.

We got the phone on, but the battery was so low that Trisha couldn't get farther than the home screen. We couldn't find a nearby charger so Jenna bagged the phone and took the passwords, telling Trisha she'd charge it at the station and take a look. I had a charging cord in the Jeep, but I didn't offer to get it because I wondered if Jenna just didn't want Trisha there when she took the first look at the phone. More tears fell down Trisha's cheeks.

"It'll be okay, Trisha," Jenna said. "We'll figure it out."

Trisha nodded and took a deep breath.

Jenna couldn't understand the bones and seemed momentarily overwhelmed at the idea of having to sift through them to look for clues to any crime. I told her I didn't think there was anything to find in the piles, that they'd been accumulating over the years, but considering everything going on, I could be wrong. I told her about Jerry's lifelong walk-and-gathers through the desert.

She blew a deep breath out of puffed cheeks. "That's just more overwhelming than I can contemplate at the moment. I'll tell Verro about these." She took pictures. "I thought it was supposed to be quiet in Black Vulture. I've never had to investigate piles of bones. Will you be available to take a close look through them? I can't imagine the reaction I would get from Tucson investigators if I make such a request."

I didn't have that sort of time, really, but I would make it if necessary. "Sure."

"I'll let you know." She paused. "I need to get back to town and log Joey's phone since it is looking like it could be evidence. I don't know what Verro will want, but he'll probably come out here too," she signaled with a wave, "and look more deeply into everything around here. I'd like to find Joey, but after what you told me, I'm worried that he and Jerry might have run into something foul out there somewhere."

"I can look around. I have the Jeep—wait, I have an even better idea."

"I'm listening."

"There's a guy camping out by the caves," I waved too, but in a different direction. "He has an ATV. I could get ahold of him, and we could do a grid search."

"Graham something or other?"

"You've met?"

"No, but Verro told me about him." She paused. "I don't think the police have an ATV. Verro mentioned he had a dirt bike, but I don't know if he meant desert-type dirt. I can't imagine why not."

I shrugged. "We didn't have a real force until recently."

She nodded. "All right. Do it, and report back later."

"Will do. Can you take Trisha back to town?"

"Yep. All right. You have your gun?"

"I do."

"Good. Call us later."

Trisha's eyes were wide with fear and question and relief that someone was taking her seriously. In fact, Jenna's attention and intelligence were good things for Black Vulture, but I wouldn't ponder that until later.

After I watched the small red car make it safely to the main road, I called Graham, who picked up on the first ring and told me that he'd get to me as quickly as he could.

CHAPTER

21

GRAHAM ARRIVED TWENTY-FIVE minutes later. He and his clothes and cap were caked in grime.

"You okay?" I asked as he came to a stop.

His cheeks and the back of his neck were rosy. "Got a little sunburned, but I'm drinking lots of water." He held up a large aluminum bottle to prove it.

For a moment, I wondered if maybe I should ask to just use the ATV and let Graham relax inside the trailer, with the air-conditioning on. Not only was the desert wildlife dangerous, so was the heat. People who weren't used to it could be caught off guard.

As if he was reading my mind, he smiled and said, "I'm good, Hazel. Let's go look for your guys."

I grabbed my own bottle of water from the floor of the Jeep and hopped on the back of the ATV, wrapping my arms around Graham.

"Which way?" he asked.

I thought about it for a minute. I had no idea where to look first.

I guessed and pointed to our left. "There and then we'll grid back and forth as we make our way back here."

"Got it."

The ride was bumpy and hot as we went way far afield. As we rode, I kept my eyes peeled, and Graham would stop the ATV every now and then. We'd call out for Jerry and Joey.

Desert silence can be loud, layered with moans from the wind as well as the conversation from the wildlife. The only animal I heard was the distant squawky calls of a woodpecker.

After almost two full hours of searching, I thought we should probably be finished for the day, maybe try again later or tomorrow. But as Graham cut the engine and we both reached for our water bottles, I thought I heard something that sounded like a human groan.

"Did you hear that?" I asked.

"Shh. Maybe."

We didn't breathe or move a muscle for thirty seconds or so. Finally, I called, "Jerry? Joey?"

Another groan sounded, but it wasn't easy to tell from which direction it was coming.

"Go right," I said.

"I think it's left."

"Shit."

"Let's listen again."

The ground cover could be thick, but there were also barren spots. There were also spots where it could be near impossible to navigate either on foot or four wheels.

I figured that if we were hearing Jerry, he would have chosen the easier route. When the groan didn't come again, I said, "Go left."

Slowly and carefully, Graham maneuvered the ATV. For the longest few beats, I was convinced we'd either chosen the wrong way or the noise we'd heard hadn't been human. But then I spotted a brown thing that looked like a boot.

"Stop!" I exclaimed as I jumped off the ATV.

I tripped and high-stepped my way toward the boot, cactus needles finding their way though my jeans and into the side of my calf. The pain only registered as a distant thing, but I knew I'd have to deal with it later.

"Holy shit," I said when I came upon the body.

Jerry Smoot was alive, but barely.

"Bring water!" I yelled.

Jerry Smoot was sixty-nine and in good shape. He'd spent his life trudging through the desert, and though he'd been searching for bones all these years, the exercise had done him good. Heat and maybe a bump on his head, however, were going to set him back a bit.

I kneeled beside him as he was going in and out of half consciousness, though he didn't seem to fall fully under. Graham moved quickly and surely, making shade for Jerry out of sticks and his shirt. He dribbled a little water into the older man's mouth and then stuck his cool water bottle next to Jerry's neck.

"I have a satellite phone. I'll call for help," he said.

Graham stood and stepped away as he spoke into his phone. "Send a chopper. We have a man who needs to get to Tucson for medical attention immediately. This guy doesn't have long—you what? That's bullshit. I've approved the chopper. You can send the bill to the university in Boulder. If you don't get out here to help this guy, I promise I will ruin you."

I blinked at the harsh words, wondering why Graham felt the need to use them and holding on to hope that help was on the way.

There was a chance we could figure out how to transport Jerry using the ATV but not safely. I would have waited out there if we could have secured Jerry to Graham and onto the four-wheeler, but we didn't know anything about Jerry's injuries. The ATV didn't seem like a good idea.

I said, "Look, you drive back into town just in case the chopper doesn't come. We need more help."

"You take the ATV. I'll wait here with Jerry."

I was tempted, and though I knew I could figure it out well enough, I'd never driven a recreational four-wheeler. My Jeep had been enough to get me wherever I needed to go.

"No, you. Hurry, though."

There wasn't time to argue. Graham nodded and hopped back onto the ATV. Expertly, he maneuvered it around and got it headed in the right direction, probably before I could have figured out how to turn on the ignition.

I sat on the ground next to Jerry and tried to figure out what to do. I kept dribbling water into his mouth and onto his cracked lips. Every time I felt his pulse, it seemed to become slower and weaker, so I stopped doing that.

"Hey, Jer, I'm right here. It's Hazel."

Suddenly, I realized we hadn't searched any farther for Joey. Was he out here too? I didn't think he was—his cell phone in the trailer made me think . . . well, I didn't know what to think.

Nevertheless, I stood. "Joey! Joey!"

The only answer was the hot and increasingly lonely wind. "Shit."

I sat down again "Aw, Jer, what happened?"

He grumbled something incoherent and seemed to be trying to roll his head so he could look at me.

I put my hand on his arm. "It's okay. We'll talk later."

"No . . . ooo," Jerry uttered.

"Shh. I'm right here."

"I saw . . . he hit me."

Jerry's face was covered in the same grime we all got covered in if we were outside long enough, but as I examined his face more closely, I saw that bump and what might be a bruise on his jaw.

"Who hit you?" I asked.

"He did."

"Did you know him?"

"No. Bones. Police. He . . ."

Then Jerry fell back to that mostly unconscious state that made me check his pulse again.

Still there. Barely.

It wasn't much to go on, but I couldn't help but think that Jerry might have seen whoever had been leaving the bone sculptures, maybe came upon him.

I looked down at the old man. "Don't you fucking die. I'll be right back."

I stood and looked around again. I wasn't searching for Joey, but something else, some sort of sign that someone else had been out there and they'd had bones with them.

The desert was so familiar to me that I was sure I would catch on to something that didn't fit, something that was out of place.

My eyes scanned, walking as far as I thought might be reasonable.

If I hadn't been afraid of being too far away from Jerry, I could have done a better scan. I'd walk a grid when someone else made it out here to take care of him.

For now, I'd have to—

Not far from where I was standing, in the dirt where the ATV had parked before we heard Jerry moan, inside one of the tire marks, something . . . sparkled? Shined?

My eyes locked on that location, I made a move to hurry to get to the spot, but my toe caught on the exposed root bunch from a long-gone saguaro. The fall took me to my hands and knees. As I looked ahead at Jerry, I wondered if the root ball had been what he'd tripped over too. Maybe he'd fallen and hit his head and chin, tumbling some distance before going to the ground. I didn't want someone to have hit him.

I turned back toward the shiny object and didn't bother standing but crawled the rest of the way, ignoring the scrapes my hands took.

Half buried in the dirt was a gold chain with a gold medallion hanging on it. It seemed like maybe the ATV's tires had stirred up the dirt enough to expose the necklace. I doubted it would have been uncovered if Graham and I hadn't come along.

I didn't have any gloves on me. Using a finger but not the pad, I lifted the chain out of its partial burial and held it up.

The pendant glimmered in the light.

"Huh," I said aloud.

Of all things, of all the possible charms in the world, I came upon one that might mean more to me than almost anyone else.

It was a carved etching of a hand—but just the bones.

"What the hell?" I muttered.

The noise of an approaching chopper garnered my attention, and I stood.

Carefully, I slipped the necklace into my pocket and waved down the rescuers.

CHAPTER

22

THE NEXT FORTY-EIGHT hours would be crucial for Jerry, but the medical team who showed up from Tucson seemed to think that with some good care and an infusion of fluids, he'd be okay.

"You found him in the nick of time," one of the men on the rescue team said. "He seems like a tough old guy."

"We got lucky."

"I think Mr. Smoot here is the lucky one."

"He has a grandson, in his twenties, who is also missing. Any chance your crew could circle around and look for sign of someone else?"

The team and the pilot conferred a moment and decided that since Jerry was now receiving life-saving fluids an extra fifteen minutes wouldn't hurt.

"We'll take a look."

They had him loaded quickly. They circled a few times, but then a crew member leaned out of the chopper and shook her head as if to relay that they didn't see anyone else. I sent her a thumbs-up and waved them away.

They had offered to take me with them, but I didn't want to go to Tucson. I hoped Graham would return soon.

My wish was granted ten minutes later. He'd put on another shirt.

"We were notified about the chopper pickup. I'm glad, because I couldn't find anyone in that police station. The sheriff's place is too far away."

"I think we're good."

"Jerry still alive?"

"So far."

"Let me get you back. It's been a day."

I hopped on the back again and tried not to fall asleep as Graham took me back to my Jeep. I hadn't even realized how tired I was, how the release of a load of adrenaline exhausted me.

"You okay to drive home?" he asked as I dismounted.

"I'm good. I'm taking a shower and going to bed, though."

"Eat and drink something. In fact, meet me at the diner. We could both use some sustenance."

"I . . . uh." I really just wanted to go home.

"Come on, Hazel. We both need some food. Meet me there." He turned and headed toward town.

I watched him go, feeling gratitude that he'd helped. It didn't change what I wanted to do, but I was willing to take one for the team and eat food, maybe drink some cold water.

"Okay. See you there," I said aloud, though he was too far away to hear a word.

* * *

I wasn't hungry, but Dixie's chicken noodle soup hit the spot, along with a few tall glasses of water.

If I looked as ruffled as Graham, it was no wonder that Dixie gathered us both as we walked inside. She led us to a booth and brought food and drink quickly.

Graham ate a full steak and a loaded baked potato. I'd been known to do that few times myself, but the soup was all I'd wanted today.

I was tired, but I didn't have time to be. I was distracted by the pendant in my pocket. I should have called Calloway or told Verro or Jenna right off, but something had stopped me. It was a curious intuition, like maybe I knew something about that pendant. It was the bones of a hand—shouldn't it mean something to me of all people? Me before everyone else?

I knew what I had to do, and a meal with Graham was only prolonging my curious anxiety.

"Tell me about the last case you worked on," I asked, hoping for something to distract me from jumping out of my own skin.

"Lead coffins."

"Oh yeah?"

A few lead coffins had been dug up in the United States over the years. We hadn't used lead in coffins in this country in a long time, and only for a short time as the colonists were placing the building blocks of the country.

"What did you find inside?"

"Nothing." He smiled.

"Oh. Sorry."

"Based upon the artistic embellishments on the coffins, I had to deconstruct the timeline. It took me some diversion to get there, but ultimately I concluded that two people distantly related to Molly Brown, the one from the *Titanic*, had been buried in the coffins, but their remains had been stolen."

"Why?"

"The best we could conclude was theft of gold jewelry, but we don't know. I was able to get some DNA, which is how I found the link to Ms. Brown. Not through the embellishments at all."

"Where?"

"Just outside Denver."

I searched my brain for the discovery. That would have been something I'd read about.

"Lead coffins in Colorado? I thought those were all on the East Coast."

"Most are, but some have also been found in Michigan."

"Really? I didn't know."

"How about your last case? What was it?"

"When it comes to bones, it was the most boring assignment you can imagine. I had to confirm that it was a bullet hole in an old skull. I guess the only interesting thing was that I could determine that the injury had come about sixty years ago. We managed to find a missing man but not his killer. Not yet, as far as I know."

"I'm not a fan of loose ends."

"The one before that, though, was interesting. I got called into Tucson. Someone found remains up on Mount Lemmon. I was called up there to take a look. By then, it was just the bones, but it didn't take me long to figure out what had happened. Female, in her late twenties, she'd been strangled to death."

"You determined that quickly?"

"I did. The hyoid bone was broken." I pointed to my jaw.

"Right."

"Anyway, a woman had gone missing a year earlier and then other things fit together quickly, so I was sure I nailed down her identity shortly thereafter. I worked with the prosecutor who wanted to prosecute the ex-boyfriend but didn't have enough evidence. I was convinced he was guilty, so I could not allow him to go free. I followed him for a few days, observed his habit of smoking cigarettes and discarding them everywhere. I grabbed a cop friend and went back up to Mount Lemmon and searched and dug and even prayed to the universe a bit for a discarded butt. We found one. Nailed the guy, who ended up confessing. You know the story, 'She made me so mad that she made me do it.' He was put away, though not for long enough. Still, we got him."

"That's great. You know that, don't you?"

I shook my head. "No. What's great are the people who intervene and help before abuse and murder occur."

"Of course, but when all of that fails, justice is good too."

I shrugged. I wasn't being modest or humble. I loved what I did, but I truly believed that more needed to be done, that I didn't do enough. There weren't enough hours in the day. There were too many problems to figure out which ones to try to solve.

"Anyway . . ." I said.

Graham sighed. "It's all about karma and justice, right?"

"Well—"

"I'm driven by it."

"Yeah?"

"Justice, vengeance, you know, those sorts of things." Graham smiled.

I smiled too, but I was tired. If vengeance was to be had anywhere this afternoon, it wasn't going to be me serving it up. Though I got what he was saying.

I didn't see as she approached the booth, but I knew the voice.

"Excuse me," Jenna said.

"Hey," I said. "What's up? Any updates on Joey's phone?"

She shook her head. "Trisha's passwords didn't work. That's why I'm here, to talk to her. Also, Jerry Smoot is going to be okay. He'll be in the hospital for a couple days. He's not coherent yet, but he will be. He'll be okay."

Tears choked my throat momentarily. I swallowed them. "That's wonderful. Thanks, Jenna."

"I'm heading up there to try to talk to him after I talk to Trisha. Did Jerry say anything out there?"

I told her his cryptic words. She didn't seem impressed or bothered.

"Where's Verro?" I asked.

"Working," she said.

There was something about the way she answered that made me think she was being evasive. She didn't owe me the truth, but I sure wondered what our new chief was up to.

Jenna took off to talk to Trisha as Graham and I finished our meal. He didn't want to let me pay, but I insisted, and he relented with an "owe you one."

He was tired too, but he walked me to my door before climbing back onto the ATV. He waved and then drove away quickly.

I made my way inside and locked the door behind me. I gathered the pendant from my pocket and hurried up to the bedroom.

I was completely exhausted, but I had a box to open.

CHAPTER

23

MEMORY CAN BE so many things. Mostly unreliable, I thought.

Something inside me knew important information. I hadn't been able to access it, but I knew it was there, behind some locked door, inside that black hole I kept sensing. I'd known it since this started, since Calloway drove me out to the first sculpture. There was a reason he thought of me, and on a level I didn't know existed, I got it. We both thought of me, though neither of us really knew why.

There should be no reason to hesitate to open this last box. There was no good reason unless there was something inside it that I didn't want to face.

As I sat on the bed and looked at it, still sealed, I closed my eyes and tried to remember what I wasn't remembering. I would have liked to have at least a tiny preview, but life didn't generally work that way.

I *knew* that Wilmot's classes had never been on my radar. I hadn't just forgotten about them. I was sure that I hadn't known anything about them. I hadn't known about Silas throwing a bucket of blood inside the studio. The abomination. That all sounded traumatic enough to create amnesia, but that hadn't been the kind of kid I was. I might have been in some shock, but I'd been a kid who'd seen so many things that others would be put off by. I'd seen dead animals, blood, gore. I'd grown up with it. It had come with the deal that was my father and his profession. Even whatever happened wouldn't have ruined me.

But it might have ruined others.

The bigger question was: What had I been doing that ominous day? Where the heck had I been?

I looked at the old tape that still sealed shut what was unknown. Was it better kept that way?

"Open the damn box," I said aloud.

I stuck the knife into the tape and tore through it. I lifted the panels and let my eyes digest the contents inside, hoping for some sort of epiphany to come forth.

There were things to learn from the items in the box, shocking things.

Inside were four items. A red scarf, a barbeque fork, a gold pendant etched with the bones of a hand, and, last but not least, a knife, like the one I carried these days, almost exactly like one I had when I was a kid.

"Shit," I uttered, knowing that these items were undoubtedly tied to the skeleton sculptures in the desert. I said it again when I realized that only three of the items had been found. I wasn't aware of anyone discovering a knife, one that happened to look similar to the one I and so many around Black Vulture carried, and almost identical to one I used to have. Was someone after me too or were knives just so commonplace around Black Vulture that they could be tied to almost anyone? To clear my mind, I shook off the wave of cold fear.

Okay. Had we missed some sculptures? Had we not searched well enough?

I reached into the box but pulled my hand back quickly.

I grabbed my phone and called Calloway.

"I need you to come to my apartment," I said after he answered on the first ring.

"Are you okay?"

"Yep, but I need you to get here."

"On my way."

* * *

"This is some F'ed up shit, Hazel." Sheriff Calloway sat on the edge of my mattress, in the same spot I'd been in when I finally cut the box open.

"I agree." I handed him the pendant. "I found this out by Jerry Smoot today."

Calloway squinted at my hand before he took the pendant. He held it in the box, comparing it to the one in there.

"It's almost identical, but not quite."

"Like the knife." I grabbed my phone and swiped my finger over the screen. "I found things like the pendant for sale at a few different places. I emailed you the links. As for the other items, you can get those almost anywhere."

"You think someone recently purchased this one?" He held it up.

"It's just a guess." I shrugged.

"What does all of this mean?"

"I have no idea. Sheriff, I have no idea what the significance of any of these things could be. Until learning about the classes my father taught, I thought I knew all there was to know about him. At least all the important things. These items are more mystery to me."

"Your life was different in many ways."

"What if I'd never gathered these boxes and opened them?"

"Maybe your subconscious knew you should."

"I don't know. Sheriff, my life was normal to me, and probably led to who and what I am now. My father wasn't strange about our life, Sheriff. I know people assign personalities to taxidermists, and my experience doesn't negate that my father might have been a little strange, but I'm sure he wasn't cruel, which is hard for some people to understand. He loved wildlife. He didn't hate it. He loved preserving its beauty, but you know how it is, people will draw their own conclusions." I stopped speaking and frowned. I'd given that speech or one like it a lot of times over the years, but this time it was mostly for me. I knew Wilmot better than anyone had. Right? Besides, Calloway didn't need to hear it.

And he wasn't wrong. If normal is the conformation to some standard that the majority of the population buys into, then it's true, my upbringing wasn't normal.

But it also wasn't murderous. I was sure of that.

"I know," Calloway said, responding not only to my speech but also to what he probably knew I was thinking. "But this is important. I'll take these things. They have to mean something." He nodded at the knife. "I wonder when we'll find one of these."

"I used to have one like it when I was a kid. I still carry a similar one."

Calloway's eyes widened briefly. "Well, lots of folks carry these knives."

"Yep."

"Still though, be on your toes."

"Always." I nodded and sat on the small chair that was tucked up against the wall next to the door. "Did you find my mother's sister?"

"Oh . . ." Calloway reached into his pocket and pulled out a small evidence bag. He took a few moments to put the pendant inside it and then seal it closed. I assumed he was thinking of what to tell me. Finally, he said, "I found her, but she's not what I expected."

"What does that mean?"

"She's not well, Hazel. She lives in a situation."

"I repeat, what does that mean?"

"When your father disappeared, we all jumped in to make sure you'd be okay, right?"

"Yes."

"When I set out to find your mother's sister yesterday, I went into it with an anger I shouldn't have had but also couldn't deny. I mean, I did reach out to her all those years ago and heard nothing, so what the hell? A relative nearby and a minor was left on her own?"

"Many people offered me a place to live. You were one. There are good people around here."

"Anyway, that's what I thought back then. Yesterday, I found her house, but when I knocked on the door, a nurse answered. At least that's what he told me he was. I verified all of what I'm going to tell you, but your aunt isn't well, hasn't been for a long time."

"What's wrong with her?"

"She has mental health issues, but the nurse didn't feel like I had the right to know the details. He wasn't wrong, but I met Susan, and she's in no shape now to care for anyone, including herself. The nurse said she's gotten worse over the years but hasn't been well for her entire life."

"That's sad."

"It is, and I suspect your father just wanted to keep you safe from having to deal with that, maybe feel like you had to take care of her."

"That bad?"

"I think so. Sometimes."

"I'm sorry to hear that." I paused. "She's at home? Not in a hospital?"

"She's living in a home, and she claimed not to remember anything at all, including helping Wilmot with any classes." He looked at me expectantly.

"What are you not telling me?"

"This is going to be a bitter pill to swallow."

"I'm familiar with that flavor."

"Her care is being paid for by money from your mother's estate."

"My mother had money? This is news to me."

"I thought it might be, and I'm sorry to be the one to break the news to you, but, yes, your mother had some money and the funds needed to take care of your aunt are from that reserve. The money Wilmot left behind for you probably came from your mother's money too, but I've never looked into it."

"Well, then it might have been my aunt's too. I mean—"

"Probably. However, I've asked an attorney to do some digging."

"Why?"

"Because, when your aunt passes, I think you should be the recipient of anything that's left."

"Calloway . . . I don't want her money. Call off your attorney."

"Hazel, you don't have to be involved at all, but I'm doing this as a part of my investigation, so you don't get to tell me to give it up."

"That's silly."

"No, it isn't." Calloway rubbed his finger under his nose. "My investigation is legitimate, and I think that something in your past—your father or even mother or Susan—have something to do with the skeleton sculptures out there. Maybe the money doesn't tie into the crimes, but I'm going to get to the bottom of everything."

I looked at the box. Would the contents change anything?

Calloway said, "I can't find Danielle Harold or Johnny Clark anywhere. Do you know anything about them?"

"Nothing. What do you mean you can't find them? No trace?"

"Johnny Clark and his father, George, seem to have fallen off the map. I can't figure out where they went then or where they are now. Danielle lived here as recently as three months ago, but she's not at her house."

"Johnny Clark was a popular kid, though the rebel type. Danielle wasn't, but they were all a few years older than me. I didn't pay much attention to them, but I did think Johnny was cute. He didn't know I existed."

"You sure?"

"Yes, Johnny Clark and I did not know each other. I'm . . ."

"What, Hazel?"

"Oh no, wait. I think Johnny had dinner with Wilmot and me one evening." My eyes wide, I looked at Calloway. Why hadn't I remembered that before now? "Damn, Calloway, that just became clear to me."

He nodded. "Why did he have dinner with you? What else do you remember?"

The words came without me thinking much about them. "Wilmot said his father was an asshole."

"George squatted on some land over by Pecan Acres, in an old shack. No one stopped him."

Pecan Acres was a two-block neighborhood that sat next to a farm that hadn't produced pecans for a long time.

"I don't remember being at his house, but Johnny was here for dinner once. He was quiet. And hungry."

"Your father was known for helping wayward folks, teenagers included."

"That could either be noble or creepy."

Calloway chuckled and said, "Your father's job was creepy, to some. Your father was odd but a good man. He wasn't a predator."

"I'm glad to hear that, particularly now since hearing about the classes for teenagers that ended with an abomination and a bucket of blood."

Calloway sobered quickly. "Right. No, Hazel. Whatever happened, Wilmot did what he thought was best for the kids. That much I'm sure of. It might have been the wrong thing to do, but he must have had his reasons."

I nodded. "So, Johnny Clark is in the wind? I can't imagine Danielle is too far away. She's been in Black Vulture forever."

"There's a rumor that Danielle and Joey Smoot have been seeing each other."

"What? No. She's almost twice his age."

"But he is of age."

"Does Trisha know?"

"I don't know what Trisha knows."

"She hasn't mentioned that one to me. Where did this come from?"

"Dixie."

"Oh. She knows more than anyone else around here."

"She usually does."

"And Joey's missing too, texting Trisha that he's in Nogales."

"Yeah. I heard from Jenna. While his phone was at the Smoots' trailer."

"Is Jerry talking yet?"

"Not really, and the hospital folks told Jenna to leave him alone for another twenty-four hours."

"Where's Verro?"

"I have no idea."

"That's not good."

"I don't know."

"How many mysteries are going on here?"

"That's a great question. I think they're all tied together, except for Joey and Danielle. That one seems different than the others except that Danielle *was* part of your dad's class." Calloway rubbed his hand over his chin. "Your father should have talked to law enforcement back then, but I can't find any record of him doing so, about anything."

"We both know that that doesn't mean he didn't. The police back then were probably worse than they were before Verro."

Calloway shook his head. "I'm meeting Graham later. Maybe he'll have some new insight."

"He was helpful today. I'm grateful to him."

"Good to hear. I'm going to send him home, though. I thought there would be more for him to do here, but for the most part, he's just searching and waiting for the next skeleton sculpture to appear. I'm sure he has plenty of other things to do."

I nodded. "I get it. We need an ATV out here. Jenna mentioned that Verro has a motorbike, but an ATV would be better."

"I'll check the budget."

"Hello?" a voice called from downstairs.

"Who's that?" Calloway asked.

"Sonny."

"Oh . . . ? Oh!"

I held up my hand stop-sign style.

I led the way downstairs. Calloway had grabbed the box and carried it behind me. Sonny stood in the museum, looking more adorable than I remembered from the night before. I wished I'd showered already.

"Hi, Sheriff," Sonny said when he saw Calloway. "Am I disturbing?"

"Not at all." Calloway stepped around Sonny and made his way to the door. With a hand on the knob, he turned back to me. "I'll call you tomorrow, Hazel." He smiled at Sonny. "Have a good evening, kids."

"Seriously?" I uttered.

"Thanks," Sonny said simultaneously.

Once Calloway was gone. I looked at Sonny. "Hey."

"Sorry if I surprised you. I've been trying to reach you. I got a little worried. Is it okay that I'm here?"

I nodded. "I guess I've been busy. I'll tell you all about it. But first I need a shower. Give me a few minutes."

"Will do." He glanced around the room. "There's plenty to see here."

"There is. Don't let it creep you out."

"I'll do my best."

"There's beer in the fridge too. Make yourself at home."

"Will do."

"Wait!" I glanced at the sliding glass door. "Have the police called you about getting prints?"

Sonny's eyes got wide. "No. Why?"

"You were looking around in here the other day. Did you, by chance, touch the sliding glass door?"

"I . . . maybe?"

"There's a print on the door. Someone broke in the other night—"

"What?"

"Well, I think. Anyway, here. Look." I angled the light from my phone so the handprint became obvious. "If it's yours, then it's not someone else's, someone who got inside."

Sonny didn't hesitate. "Oh. Sure. Let's compare."

Carefully, and without touching the glass, Sonny hovered his hand above the print. "It might be mine. Want me to give the police my fingerprints? I did have to give them to The Institute, so they're in a system somewhere."

He was correct when he said the print could be his. It could also be someone else's. I wanted it to be Sonny's because I would understand how it got there. "Let's just let Calloway know."

"You got it." He pulled out his own phone. "Want me to call him now?"

I nodded. "I'll grab that shower." I turned.

"Hang on," Sonny said.

I turned back around as he took somewhat tentative steps toward me. When he was right there in front of me, I could smell his soap and shampoo, and I couldn't help but wonder what he smelled coming from me.

Slowly, as if he was making sure it was all right, he put the hand that didn't hold the phone on the side of my face and then leaned forward and kissed me. I kissed him back. The thought of asking him to join me in the shower passed through my mind, but I wanted my own shower for now.

Sonny smiled as he pulled back. "Have a good shower."

I sent him a side-eye, wondering about the spell he was casting. What in the world was happening here? "Okay."

"Are you hungry?"

He meant for food, I knew he did, but I answered quickly. The soup hadn't been enough. "Yes."

"Dinner after shower?"

"I have the perfect spot."

"I can't wait."

After I was cleaned up and Sonny confirmed that he talked to Calloway, I offered to drive us in the Jeep, but Sonny held up his keys instead and claimed he'd didn't need the open-air life this night. The Jeep was a sad sight anyway. It was hard to tell the paint color under the dirt. I should have been embarrassed, but Sonny said I should be proud instead. I used the Jeep the way it was supposed to be used.

Two I-19 freeway stops up from Black Vulture was place that served the best fried chicken and the most mouthwatering banana cream pie.

It was also located inside a gas station convenience store. We dined at one of the three booths, enjoying the smells from the food as they mixed with the scents of motor oil and gasoline when the doors swung open. A sickly sounding bell dinged every time, but I tried to put both out of my mind and focus on my date and the food.

I usually spent my days working. My nights, going over things I'd worked on during the day or doing more work. I liked my life.

My mind and body weren't quite sure how to handle the good distractions and relaxation, not to mention the company of a man who didn't irritate the crap out of me.

It was what it was.

We'd already discussed that we were both only children. The night before, I'd delved into my childhood and my father's disappearance, which Sonny had found interesting enough to ask a lot of questions. I didn't want to talk about me again.

"Your parents?" I asked after he gave his approval to the chicken.

"What about them?"

"What do they do? What are they like?"

"They are from Wisconsin," he began.

When he didn't continue right away, I said, "I'm going to need more."

"Right." Sonny set down his food and wiped his mouth with a cheap paper napkin.

"Uh-oh, I've spoiled your appetite. That can't be good. I'm sorry. If you don't want to talk about it . . ." Though I was extra curious now.

"It's okay. My mom died when I was young. My dad drank himself to death a few years ago."

"Oh no." I put down my food too. "I'm so sorry. That had to be rough."

"It was rougher when he was alive. Man, he was a mess."

"You took care of him?"

"I wasn't left with a lot of choice. No one else would, and I could never bring myself to abandon him."

"Oh. Not good."

"No, but it's good now." He smiled sadly. "Isn't that horrible to say? My life is better without him. There are countless people who would give anything to still have their parents."

I nodded. "Well, that's true, but who knows what my relationship with my father would be like if he was still around? We can't predict."

"But you'd like a chance to know, right?"

"Sure."

"We all have old bones."

"That we do."

Sonny waved off the line of conversation and picked up a drumstick. "So, tell me something you can about the investigation. Has anyone got any clue what's going on or who's doing it?"

I shook my head. "No, and it only keeps getting more mysterious. I mean, I didn't even know I still had an aunt, but I do."

Sonny's eyes got big. "What does that mean?"

"My mom's sister is living in the same county as we are. I met her once a long time ago, but I don't remember her well, and I didn't know she was nearby."

"Why not?"

"Well, to be fair, she's not well apparently. However, I'm going to go see her tomorrow, even if I've been told not to."

"What's wrong with her?"

"Mental health issues."

"Your visit might turn out to be a big disappointment."

"I know, but I have to try."

"That's a twist."

"Or it's nothing."

"Yeah. Maybe. Want some company? I have tomorrow morning off."

"When do you sleep?"

Sonny smiled. "I get plenty. I'm wired differently. I only sleep four hours a night."

"That's not right."

"Even when I was a kid and even when I was sick, four hours and I'm wide awake."

"You seem healthy."

"I am. It's called short sleeper syndrome."

"Is that real?"

"Yes, it is."

I thought for a moment. "I'd like to see Aunt Susan alone, but do you want to hang out in my bed for five or so hours?"

He put the food down again. "That's a good surprise invitation."

"Is that a no?"

"No, that is most definitely not a no. You done with dinner yet?"

I smiled. "I think I need some banana cream first."

"Deal. Let me go get that." He paused. "Should we take it with us?"

I laughed. "Maybe."

As I watched him make his way up to the counter and order the pie, my eyes landed on a spinning hat display. I stood and walked toward it, noticing a Mobil Oil cap, almost exactly like the one that Graham wore. I realized the gas station's signage was also Mobil Oil. It had been that way forever as far as I knew, but I'd never given it much thought.

The last time I'd seen Graham's cap, it had been covered in desert grime. Would it be nice of me to purchase him a new one or would it be rude—"Your cap is filthy, and you should throw it away."

Sonny joined me. "Need a hat?"

I shook my head and decided not to make the purchase right now. Buying a gift for a guy when I was with another one seemed rude. Maybe later. I had more important things on my mind.

I'd never thought about having sex so much in my entire life. Was that good or bad, the product of stunted growth or a late bloomer?

I decided I didn't much care as we took the banana cream to go.

He'd been derailed again. Things hadn't gone as planned.

Had no one figured out who the second set of bones belonged to? Why hadn't Hazel, someone, told them how old they were, how long they'd been free of skin and tissue? It's simple after that. Well, maybe not simple, but not too difficult to figure out.

Old bones. He remembered watching the blood pool come from the veins, and then soak into the ground. He'd buried the bones along with everything else long ago.

If Hazel hadn't been out in the desert today, he would have killed her in her apartment, hopefully in the museum. He'd been torn—maybe he would deflesh and leave her bones right there, underneath the owl with the terrifying eyes, right where . . . no, he couldn't let his imagination see the horror of it.

From the first moment a year earlier when he saw Silas Reynolds standing on a street corner in Tucson, begging for money, he knew what he had to do.

To get back to Black Vulture, he'd had to make up a backstory that would unravel if even the tiniest thread were pulled, but no one seemed to be interested in his past. They just wanted to know what he could do for them now. They'd learn everything later, when it was over, but time was ticking and someone would become curious.

Accepting that he might have to wait until tomorrow, he sighed heavily and reached into his pocket.

His fingers didn't feel the tiny golden pendant or the chain. He dug around as panic rushed his movements. He reached into his other pockets, but there was no pendant.

Where did it go?

He reassured himself: "If Hazel doesn't see it, no one will understand it anyway. It won't matter if someone finds it out of context," he muttered aloud. "It just won't matter."

But what did matter was the fact that he didn't have it anymore, and it was important. He'd planned it all out and there was no substitute for that pendant. It wasn't like he could stop by the small Black Vulture grocery store and buy another one. It had taken him time to find and then order it.

Should he order another one? Could he get it sent overnight? How would that work? Was he going to have to deal with that old woman at the post office?

Inadequacy, failure spread through his limbs, leaving him both hot and cold at the same time.

He knew he'd been faking it until he could make it, but he'd thought things were going well. Now he was sure he was just an imposter, even with a grudge he couldn't deny.

He bit down on the inside of his mouth, just to the point before his molars would break through skin. He liked to taste the blood, and the pain was sometimes the only thing that could cover up the soul crushing ache, the real pain that would truly never go away.

Until he killed and posed Hazel Dylan.

CHAPTER

24

"ARE YOU FUCKING kidding me?!" Trisha slammed the empty ceramic coffee mug down on the counter. "Joey and Danielle Harold? That's the wildest thing I've ever heard."

Calloway and I sat at the counter. It had been by chance that I'd seen him walking into the diner. I suspected he was going in to talk to Trisha, and I didn't think it would go well. I wasn't sure I could make it better, but Trisha liked me enough to maybe not throw something at Calloway if I was with him.

"Trisha, watch your language!" Virgie said from somewhere in the kitchen.

I didn't see her or her hair. Trisha ignored her, keeping her angry focus on Calloway and me.

"I know, Trisha. I'm just asking," he said.

"No, you're not just asking. You've heard something. I want to know what it was and who said it."

"I'm trying to find Joey. I'm exploring every lead, no matter how small or ridiculous."

He wouldn't bring up Dixie's name. Neither would I.

The bright anger in Trisha's eyes calmed a little, but her pursed lips remained tight. "Okay, okay. Look, I know how rumors go around this crazy place. Joey did some work for Danielle out at her place. Her water heater busted, and she paid Joey to drain and remove the old one and then put in one she bought off some online marketplace. Joey had to go out to her place a couple times because the one she bought needed some new parts that he had to go buy. He was at her place a lot, trying to get that damn water heater to work."

"Did he?" I asked, surprised that Joey had any useful skills.

"Yeah. Joey can fix anything."

I had no idea. "Okay."

Calloway continued, "Trisha, is there any chance at all that they went to Nogales together? She's not at her house."

"No. And, there's no chance that Joey went to Nogales by himself, Sheriff. He for sure didn't go with Danielle. She's . . . old and strange. He told me."

"What? Talk to me, Trisha," Calloway said.

Trisha grimaced as if she wasn't sure what to say, but she continued, "She's paranoid."

"How so?"

"She made him knock on the door a certain way. I don't know. It was something like two long pauses and then two short. He said she answered the door by just peeking out first. Joey said she kept looking outside, like she thought someone was coming after her."

"Is there anything else he said? Anything at all, Trisha? What you've told us so far might help. Can you remember anything else?"

As Calloway asked the questions, I thought back to the last time I'd seen Danielle. It had been in the grocery store a few months earlier. She'd always kept to herself, wasn't polite. I never thought much about it, but I wondered if Joey had misinterpreted misanthrope-ish to mean paranoid.

"She didn't say a thing to him, but while he was there, she listened to Minnie's podcast, on loud. He could hear it from inside as he worked in the garage. He wondered if she was losing her hearing or something."

"Which episode?"

"Joey wouldn't have had a clue. He just recognized Minnie's voice."

Calloway and I shared a look. He confirmed that Trisha didn't have anything else to add before we left the diner together.

"Maybe something scared Danielle. I mean, before all the recent events," I said as we stepped outside.

"I agree. I'm going back to Thalia's, see if something might have spooked her too."

"I want to come with you."

Calloway gave me a long look. "Okay. All right."

I didn't even go back to my place for my pack, but I'd already grabbed the gun.

We hopped into Calloway's SUV. As we made our way, fear and concern built inside me. Had we missed something, or were we possibly too late for something?

Calloway got us to Thalia's quickly. She wasn't outside this time. The front door was closed tight. There was something about the place that elevated my concern.

"Stay here," Calloway said.

"Sheriff, you know I can't do that." I got out of the car.

"Stay behind me." Calloway came around and placed himself in between me and the house.

"That I'll do."

"Thalia? You there?" Calloway called.

There was no response, but I didn't expect any.

"Sheriff," I said, my voice tight with concern. I wanted him to be careful, but I couldn't bring myself to finish the request.

"I know." He knocked on the door. "Thalia, you in there?"

When there was no response again, he tried the door. It was locked.

"We have to get in there," I said.

"I know. I'm going to check the back."

"I'm coming with you."

"I wish you'd go back to the car."

"No."

Neither of us drew our guns. Our quick steps stirred up dust as we navigated over a few toys on the way to the backyard. We took two stairs up to a deck, toward the back sliding glass door. Calloway tried to pull on the door, but it was locked. He put himself up to the glass and peered in.

"No one." He seemed to deflate a little, in a good way. "There's no sign of trouble either."

"We still need to get in there. We need to confirm."

"I don't disagree, but I don't want to break the glass if I don't have to. Let me get something from my car. Come around with me."

I hesitated, but only for a few seconds. A few minutes later, without taking any time to see if we were being watched, Calloway picked the front door lock and opened it wide.

"Thalia? Anyone home? It's Sheriff Calloway and Hazel Dylan."

No answer.

I followed the sheriff into the house. He looked all around as he called for Thalia, anyone. No one answered.

It seemed like a long time, but it was probably less than a minute before we'd searched the entire house. No one was there, dead, alive, or hurt. Beds were made. The kitchen was clean and free of dishes in the sink.

They'd left the house, but not in a hurry or under duress.

"But they've gone somewhere."

"I don't know, but the house does feel like they might have wanted to make sure it was clean when they came home."

Calloway grabbed his cell phone and scrolled to a saved number. He put the phone on speaker. I heard Thalia's voice. "Not me. Leave a message. I'd suggest texting."

"Thalia, its Sheriff Calloway. Could you give me a call as soon as possible? Thanks. I just need to confirm that you are okay." He ended the call and then texted her the same message.

We both watched the phone for a moment, but there was no indication that she received or read the message.

"Do you think she's running scared?"

"I have no idea, Hazel. People leave Black Vulture all the time. Trips to Tucson, trips anywhere. It's impossible to know until I talk to her, but I do want to talk to her."

"Should we check with Jeff, maybe try to find Danielle again?"

Calloway sighed. "No, I'm taking you home. I'll check on Jeff."

"I can come with you, Sheriff."

"No, we're not going to do that, Hazel. I don't know what's going on here, but I need to do my job without worrying about you."

"This has something to do with my father."

He sent me a sideways look. "Now's not the time."

"What do you mean?"

"Look, Hazel, I don't know what happened to Wilmot, but I know that if there had been any way to get back to you, he would have. He was a good father and he adored you."

A swell of emotion hit me in my gut again, but there wasn't time for that now. "So whatever involvement you think he has in this, it's posthumously?"

"I do think he's dead, Hazel. I'm sorry."

I let his words settle a bit. "I guess that means he can't be the one killing and skinning people then."

"I agree, but I do think his reputation or something that happened in that class is behind all of this. I just need to figure out what it is. I do. Me. You need to stay safe. Spend more time with your boyfriend."

"He's not my boyfriend."

"Right. Whatever. Hang out with him. Do your work."

I nodded disagreeably.

"I'll take you home."

The brief ride back to town was silent, but as Calloway came to a stop in front of my place, I said, "Call me later."

"Absolutely."

I got out and watched him drive away. I thought he might turn right, but since he didn't, I knew the first place I was going to explore on my own.

I grabbed my pack from inside, locked all the doors again, and hopped into the Jeep. As I passed the diner, I spotted Trisha in the window. She was taking an order at the front table. She sent me a frown and then a nod. She knew I wasn't going to be able to just sit back and wait for someone else to solve these mysteries, and she knew Joey's whereabouts was one of them. She was glad I was on her side.

I sent her a return nod and steered the Jeep back toward The Wild.

CHAPTER

25

FROM ALL OUTWARD appearances, Danielle Harold despised the human race. She loved horses, though, which had given me pause a few times over the years. Since I was somewhat of a misanthrope myself, I wondered if maybe she was on to something.

I was fond of horses, all animals, but I wasn't in a position to take proper care of any creatures. Or plants.

The mounts in my father's museum as well as Jack, the wild owl who visited me, were as close as I would probably get to caring for other creatures.

Thoughts about Jack made me hope again that he was okay and just taking time away.

I stopped in front of Danielle Harold's house. I put my concerns over Jack on a back burner and took in the dilapidation around me.

If there was ever a place that belonged to Black Vulture, it was Danielle's house. The downtown could blow over with a strong wind, but her house gave the impression that a good sneeze would be enough.

The barn and corral, however, were in good enough condition. There was no indication that those structures would crumble anytime soon. Horses would be okay.

There were none there today, though. I hadn't thought of asking Calloway about the animals, but I should have. If he'd told me that there were none on the property, I would have known for sure that Danielle was gone, maybe never to come back.

Thalia was gone too, but her empty house didn't seem so permanent.

The good news was that if the horses weren't there either, Danielle was most likely okay. But where had everyone gone? The same place or different locations?

I did a quick walk over the property and peeked into a front window, confirming that there was furniture inside but no one was around. I came to no clearer conclusions as I hopped back into the Jeep and turned to head to Minnie's trailer.

But I changed my mind and pulled a tight U-turn.

There was someone else I wanted to talk to first.

It was easier than it should have been to find my Aunt Susan. An internet search and then some guessing sent me to a house on the edge of the county. In fact, it was in a small township that straddled the border of two counties. Like the traffic signs in kilometers, things in this part of the world didn't run on normal rules.

You couldn't see much of the house from the road because of the thick overgrowth. There was no welcome sign. There was no sense of invitation at all. Whoever lived there amid all the desert plants didn't want visitors.

Too bad.

I parked the Jeep and stood in front of the property a moment, my hands on my hips. I didn't spot any cameras, but I suspected there was at least one trained right on me. I wanted to give whoever was watching enough time to size me up, and see the bulge of gun in my back waistband. Maybe realize I was related to the woman inside.

I wasn't law enforcement, but most people around here thought of me as adjacent to law enforcement. I was going to use that and hope no one thought they even had the option of turning me away.

I found a small break in the foliage and took the walkway up. Creosote, sagebrush, all kinds of cacti filled the space. I found it wild, out of control, and beautiful.

I knocked on the door, hearing footsteps only a second or two later. A young man opened the door and frowned.

"Can I help you?"

"I hope so. I'm here to talk to Susan Shaw."

"Do you have an appointment?"

"I do not."

"We are a private medical facility, and we require advance notice and appointments." The door started to shut.

I stuck my boot-clad foot in the opening.

"I work with the Sheriff's office."

"Do you have a badge?"

"Nope. I'm their bone expert."

The young man blinked at me before his eyes widened. He was probably in his late thirties, pale and tired. "Are you Hazel Dylan?"

"I am."

"Oh." He opened the door wider and cocked his head as he looked at me for a long moment. "Interesting. Well, without a badge, the rules apply. You need to be cleared, and an appointment needs to be made."

"Do you know me because my aunt is Susan Shaw or is there another reason?"

"I'm not sure."

"Look, I can go get the sheriff and we can come back together, or you can let me talk to Susan for just a few minutes and I'll be on my way."

"You should get the sheriff." The door started to shut again.

"David!" A shrill voice called from behind him.

He frowned at me as if to say, "Now you've done it," but he opened the door wider.

A woman stepped around David and filled the space in the doorway. If I'd seen her in public, I wouldn't have immediately pegged her as my mother's sister, but since I knew who she was, I could see the resemblance to the picture of my mother that I'd seen. We all had long, dark brown hair and light brown eyes. Our noses weren't cute and petite but made a statement along with our strong chins.

"Hello, Hazel," she said as a single tear rolled down her cheek. "I've been wanting to talk to you for so long. I'm glad you found me."

I wanted to say something like "I didn't know you were lost" or "I haven't been all that far away" or "Are they keeping you hostage?" but I simply nodded and said, "Nice to meet you."

She smiled. "Oh, we've met before, but I understand why you wouldn't remember. You were very little. Come in. Let's chat."

She turned and walked into the dark depths of the house. David, straightening even more, stood his ground as I stepped inside.

"She's not well," he said quietly but with gritted teeth. "Do not upset her."

"I wouldn't dream of it," I said.

She seemed fine to me, but what did I know. I wasn't even sure what questions I had for Aunt Susan, but I was sure something would come to me.

I took off my hat and followed her confident footsteps.

CHAPTER 26

The house was a mishmash of décor. Bright, colorful art filled the walls, and an overload of knickknacks decorated tables. The floor was made of red clay square tiles with tan grout. It was as if the house was first put together with a southwestern flair in mind, but other things like porcelain cats and Asian fans just couldn't be ignored, so they were included too.

The place was enormous, but I didn't see much more than the rooms off the long hallway as we walked down the middle of the expansive home. I glanced into four open doorways that we passed before we walked through a fifth. I didn't see anyone else in the house, but I saw a lot of stuff, too much to take any sort of quick visual inventory.

The room that Susan led us to was like the rest of the house, colorful and packed with things. The house was one tipped over ceramic cat away from being classified as a hoarder's.

But it was clean, everything dusted, the floors spotless.

I didn't know the right or polite way to ask Susan what was wrong with her. So far, I hadn't noticed anything.

She offered the answer anyway. The words sounded scripted. "I will not go into detail, Hazel, but I'm going to call what I have a mental health disorder, which, for some people isn't debilitating, but for me it isn't good. Sometimes I deal with psychosis and violent behavior, and that's why David will sit here with us. Lots of people do much better than I do on medication. In fact, many people can function in the real world just fine. I'm not what you could call functional. Medication has changed over the years, but I've been unwell for so long that there's not a lot of hope for me."

"I'm sorry."

Her eyes locked on mine. "I don't bother with apologies. Ask me what you want. Get to the nitty gritty. Let's not waste time feeling sorry for ourselves and the impossibility of having a relationship. You can deal with understanding things if you want on your own time. I've come to terms with everything."

I nodded. "Right. Okay. Um. What happened during some classes my father taught all those years ago, shortly before he disappeared?"

"The sheriff asked me the same."

"What did you tell him?"

"I told him that I had no idea, and at that time, I didn't. Since Sheriff Calloway's visit, some things have come back to me. David and I have been taking notes." She looked at him. "David, let's give those to Hazel now."

"I don't think that's a good idea, Susan."

"I don't care what you think. We are giving the notes to Hazel."

David sighed and made his way over to a simple desk. Made with blond wood, the legs were spindly and there was one drawer in the middle of the slim top. David opened the drawer and gathered a yellow notebook. He held it for a moment.

"Give it to her."

"I haven't cleaned it up."

"It doesn't matter. She can sift through it herself to find the truth." Susan looked at me. "There is truth in there. Horrible things happened, but my memory isn't to be completely trusted."

"Okay." I wasn't sure how I could figure out the difference, but it was something.

David handed me the notebook. As much as I wanted to read it, I was also afraid to take it. Only five minutes earlier, I hadn't known this woman. It was like I'd been forced to swallow all the years that had passed and deal with the indigestion, while she'd tasted them along the way.

"Read the first few lines aloud," Susan commanded.

I took the notebook and looked at the first page. There were notes down the page, done in blue ink. But there were also illustrations made with sharp points and unintelligible scribbles. There was no way to see anything clearly. Just looking at the page was unsettling.

I cleared my throat. "Rogue taxidermy! Rogue taxidermy. That's what he called it. It was good at first, but he pushed it too far and he cracked . . ." I looked up at Susan. "Cracked."

"Went psychotic. Lost his mind. I drew sketches."

"Who?"

"Keep reading."

I never understood if mental illness contributed to creativity or if creativity could just be a part of an ill mind, but Susan was a gifted artist. I knew who the sketches were supposed to be.

My father was at the top of the page. His dark hair was always short, but the front seemed to fall onto his forehead. His dark eyes appeared angry in the sketch, his thin lips even tighter than normal.

Minnie looked almost the same—a beautiful, exotic young woman. Susan had drawn her with a hesitant smile and big eyes.

But everyone else had been given less than happy expressions. Still, though, I could recognize them.

Jeff Ranke looked like the younger version of the grease monkey that I knew now. Thalia had been stunning, even with a sour expression. I remembered Silas now even better and felt a wave of sadness over the fact that the first set of bones had belonged to him and, from all indications, he'd been living as a homeless man in Tucson. Danielle had been cute—but her decades-long constant frown and attitude toward everyone else had made her only unpleasant to be around, no matter what she might look like. I didn't remember her being cute. Johnny Clark, his long brown hair kind of greasy, just like I remembered it. From this vantage point, I couldn't understand why I thought he was cute. It wasn't that he wasn't, but his look did scream rebel.

I remembered the people almost like the sketches in front of me, but it was the last sketch on the bottom corner of the page that I thought the most interesting. It was the most detailed rendering and illustrated a beautiful woman.

"You are good at self-portraits."

Susan's focus was on me, but her foot had started tapping nervously. "That's not me, Hazel. That's your mom."

I was tired of all these emotions coming at me like horror movie jumps. There was no time for a discussion about my mother, but I sure did think she'd been pretty.

"She was the best of everyone, all of us," Susan said.

I nodded.

"Your father loved you, but he was somewhat lost without her."

"I'm sure." I pushed away things I wanted to feel, the memories I didn't have because I'd never known my mother, but that didn't mean I hadn't wanted to hear the stories. Just not today.

"Maybe someday we can spend some time talking about her," Susan said.

"I'd like that. Why is she pictured here? She was long gone by the time everything happened."

Susan nodded. "She was, but it was . . . her things that were taken and used by that boy, Silas."

I shook my head. "Can you explain that better?"

"When it all fell apart, Wilmot called me to help that day. He knew he could trust me not to tell anyone what happened, and I was doing okay, so I agreed. I helped get everyone and everything cleaned up—"

"Susan, where was I?" I interjected.

"Oh." She fell into thought. "You were never around. I can't remember what you were doing, but your father made sure to hold the classes when you weren't home. The kids who took the classes did so without parental approval, not that that really mattered until the end anyway. He didn't want to put you in an uncomfortable situation. When the last class happened, you were in Tucson for a workshop."

I remembered a week in Tucson, working with the university at a fake archeological dig. It was something they set up to give teenagers a chance to see if they might like archeology. I hadn't, but that's where I'd met my future mentor, Dr. Fulgi. She'd seen my keen interest in the bones, but not the tedious digging. Meeting her had been fortuitous.

I laughed once. "I was away from my father for one week during all our years together, and that was when all this happened?" I didn't remember that the workshop had been right before he'd disappeared either.

"I believe so." Susan lifted her hands and then dropped them back onto her lap.

I sighed. I was glad I hadn't forgotten the things that had taken place in my father's shop. I'd been away, and as that week came back to me, so did returning home from it and finding

Wilmot leaving doors open and unlocked again for the few days he was still there.

"Okay," I continued. "What happened?"

"A few days or maybe a week before that day, one of the kids snuck up to the apartment, took a box of your mother's stuff that Wilmot had up there. Then the things were added to some gruesome thing he created—"

"Let me guess the items in the box. A red scarf, a barbeque fork, a gold pendant, and a knife."

Susan shook her head. "No knife, but the other things were Catalina's."

"A barbeque fork?"

Susan laughed. "Yes. She would take it with her on hikes. She killed scorpions with it."

"That's strange."

Susan fell into thought. Her eyes glazed, but she smiled this time.

"Hang on," David said. "Just give her a minute."

Susan continued, "Your mother was a character. She grabbed the fork one day when she was out on the patio. She speared a scorpion. Your father thought it was so funny. She liked his laugh." Susan sighed and then waved away the memories. "Anyway, your father was so angry when the box was taken."

"The box was taken before the last class, so the items inside were used on the creation?"

Susan nodded. "Yes. If I remember correctly, Wilmot told me that he should have just let the box go, not mention it. He went to a few of the kids' houses to ask about it, and one of the fathers was particularly upset that his son might have stolen something. Then things about the class came to light. It got ugly, but the box was never found. Then the thing showed up with the items included, and one of the kids had a bucket of blood. He was so angry about being found out by his father—"

"One of the kids? Wait. Was this two separate kids?"

"I don't know. I didn't ask. When Wilmot called for help, I just went out and helped." She looked at David briefly and then back at me. "It gave me something to focus on, and sometimes that's good, though not all the time."

"Your aunt had nothing to do with anything that occurred," David said. "She just helped in the aftermath."

He looked young to me. "Were you with her back then?"

"No, but I know Susan."

"I'm prone to . . . outbursts sometimes," she said. "But not . . . not what happened there."

"You screamed when you went back inside and two girls were left on the patio?" I asked.

For the briefest of instants, I saw that I'd surprised her, but she covered it quickly. "I don't remember screaming."

She was lying, but I didn't challenge her. "You didn't remember any of this when Calloway stopped by?"

Susan looked at David again.

"See, this is why I don't want anyone talking to her. People hold Susan to a standard of a mentally healthy person. It's not fair."

"Okay." I looked at her. "But you didn't remember?"

"I wasn't in a good place that day, but David has helped me get these things out." She nodded at the notebook.

"Were you at the apartment other times too?"

"Right after you were born."

And my mother had died. "Any other time?"

"I have visited a few times, but not for long and not when you were there. Wilmot and I didn't want to confuse you. I wanted to be in your life, but we both thought it best that I wasn't."

"I hate that. It doesn't really make sense."

"You shouldn't hate it. It's a good thing."

I disagreed, but maybe she was right.

Susan's fingers started to flutter, and the blank look filled her eyes again.

"Take the notebook and go, Hazel. Susan needs to rest now."

"No . . . I have more—"

Somehow, he herded me out of the room and saw me to the door quickly.

"Sheriff Calloway will want to talk to her again," I said.

He opened the front door. "Hazel, I'm not trying to make your life difficult. I'm your aunt's advocate. She hired me to be her caregiver and with that came advocacy. I will fight until the end for her to be left alone. That comes before everything else. Got it?"

"I'd like to see her again too."

"Goodbye, Hazel. Good luck." The door shut decisively.

I stood on the stoop for a few seconds. When I was back in the Jeep, I called Calloway.

"I have something you need to look at."

"What is it?"

"It's a long story. Where are you?"

"I'm in town, with Verro and Jenna."

"That'll work. I'm on the way."

CHAPTER

27

I MADE MY WAY back to town, parked, and hurried inside with the notebook.

Calloway, Verro, and Jenna were there. Tension seemed to fill the air, but if it was because of something other than the recent mysteries, I didn't have time to pay it any attention. Weirdly, Verro had a few cuts and bruises on his face.

"What happened?" I asked.

"Nothing," Verro answered quickly.

"Are you okay?" I asked.

"My pride is hurt worse than anything."

I nodded but didn't push him further. I told everyone about my visit with Susan. Calloway flashed a look when I mentioned that she hadn't remembered the things she'd told me today when he was there, but he didn't have time to ponder that either.

We took an hour to look at the notebook. Jenna rolled the whiteboard next to the desk and transcribed our interpretations. Ultimately, we had a story, but none of us could be sure it was the right one. A lot of it was made of "filled-in assumptions."

Had Silas been the one to bring in the abomination and the bucket of blood? I thought we were wrong to assume he'd done both.

"Remember, Jeff wasn't sure, and he got there after the blood was all over," I said. "The people in the class didn't want to talk about it again, even to get their stories straight. They moved right to making a vow not to. And Thalia wasn't so sure either. Also, I think Susan and David kicked me out before telling me everything that went on."

Calloway nodded.

"We need to know what happened to Johnny Clark," Verro said.

"I can't find anything," Calloway said.

"I remember where he and his father lived," I added. "Out near the caves, Pecan Acres, in an old shack. Maybe a hunting cabin. I never visited them, but I just knew the location."

Calloway nodded. "At first, I thought they owned the place, but I couldn't find any record of ownership or rental agreements. I suspect they were squatters. I did find record of George Clark filing unemployment up in Tucson shortly after Wilmot disappeared, but that was the only trail, and it ended quickly. Johnny never was enrolled in any of the public schools up there."

"He might not have finished high school," I said.

"Probably not," Calloway agreed. "I ran out to the shack, looked through the windows. It's bad. Other squatters have been there, and animals too. There's nothing there that will help us."

"Who else would have known them well back then?"

"You would know that better than any of us, I think," Verro said.

"I have no idea," I said.

But I had vapors of an idea. I couldn't make all the dots fit together, but having the first bones identified as Silas Reynolds helped formulate something in my mind.

"I need to talk to Minnie again. Who has her number?" I asked.

Calloway reached for his phone and scrolled through his contacts before handing me the phone. A voicemail picked up.

"Should we go out there?" Calloway asked.

I thought about it for a long moment. "No, but I know what I need to do." I looked at Verro and Jenna. "There are two dentists up in Sahuarita. All of us around here see one or the other. Can you two give them a call and ask if they have George's or Johnny's dental records?"

"Okay," Verro said.

I looked at Calloway. "I need to see the second skeleton right away."

"Pictures won't do?"

I looked at the sketch of Johnny that Susan had drawn. "Nope."

"Let's go. I'll drive.

The bones had been taken to the Tucson medical examiner's office. I knew the chief medical examiner, Gretta Hess. She was good at what she did. So was everyone who worked with her. There had been a rush on the first set of bones. The second, clearly older, set was still being tested, though it had been moved into a priority position too.

When there had been no dental or DNA match in any of the systems, the investigation was still going on via lab tests that would help with, among other things, precise aging of the bones, telling us how long they'd been in the ground, maybe even give us a clue as to the location of their burial. I wondered if Verro and Jenna might find some information that would help regarding the teeth, but I doubted it.

Mostly, I wondered if I could help.

I resisted looking at the pictures I'd taken as we made our way north. I remembered what I'd seen, but I knew about memory and how it wasn't always accurate. I also knew that if the pictures didn't match my memory, I'd be disappointed. If they did match it, I'd want to see the bones again anyway just to confirm.

This wasn't as easy as a picture. I didn't even want to ask clarifying questions over the phone. I needed to see what I needed to see.

"Dr. Hess isn't here," the receptionist said as Calloway and I entered.

"Could I still take a look?" I asked, thinking I might be compelled to break down a door if I wasn't granted permission.

At that moment, one of technicians came out from the lab.

"Hey, Haze, what's going on?" Brady asked. He was young and smart and had a wicked sense of humor, which could be helpful in such a serious profession.

"I need to see the second set of bones found down near Black Vulture," I said. He'd know exactly what I was talking about.

Brady and the receptionist exchanged a look. Relief spread through me when Brady said, "Gown up."

I put on a gown, footies, and gloves before Brady led me into the lab.

"I can't let you touch anything," he said.

"I just need a good, close look."

"Have at it."

The bones, still formed into a scorpion shape, had been placed on one exam table. The other sculpture was in the room too, on another table. The coyote.

Seeing the sculptures inside the autopsy room was different than out in the desert. The desert was the creatures' natural habitat. Even as models, they felt out of place in this sterile room. And something else—more human.

I tried never to forget about the people who left their bones behind.

The bones belonged to people, once with flesh, bones, and a soul. Wilmot had preached this, even about animals. I always wished I could relay that to the people who despised what he did and him for doing it, but words weren't enough. You had to live it. And I had.

I made my way to Silas's bones first, allowing my eyes to roam over the whiteness, so clean and pristine, unless you looked closely or knew what to look for. I thought about the kid, the sketch in Susan's notebook. I remembered the bullying he'd endured.

I muttered quietly, "I'm sorry, Silas, for . . ." I didn't have a specific reason, but I was sorry for that little boy.

Brady came up next to me and nodded toward a femur. "We wondered about that slight bowing. We did some tests and found osteomalacia."

"Really?"

Osteomalacia was a bone disease that caused bones to soften and weaken from inadequate mineralization, usually a vitamin D deficiency. Even in the sun-drenched state of Arizona, it could happen.

"I believe he was homeless for a long time. Poor nutrition," I said.

Brady nodded.

The coyote and little boy shapes faded in my mind, and I tried to imagine Silas as a grown man. It was difficult to see anything but struggles from his time on the street. It was a rough life, but I knew that some people lived it as a choice. I had no way of knowing all that had led to Silas's circumstances, but I hoped he found peace somewhere along the way.

"So, so sorry," I whispered.

I sighed and walked to the scorpion sculpture, pushing away the desert creature image again and focusing on the bones.

I kept my eyes away from the spot I wanted to inspect most of all. I wanted to take in the whole skeleton again, just in case there was something else I wanted to see. Immediately, my heart ached at the age. Clearly this was a younger person than Silas.

"Do you have an age yet?"

"We X-rayed. The growth plates were almost closed. He was probably about seventeen, give or take a little," Brady said.

A kid, just like I'd thought.

I had to shake off the melancholy and focus. The bones were stained throughout with stripes of red that must have come from the dirt they had been buried in, I wondered if it had been dug up in Sedona, which was a lot farther north than Tucson and Black Vulture. The shape was unmistakable. Whoever put it together had been patient and meticulous. Respectful. Thorough. The barbeque fork, looking exactly like the one I'd retrieved from the box, sat on the table behind the bones.

"The fork wasn't secured well?"

"I don't know," Brady said. "It came in as a separate piece."

"Sedona dirt?" I asked.

"No. Definitely down where you are, out by the . . ." he grabbed a clipboard from a table, "Tumacácori Mountains. That's down by you, right?"

"Yep." I was surprised to hear the location, but I shouldn't have been.

"I don't see anything more specific, though. We'd like to find the burial site, but no one's gone out looking yet."

"Why not?"

"Apparently, the Tumacácori Mountains cover a lot of ground. We need to narrow it down some or have more to go on, before the investigators will go out."

I nodded. All the bones had been supported by wire and wood pieces. "Anything on the nonorganic pieces?"

"Not a thing. That wire, that wood, you can get stuff like that everywhere. There are no prints anywhere."

"What else do you have?"

Brady nodded. "Not great nutritionally but functional. Blunt force trauma to the head seems like the obvious cause of death, but I wonder about a nick on a rib, so maybe a stab wound. We'll figure it out. There is no presence of poisons, no obvious disease. Bones are pretty strong, despite nutritional challenges. No sign of infection."

My eyes finally went to the skull. The hole with ragged edges along the forehead. The skull was cracked but not with a pattern that I could recognize.

"That doesn't look like something hit it too hard. Maybe a fall?" I speculated.

Brady nodded. "I think that's possible, but the edge of what it hit was—"

"Sharp," I supplied for him. "Like maybe from a fall on a rock with a sharp edge?"

"Or the edge of a table, but I think your idea is a reasonable possibility. I don't think we've taken a closer look inside the gash. Do you want to?"

"Sure. In fact, I want to take a closer look at the skull. May I use a magnifying glass?"

"Of course." He reached into a drawer and grabbed one.

I stepped close to the skeleton and brought up the glass. This was it, the thing I'd come here to see.

First, though, I took a look in the gash, hoping to find something that might be debris from a rock or something else. I didn't spot anything, but that didn't mean there wasn't something there.

"You'll have to test it," I said.

"We will."

I pulled back and looked at the eye sockets as if there were eyes in there. "Okay, my friend," I said. "Are you ready to talk to me?"

He was.

I'd looked it up. The kind of piercing that Johnny Clark had below his lip was called a lowbret. Piercings didn't go through bone, but the placement of them could affect the bone underneath. A lowbret could affect the teeth and gums too, which would be helpful if Verro or Jenna could find someone who'd looked at these teeth.

But my eyes went to the mandible, below the teeth, on the right side. I could see it in my mind. Susan had sketched it: Cool Johnny, in his black leather, his eyes sharp and suspicious, a silver post though the skin below his bottom lip.

And there it was. There was most definitely some unusual wear to the mandible. It wasn't much, but it was enough.

"Come here, Brady." I handed him the glass. "Look there. Wear from a piercing?"

"Oh. Yeah. Maybe." He moved even closer. "There's not much, but enough to make me think we should have noticed it already."

"I don't know. He was young. Given a few more years, the wear would have been more apparent."

Brady looked at the mandible again. "It's undeniable, though." He dropped the glass and looked at me. "Good job, Hazel. Do you know who this is?"

"I think so. I think his name was Johnny Clark."

"Did you know him?"

"Not well, but I did. He lived in Black Vulture, though a long time ago."

"Wow. This is great. I'm glad you came in."

Brady had me write down the particulars, then he led me toward the reception door. On the way, I noticed a bag of bones on another lab table. Curiosity got the best of me, so I veered that direction.

"The extra phalanges," I said as I looked at the bag.

"Phalanges?" Brady said. "No."

"No?"

Brady's eyes narrowed over his mask. I returned the expression.

"Did you think they were phalanges? Human finger bones?"

I nodded a bit too exuberantly. "Yes."

I had the history. I knew what my father had carried in his pocket. I'd seen it, witnessed him rolling a phalanx through his fingers. I'd seen the bones stuck between the sculptures' finger bones and the turtle foot.

"No, they're equine," Brady said as he reached for the bag with his gloved hands. "Just look through the bag."

As I held it up, it was as if a filter cleared. "Oh," I said desperately.

I knew bones. I could read them. I had just figured out the scorpion was probably Johnny! But I'd let my personal experience interfere with my professionalism.

If I'd had them in my lab, if I'd picked them up and looked at them closely, I would have known that the bones in the bag had originated in horse tails. They'd been tucked in between or under other things. The tail bones can resemble phalanges, kind of, but they were more robust, with bony protuberances that human phalanges don't have. Any other time, any other situation, I would have spotted the differences immediately. Now, I just felt . . . careless. Maybe a part of me was just looking for an excuse, but I allowed myself a little cold comfort by rationalizing that Graham hadn't noticed the difference either.

"What's going on, Hazel?"

"Any prints?" I asked.

"No, they were wiped clean of everything. You okay?"

I shook my head. "It's all good, Brady." I set the bag on the table and thanked him again as he walked me out.

Calloway looked at me with raised eyebrows.

"I think I know who the second sculpture is, and . . . well, I learned even more. I'll tell you on the way home."

"Any clues as to who's been doing it?"

"No."

"Come on, let's get home." He held up his phone. "Black Vulture's made the news."

"That's never good."

* * *

He was surprised and impressed by the news story.

"What's Going On in Black Vulture, Arizona? Bone Sculptures, That's What."

When it came to the sculptures, no one knew much of anything, but someone had obtained a picture of the first skeleton. The reporter mentioned the two poses, but the media hadn't tied any of it to taxidermy positions and mounts.

It was like they weren't paying attention.

No one had talked about his trickery either. He'd heard the investigators had figured out that the first sculpture was Silas, but the reporter didn't mention the ID. The whole story was speculation and mystery, which wasn't terrible. But he would like more credit, even anonymously.

How could they not mention how the poses looked like taxidermy? Was it not all as obvious as he'd intended it to be?

Was it all just random?

He'd spent so long preparing, and they just weren't "getting" it. Or they weren't fully talking about it. They would. Soon enough.

He knew it would all be so much more difficult to ignore when he was done. He knew he shouldn't have waited so long, but damn it, he liked her. He'd let himself get to know her just enough that she wasn't the same ghost she'd been.

"Keep Hazel out of this," Wilmot had said. "I'd do anything to protect her. Don't test me."

You out there, Wilmot?

Where did you go? Are you seeing this? I don't care. Either you're dead or you're watching, and you'll see what you deserve to see.

He considered calling a news outlet and giving them some better clues, just so the stories could beef up some. Maybe he could tell them about Wilmot Dylan and the day the taxidermist killed the boy.

That would be something.

Not yet. He'd finish tonight, and then maybe Wilmot would reappear so he could face the man who'd ruined his life all those years ago.

They were destined to ruin each other's.

CHAPTER

28

THE HOSPITAL PERSONNEL were not thrilled we were there. With Calloway in his uniform, we appeared to be official, but our visit to Jerry Smoot was mostly personal. Maybe twenty percent business.

He was in a regular room, receiving fluids and being watched over for a day or so more, but they didn't want him agitated. We told them we wouldn't agitate him, but it was possible that we would. Jerry's normal was a state of agitation.

"Damn it, Hazel, Calloway, bust me out of this place," Jerry said as we walked into his room.

He looked great, back to his normal scruffy self. He didn't even appear to be as skinny as I thought he'd seemed when we found him. His color was good—that same old leather tan he'd built up over the years was back. It was no longer red and burned, white around the mouth. He'd recovered well.

"They said probably tomorrow," I said.

"Damn, one day early wouldn't hurt. Ask 'em."

"We will." Calloway put his hand on Jerry's calf. "We're glad you're okay."

"Shoot. I'm right as rain. Nothing even bit me."

"What were you doing out there?" I asked.

"The same I'm always doing, I guess. Cleaning up the damn desert."

Also known as looking for bones.

"Do you remember what happened?" Calloway asked.

Jerry frowned. "Not really. I mean, some of it."

"Tell us what you can," Calloway said.

Jerry nodded. "I don't think it was anything criminal, Sheriff, but I just can't be sure. I think I saw a man. He had bones. I don't think he was happy to see me. He could have hit me, but maybe I tripped and fell as I was walking toward him. That's all I remember. When I woke up, I thought maybe he's the one who got me here, but then I was told how long I was out there. Now I wonder if I dreamed the man. Surely, a man wouldn't leave another out there to die. Right?"

"What did he look like?" I asked.

"I don't know. Baseball hat. Sunglasses. Medium build, white. Not even a little bit of a tan." Jerry paused. "But I can't be sure of any of it. Like I said, maybe I dreamed it."

"Good to know, Jerry, but I want you to call us if you think of anything else important."

"Sure. Sure. Have you found my Joey? Trisha told me that you're looking for him. She said she'd come get me if I needed her."

"We haven't. We do have his cell phone, though."

"The one in our place, in the drawer?" Jerry asked.

"Yes," Calloway said. "What was it doing there?"

"That's where he likes to keep it when he goes down to Mexico. He doesn't like Trisha to know where he's gone, and they have that tracer app." Jerry sighed. "I'm not to let her know. She'll probably break up with him, and he'll be heartbroken, but the boy has to learn that he shouldn't lie to his people."

"Who might have been in your trailer and turned it on briefly?" I asked.

"Joey's the only one I can think of. Dang him. He keeps finding a good path, but then he veers. I love him with all my heart, but I want him to be a better man. Trisha is the best thing that ever happened to him."

I nodded. Neither Calloway nor I knew how much Jerry knew about everything else that had been going on near Black Vulture. Without discussing it, we both must have decided not to bring it up or question him further. He seemed fine, but we'd promised not to agitate.

I did have one more question for him, though. "Jerry, was Joey seeing Danielle Harold?"

"Romantically you mean?"

"Yes."

"Good Lord, no. I know he did some work at her place, but no, not romantically. That boy loves Trisha, even if he does end up screwing it all up."

We thanked him for his time. I hugged him and told him we'd have dinner when he was home. Tears filled his eyes as we left, and he thanked me for finding him, but we confirmed that they wouldn't let us break him out early.

We were almost to the doors at the end of the hallway when we heard him yell, "Hazel! Calloway!"

We hurried back inside the room, a nurse on our tail.

"The man. He had a motorbike thing, I think," Jerry said when we got there.

"Describe it." Calloway pulled out a notebook and a pen.

Jerry closed his eyes for a moment and then opened them again. "Silver. That's all I got. I only saw it briefly before I went down. No, no, no, wait!"

We waited as patiently as we could.

Jerry looked up again. "Yes, I went down, but that was because he pushed me. I was trying to help him. Was he hurt? I . . . I'm not sure. Maybe he was. Was there a cut on his face? I don't know. Maybe. I think he had wrecked or something, but he didn't want my help. That's what I got. I don't know."

"Okay, so you said motorbike. Two wheels or more, like an ATV?" I asked.

He looked confused for a moment. "I'd'a said two, but now that I think about it, I don't know for sure."

"What else?" Calloway asked. "Take your time."

Jerry fell into thought again but only frowned when he looked up this time. "That's all I've got."

"That's great, Jerry. Really great," Calloway said.

Jerry smiled, pleased to be helpful.

We left again, and I said to Calloway, "A cut on his face, like Verro has?"

"I don't know, and the timing isn't right."

"I know, but Jenna mentioned Verro's motorbike?"

"Lots of people have those, Hazel."

"I know, but . . ."

"Yeah. I'll look into it."

I trusted that he would. On the way to the car, I realized how devastated I'd be if Jerry's outcome had been different. What if he hadn't made it? When he got home, I wasn't going to let another big swath of time pass before I brought out some whiskey, and we got drunk under the stars.

CHAPTER

29

"THAT'S THE SPOT. Yes, turn there," I told Calloway. "This is a good half mile back from the shack."

"Right. Not easily accessible. Can't see it from any road other than one we're on, if you could call it a road."

The ruts and divots kept me holding on tight as Calloway kept the Tahoe under ten miles per hour or we'd risk damage to the vehicle and us. We were headed toward half a boulder that stuck up from the ground. Getting to it was next to impossible. It was one of those high school dares, a place kids try to hike to without getting bitten by something or legs being stuck with cactus needles. I'd never been much of a part of any high school group, but I'd heard all about the things kids did around town to try to make Black Vulture a little less boring. The view was apparently great.

Frequently, the trips turned into someone needing some sort of medical attention, so I figured I hadn't missed much.

But I had heard about the red dirt. And the boulder was at the foot of the Tumacácori Mountains.

There was a tinge of red to the brown desert floor in this area, but in this part of Arizona the iron-rich red that could be found in and around Sedona was rare.

Somehow, though, millions of years earlier, the boulder pushed some up from the depths that must have been replete with it.

When we found the boulder, I said, "There it is. Oh my God, Calloway, there it is."

"I'll be damned. Be careful." He parked the Tahoe and we got out.

It was still treacherous walking to reach the spot. Red dirt surrounded the stone, about ten feet all around.

The dirt was stirred up, as if it had been dug recently.

"Shit. This must be the place." Calloway looked up to the boulder, at the rock face of the mountain not far away. "What do you suppose happened out here?"

I said, "I don't know."

The heat was searing. I adjusted my hat as we stepped even closer.

Calloway stood next to me. "Damn."

"Yep."

There was nothing inside the hole. It wasn't six feet deep, but maybe about four or so. There was no doubt in my mind that the second skeleton, Johnny Clark most likely, had been buried here, but testing would still need to happen.

I looked down toward the old shack where George and Johnny Clark had lived. It was about half a mile away, through a misery of desert landscape that would have made it impossible to carry a body.

"Was it like this out here twenty-five years ago?" I asked aloud, but it was more a thought than a real question.

"I think it's always been like this." Calloway looked at me. "Hazel, what are you thinking, really? Do you think Johnny's father . . . killed him or buried him here?"

I swallowed hard and locked eyes with the sheriff.

It took some courage to speak the words. I didn't like the thoughts I was having. I didn't want them to be true, but we were after the truth, and there was simply no other way to get to it but saying all the words.

Finally, I said, "Or mine did."

CHAPTER

30

AFTER A SHOWER, I texted Sonny and told him I'd be hanging out on my patio if he wanted to join me. He answered almost immediately saying he was stuck at work for at least two more hours. He'd let me know when he was finished.

I grabbed a bottle of beer from the fridge and made my way outside. It was still warm.

I glanced at the tree, hoping Jack would stop by. I had a lot I wanted to run by him. The other side of the wall was teaming with potential gourmet meals made for owls, though, and I wasn't ready to tempt him with any sort of bait. He'd have to make his own decision to return to the tree. Nevertheless, I asked aloud, "Where are you?"

I sat on the cushioned chaise and looked up at the sky, trying to clear my brain of everything. It wasn't that I didn't want to work toward answers, I just knew that not thinking about all of it for some time might offer answers much more quickly than all this focusing on it.

I grabbed my phone anyway and found the app connected to the camera.

"Shoot," I said when I saw that the camera hadn't picked up any new videos. The battery was fully shot now. Calloway had been holding the phone as we looked at the original three videos that the camera had managed to capture. As I held the phone now, I watched the dog trot by, and then Pearly leaving the diner, cutting a path toward the post office. But as I watched Trisha walking into the diner, something else caught my attention.

Trisha stutter-stepped as she made her way, her attention drawn across the street, seemingly at my front door if I had my angles right. She squinted at something before she hurried into work.

I knew she wasn't at the diner tonight, but I had her number. I dialed it.

"Hazel, what's going on?" she answered.

"Quick question, Trisha. Do you remember walking into work recently and looking over toward my place, maybe seeing something that caused you to pause or wonder what might be going on?"

She was silent for a long moment. "Yeah, I can't remember the exact morning, but I saw a guy at your door, turning the knob."

I sat up on the chaise. "What did he look like?

"I have no idea. Just a guy in a jacket and a cap. It was early, so it was still a little dark. I figured it was just someone who wanted to see the museum. When the door didn't open, I figured he would just be on his way. I forgot all about him about three seconds later."

"Okay. Can you give me anything, like a color of clothing, height, something?"

Again, she was quiet for a long time. "No, Hazel, I'm sorry. Want me to let you know if I remember anything?"

"Yes. Please."

"Sure. Any word on Joey?"

"I'm sorry. No."

"I'm going to bring Jerry home tomorrow."

"You're a nice person, Trisha."

"Yeah, well, a lot of good that does me. I'll call you if I remember anything."

"Thanks."

We ended the call. I thought about letting Calloway know what Trisha had said, but there wasn't much to it. I needed that new camera, but the post office was closed by now.

A familiar rustle pulled my attention back to the tree.

I smiled uncontrollably and lifted the bottle in salute. "Well, there you are. Where have you been?"

I was always surprised not to hear a whop-whop of wings or any sort of warning noises. Jack simply glided in and landed, his long talons gripping the soft wood easily and with immediate balance. The shimmy of the leaves was all I ever heard to announce his arrival. His orange eyes, in the moonlight, sparkled.

"What, no dinner?" I noticed his empty beak.

He blinked.

For a long few moments, we did what we always did. We looked at each other. I knew our conversations were things of my imagination, but sometimes all a person needed was a silent response punctuated with wise eyes, even if words weren't exchanged.

He looked well. I now had complete confirmation that he hadn't been hurt, and I was happy about that.

They were wicked creatures, owls. The top of food chains, they were extraordinarily good at catching their prey. Both of us were creatures of the night, but owls came by it honestly. I had grown up in the heat, around people who spent many months of the year waiting for it to cool off enough to go outside. Those cooler times were usually in the dark.

The weather didn't alter my love for where I lived, but I knew not everyone spent so much time under the stars simply because they wanted to be outside after a hot day had kept them in.

I thought back to when Jack and I first met. It had been seven or so years ago when I'd gone out to the courtyard, spotting something out of the corner of my eye. I'd gasped and jumped but became quickly intrigued when I could see the owl.

"Hey," I'd said.

He'd looked at me.

"I don't have anything for you, but you sure are pretty."

I'd watched as he watched me. The visits became frequent and more filled with me speaking as he continued to strike a sage pose while he listened. He probably thought I was brilliant.

"Well, I'm glad you're okay," I said tonight.

Before I could say anything else, the owl took off.

It had been a literal and quick flyby.

Was this a turning point? Was he going to visit with less frequency? What had been the catalyst? Was there a family out there in a nest in a cactus? Did he have other commitments?

I smirked at myself, wondering why I was attempting to figure out the actions of a wild animal that didn't owe me anything.

My phone buzzed with a text from Sonny.

"Things are wrapped up. Your invitation to come by still good?"

"Absolutely."

I lifted myself off the chaise, thinking I'd check the fridge for potential snacks. As I reached the sliding glass doors, I turned to look back at the tree one more time.

Jack wasn't there, but a flash of movement at the top of the wall caught my attention. Had the owl moved to the wall, or was I seeing something else?

I hesitated. Normally, I would take a closer look, but something froze me in place. I didn't know if what I'd seen had scared me or if I was just anxious to get ready for Sonny.

"Hello?" I said, though I knew that no one would answer even if someone was there.

The silence was punctuated by the distant shriek of an owl. Horned owls mostly hooted. Shrieks were used as warnings.

Chances were that Jack wasn't talking to me, warning me about some threat, but I took it for that and decided to listen.

I closed and locked the door. I didn't, but I really should have just taken a look out there, into that place that was familiar but also always surprising, my backyard AKA The Wild

C H A P T E R

31

THE NIGHT WITH Sonny had been a perfect distraction, but as I stood next to the kitchen counter and sipped my first-of-the-day cup of coffee, I pondered what I thought I'd seen the night before.

Sonny had left before sunup because of some technical problem with the alien computer. I joked that they kept getting a busy signal.

After he left, I fell back to sleep, my subconscious telling me things I needed to know.

Something occurred to me and woke me again.

Had someone on the other side of the wall kept Jack away? Had someone been watching me from back there? The rock had come over. Someone had broken in. Bones that I'd thought were finger bones had been left behind with the sculptures as well as the turtle.

I gave one humorless laugh as I realized that I might not only be a part of what was going on but also maybe I was being targeted—for what exactly wasn't clear. The random appearance of defleshed bones wasn't good, but just how personal were they

Who would it be? The man who'd attacked me? If so, where had he been the rest of the time? It was like he'd knocked me over and then left town. Had he pitched a tent somewhere in The Wild?

I threw on some jeans and my boots. I left through the museum's front door so I could get around the building and into The Wild.

I hadn't spotted a tent anywhere, and there were frequently a few in sight. It was already hot, and I forgot my hat as I lifted my boots high to get through the landscape.

I didn't get far before I realized this was a bad idea, but as I scanned again, I spotted something that kept me going. I trudged toward a clearing of sorts. Someone had forged a trail out here. It didn't lead all the way to my patio wall but stopped about twenty feet away. No one could watch me from this far out.

I spun around and scanned yet again, but didn't see anything suspicious.

I wasn't ready to give up. I made my way back to the patio, grabbing a ladder from a small shed off to the side.

I set the ladder next to the wall and climbed up. There were worn spots along the bark of Jack's limb from his sharp talons. I glanced outward but didn't see him anywhere. It was daytime, though. I wouldn't expect him.

As I turned to make my way back down the ladder, my eyes landed on something on the ground on the other side of the wall. It was a small brown metallic box of some sort.

I wasn't going back out there to retrieve whatever it was, but if there was another way . . .

I needed a long scoop of some sort. A fishing pole with a sure hook. I remembered an item that my father had used years earlier. It was a grabber, something he'd bought when he hurt his knee and spent some time on crutches.

It only took a few minutes to retrieve it from one of the shelves in my lab.

With the grabber, I climbed back up the ladder and leaned over the top of the wall, reaching down for the item. I got close but not close enough. I leaned a little more. I hoisted more of my body onto the top of the wall.

My father had been careful and wary. He'd commented about my lack of self-preservation and how I should take everything just a little slower than I did.

I had slowed down some, particularly when it came to my work. But as I reached for the thing on the ground, I knew I should try to find something else to use—but I was so, so close.

I wasn't even all that surprised when I went over, landing awkwardly on my arm and into a bed of cacti. But there was a surprise to come. For an instant, and since I was still conscious, I recognized that the pain I wasn't feeling quite yet was going to be brutal. The cactus needles themselves were going to be torturous, but, even worse, I'd broken my arm.

My humerus, at about the greater tubercle, I was sure. And not only did I not have my hat, I'd left my phone inside too.

Shit.

CHAPTER

32

I REALLY NEEDED TO get myself up and out of this mess. As I took a quick body inventory, I realized that minus the cactus needles and the broken arm, nothing else was hurting too badly.

I'd never been in such a spot. Young and agile, I knew how to make my way through the desert safely and intelligently. I didn't do foolish things. I'd found a grabber, for God's sake.

First things first. I would crawl out of here somehow some way, but I might as well find the item that had brought me back here in the first place. I looked around on the ground, patting with my one good arm while the other one flared and throbbed with pain that was going to get worse quickly.

I found the item next to my head. It was a camera, something like a GoPro. It wasn't like the camera I'd had. This one was beefier, but it was also probably attached to an app.

I looked up at Jack's branch. At the end of it, hidden from me on the patio side, was what was probably the mount for the camera, its rubber ring torn up by something that had made uneven cuts.

Possibly a talon.

The camera in my grip, I gritted my teeth and tried to figure out which way to turn now. I rolled onto the arm that wasn't broken and screamed, yelled. Maybe someone would hear me, but it was doubtful. Unless someone was right on the other side of the patio wall, no one would have a clue I was back here. Even someone in the museum might not hear me.

I took three quick, deep breaths—in and out—to steel myself as I sat up.

That resulted in another scream, this one made of pure white hot pain. I was going to have to get myself out of there, though.

Three more breaths, I lifted myself up to my knees. This time it was all the cactus needles in my arms, back, and legs that sent searing pain throughout me.

As I worked to build up more breaths, I heard something. Was that the distant noise of an engine? Had someone heard me? Was I going to be rescued?

I squinted out into The Wild and spotted dust flying up as if behind a moving vehicle. Yes, that was it! Graham was out there looking for the next sculpture.

I just had to make sure he saw me. I opened my mouth to yell, lifted my good arm to wave, tried to stand, tried everything.

And then I fainted dead away.

CHAPTER 33

I SMELLED FIRE. I felt warm. Was it fire or was it just hot outside?

The pain came next and nothing else mattered. I yelled and groaned, my eyes propelling open and staring right into the flames of a campfire in the line of my vision.

What . . ?

"Hazel," a man's voice said.

Panic choked me as I tried to figure out where I was and who was with me.

I looked down at my jeans and shirt. I was covered in bloody spots, but I didn't see any needles. My arm had been put into a tight sling. My whole body throbbed with pain once the immediate confusion mellowed, and I was woozy, like I'd been drugged.

"You're going to be okay." The man came into my view.

"Graham?"

"Yes, I got you."

I looked around again. "And you brought me here? Where are we?"

"We're right where we're supposed to be." He smiled.

My brain was muddled, my stomach roiled. The pain. The pain. I tried to focus on Graham's face. He didn't look exactly right. He was still him but different.

Were the flames, maybe bacteria from the cactus needles, playing tricks on my mind, or was it drugs?

"Can you help me sit up?" I asked.

"Of course."

Graham moved to my side. He hoisted me to mostly upright. My head swam, but I worked to keep from falling over.

"You okay there?" Graham asked quietly into my ear.

"I . . ."

I wasn't okay, but I couldn't grasp all that was wrong with me. I didn't have any energy. I wanted to lift myself up and run, but I knew that wasn't possible.

Okay, focus.

I squinted as I looked around again. "Are we in a cave?"

Graham sat down next to me. "We are. The Vulture Caves."

"Why?"

"Because it was one of your father's favorite places."

"Okay. That's true, but why are we here?"

Graham's smile fell. The flames played tricks over his face, but now the smoke from the fire was becoming thicker. You shouldn't have a fire where there was little ventilation. I'd explored the caves plenty of times, but all the "rooms" looked the same to me. I wondered how deep we were.

I coughed. "The smoke is getting bad. Can we get some air?"

"I will be leaving in a moment, but you won't be going with me, Hazel. I'll be back for you. Later."

"Graham . . ."

A part of me knew I was in deep trouble. This was bad, and though my own stubbornness had been the reason for the fall, everything that happened now was going to be his fault.

A string of drool fell from the corner of my involuntarily slack mouth. I tried to suck it back in, but it didn't work. My eyes caught a glimmer on the ground on the other side. I leaned to look but thought I would fall over, so I straightened and then tried again. Spread open on the floor was a felt case, its pockets stocked with knives of various shapes and sizes.

Though adrenaline zipped through me and made a part of me more alert, my head made a wobbly swivel as my eyes sought out Graham again. He was still there. The flames from the fire suddenly illuminated the underneath of his jawline more than his face. I thought I saw something I hadn't noticed before, though it was now obvious. A small cut, maybe? Jerry's words about the man he'd come upon in The Wild, and the cut on his face, rang through my mind. I said, "You?"

Graham chucked. "Yes, ma'am. Me."

"Why?"

What I wanted to say was, *what did we do to you*, but something clunked into place in my head instead.

"You're not Graham!" I said. "Not your name."

I'd never looked him up. I'd wondered about the lead coffins story, but I hadn't researched it or him.

"I am not."

"Is there a real Graham?" I said.

"Kind of."

"Did you kill him?"

He chuckled. "No, Hazel. He's still alive, but he's not well. He doesn't have a professional presence anymore. My God, the man loves talking about his bones. I bet you and he would hit it off." He rolled his eyes.

"Who are you?"

"My name is George Clark. You met me a long time ago."

"Johnny's father?"

"Yes."

"I don't remember you looking like this."

Waves of images played through my mind. My memory wasn't bad. Yes, I'd been in shock when Wilmot disappeared, but other than that, I hadn't forgotten more than anyone else would over time. Something in my system was muddling things, but now I worked hard to remember George Clark. While his son might have been on my radar, he hadn't. He was a grown-up. When I was thirteen, grown-ups were part of that world that I couldn't, didn't want to, be a part of. I'd been forced into growing up, of course, but by then George hadn't been around.

I could see a faint image of a memory of him now, though—long, dark hair.

"Did you cut your hair?" I asked.

He chuckled without humor. "I did it myself. I don't look like the younger me, but my hair might have been a giveaway, so I had to chop it off."

"Your Mobil cap . . . I think I remember it too."

"I worked at that Mobil up 19. Got the cap back then."

"You wanted to be recognized," I said without thinking. "It was a clue."

George sighed. "No, Hazel, not really. I guess . . . maybe I just wanted to see if anybody cared enough to recognize me. I'm not surprised that they didn't."

"I'm sorry I didn't." I was but not for reasons that had anything to do with his ego.

"You were young, and things were crazy . . . it all got out of hand.".

"You killed your son?"

"What? Of course not."

"What got out of hand?" I asked. "I didn't know about the classes."

George's head pulled back a little as if he was surprised. "Yes, you did. It was all about you in the end anyway."

I sucked in another thread of drool before it left my mouth. Whatever was debilitating me was fading some, but not fast enough. "George, I don't remember the classes at all." I paused. "I remember Johnny, though."

A strangled noise came from his throat. "He liked you."

"I liked him. He was a nice boy." I paused, wisps of fog clearing a little from my brain. "Were you watching me with the camera?"

"It fell off the tree shortly after I put it there, so no. I saw you struggle on the ground though. That's why I came for you. Hazel, what do you remember about Johnny?"

"What?"

"Johnny. What do you remember about him?"

I had no memory of any specific moment with Johnny Clark other than a flash of when he had dinner with us, but for a reason I still didn't know, I suspected his father had killed Silas and created bone sculptures around Black Vulture, one made from his son's dug-up bones. I didn't think he was doing any of it for any other reason than some sort of tribute or revenge for Johnny. Even with a muddled mind, I figured I could pretend like I had something to tell him that he might find interesting, and maybe he'd keep me alive long enough for the effects of whatever was slowing me down to wear off. A clear head would surely help me figure something out.

I started coughing, pretending it was uncontrollable. "I need air." I coughed harder.

"Tell me about Johnny!" George said.

I kept coughing. I was working so hard, I fell back to the floor again, on the side that didn't have the broken arm. It still hurt. The cries of anguish that came then were genuine.

"Oh, God damn it!" George exclaimed.

He put his hands under my armpits and started to drag me out of the cave. The pain was so horrific that, as much as I tried to fight it, I passed out again.

CHAPTER 34

I HAD NO IDEA how much time had passed, but when I woke up, we were outside under a black sky even thicker with stars than the night Sonny had taken me up to the satellites. It had been morning when I'd explored behind the wall. It was night now. A long day.

I sucked in as much oxygen as I could. The air was clean, tinged with sage and creosote and the lingering scent of smoke that probably came from the lining of my nose.

"Tell me about Johnny," George demanded.

"What about him?" I pretended not to remember what I'd said in the cave.

George gritted his teeth. "You were going to tell me something you remembered about Johnny."

I was still on my back on the ground, but I turned my head to look at George. He was crying silently now, tears running down his cheeks.

"What happened to your son?" I lightened my tone. "George, what happened to sweet Johnny?"

Johnny Clark might have been sweet, but I didn't know one way or another.

George blinked away what I thought might turn into more tears. "Hazel, Johnny's death is on your hands, your father's."

"What?!" I tried to sit up, but my stomach roiled. I went back down.

My father had been strange, but I didn't want to believe he was a killer. I wasn't either.

"You really don't know?"

"George, you need to tell me what happened," I said. I'd sobered a little more with a blast of adrenaline, but I couldn't be sure if my words were coming out slurred or not. I tried to sit up, but I couldn't manage it.

"You weren't a part of those classes?"

"No. I didn't even know they were happening." I paused. "The students were all under eighteen. I was younger than the group by a few years. I was in Tucson part of the time too. Considering what the classes were about, the parents should have been notified. They never were. Right? Did you know about them?"

"I didn't know until the day your father came to my home and asked about a box of your mother's items. I was so mad at Johnny because I knew he'd taken the box. I'd seen it in his room. I . . . he had to be disciplined for stealing, didn't he? I disciplined him hard. Too hard." George cried harder now. "He put together that . . . thing just to prove a point. He thought Silas would like it. He thought Silas would like it!"

I just wanted to sit up, but I still couldn't quite manage it. "Jesus Christ, George, what happened?"

"Your father blamed you."

"For what?"

"He said it was your knife."

"What knife? I wasn't there," I said. "Ever. I swear to you, George."

The flash of a memory came back to me. It was so vivid that I could almost smell the eggs cooking on the stove.

"Hazel. You left your knife in the museum again."

"I did? Sorry, Dad."

"I think I'm going to keep it for a while. You need to grow up a little more before you can have it back."

My feelings had been hurt, but his reprimand wasn't mean. As I looked back on it, he'd been sad, so very sad. I took his words and didn't challenge him.

I'd just come home from Tucson. I remembered the moments now, but there'd been no reason for them to have stood out over the years. Until now. And then Wilmot was gone the next day. I'd never seen the knife again. Until I saw it in the box. That was surely the knife I'd had back then. Wilmot packed it away with my mother's things. I wished he'd just thrown them away.

Damn.

George continued. "He thought Silas would like it the best, but he didn't. He freaked out and grabbed the bucket of blood your father had accidentally left in there—some hunter brought it with a deer carcass and Wilmot hadn't dumped it yet. Silas threw the blood. Chaos. It was chaos, apparently. Wilmot told me that Silas found your knife in the museum and he . . . stabbed my boy."

No, no, no! "No," I said as tears flooded from my eyes now too.

"You left the knife in the museum," George said.

"Not so someone would kill with it. I was just a kid, George. An oblivious kid."

"So was my Johnny! He was a *good* kid." Tears streamed down his cheeks even harder. Mine too.

Whose fault was it? It didn't fucking matter, because it was horrible no matter how you looked at it.

I said, "Did you kill Wilmot?"

"No."

I tried to understand what Wilmot would have done next. "My father brought Johnny's body to you?"

"We buried him right over there." Johnny nodded. "Wilmot said he'd never be found out here."

"Why? Why didn't someone call the police?"

"Because Silas was a kid too. Your father convinced me that the only way Silas might have a life was if we didn't report him."

"That wasn't the right thing to do."

"Silas's life was horrible as it was. Wilmot didn't want to make it worse. We buried Johnny. Your father gave me money, and I left town."

"What happened to Wilmot?"

"I don't know, Hazel. He was torn apart by all of it. None of it was easy for him either. I always thought he took his own life somewhere out here. I've looked for him over the years. If he was alive, I . . . well, I had to finish things here."

Me too. "So, what is this? Vengeance? For leaving my knife out."

"That, and if Wilmot is alive, he needs to know the kind of pain he put me through. Here at a place he loved, you will die too."

I squinted at him, knowing I needed to run. But I needed to get up first. "You killed Silas. He was living on the streets of Tucson?"

"I did him a favor. His life had been pathetic ever since he'd killed my Johnny. He'd've been better off if the police arrested him."

I could only imagine the scene inside my father's studio, the place where I now worked. Blood, a stabbing. Death. Twenty-some years later, here we were. However, I found it hard to believe that George was going to be able to kill me. We were chatting. We'd become friends, kind of. We'd bonded over bones.

"Look at you, George. You don't even look like the same man you were."

"You were a part of my inspiration. I changed who I was so I could get away with what I needed to do." The blade of a knife glimmered in his hand.

I needed him to put it down.

"I was just a kid, George," I repeated. "We all were. Johnny didn't deserve what happened to him. I'm sorry for all of it."

George made a move to stand.

I tried to gather my bearings. I was going to need to run. George knew The Wild but not as well as I did.

He had the knife, though, and I was hurt. At least none of the bones in my legs were broken. I could still walk, maybe run. I was going to have no choice but to try.

An idea came to me like a laser to my brain.

I sucked in as deep a breath as my lungs could pull and let it out with the loudest scream or yell or whatever it was that I could muster.

George seemed perplexed. "No one will hear you out here. You know that."

I knew full well that no humans would hear me.

A few seconds later, though, the noises came. Fluttering wings that were kind of like rain on a roof as well as some high-pitched squeaks and chirps.

George stood. "What the . . . ?"

He'd mentioned that the bats had scared him before. I counted on it happening again. The air became black with the flapping of wings as the colony of bats that had somehow heard my plea came from the cave. My father loved them. I wasn't a fan, but if they helped me I could change my mind. I used them as cover as I made my way up into a stoop and ran into The Wild.

It was ugly and uneven and painful, but I kept going. A few ticks of time later, the sounds of the bats dissipated. They were gone, on the hunt for their nightly fill of insects.

"No!" I heard George yell. "Stop!"

I hadn't made it far as I fell behind a big saguaro. It was dark enough that he wouldn't spot me immediately. He would catch up soon enough.

I know this place, I told myself. *I can do this.*

"Hazel! Hazel! You and your father killed my son!"

Of course we hadn't, but I understood his anger. I knew the pain of being left, even if I didn't know what it was like to lose a child. I hoped I never would, but I could imagine that it was unquestionably the worst pain ever. Worse than losing a parent.

The guilt I felt now about leaving the knife out was real, but not enough for me to want to die in payback.

Not only had I just been a kid, but I'd lived in Black Vulture, where everyone carried knives or guns, some sort of weapon. With the continually encroaching wildlife, it was a smart thing to do. This had been the Wild West. In some ways, it still was. Apparently, my mother had carried a barbeque fork. I eyed the cactus. Sharp things were everywhere around here.

I hadn't left my knife out so someone could use it to hurt someone else. I'd just been a lazy, thoughtless kid.

Wait! Did I?

With my good arm, I reached into the opposite side back pocket of my jeans. George hadn't looked in my pockets. I had my knife with me now. Earlier I'd missed my hat and my cellphone, but now I knew what was really important. Awkwardly I grabbed it, unfolded it.

I ratcheted my legs back up again and took off toward town. I tried to be quiet, keep my breathing as silent as possible, but I could hear George behind me, probably seeing my shadow moving now. He was gaining.

I took a turn that I thought would eventually take me to a path toward the far side of town. The terrain was unwelcoming at best, deadly at worst, but I could only hope for the best at this point.

My route must have been obvious because George continued to close the space. He'd be on me in just a few seconds. I found a patch of Ocotillo cacti that I might be able to hide behind, so I propelled myself behind it and held my breath as my heart pounded in my ears.

"Hazel, I know exactly where you are. I will catch you. You can't get away. Let's just get this over with. It's only fair."

I put my hand over my mouth and hoped he didn't hear my heart beating.

Suddenly, I heard Wilmot's voice. "Move right, little bit. Right!"

Though confused by where the voice was coming from—was it real or my imagination? I moved to the right.

"Good, now get ready." It was Wilmot again.

I knew now that I was imagining his voice, but that didn't mean I would listen any less. No one knew The Wild like my father.

After a strange play of fast and slow time later, George appeared, the orb of a flashlight landing in my eyes and blinding me with bright yellow light.

"There you are."

The light moved closer. I imagined his knife being held high in the air, ready to take me out. I readied mine.

"Oh, God damn it!" George yelled as his light went flying into the thicket.

I scrambled to stand again and tried to understand what was happening. The light was now on the ground but aimed toward George who was on his back, grabbing his leg.

"I've been bit!" he yelled.

I knew exactly where to look, and my eyes caught the disappearing rattle of a snake. George had been bitten by a rattler, one that would have gotten me if I hadn't moved to the right.

"Oh my God!" He yelled. "Jesus, it hurts. Hazel," he choked, "I can't . . . breathe." The last word came out muddled and strangled.

I knew the pain, and it was horrible, the worse thing I'd ever felt. But with some antivenom and time, I'd recovered. I wasn't allergic to the poison, but some people were. George was. Based upon his breathing and quickly swelling face, George was moments away from dying. I knew how to cut and suck out the poison, but I'd never done it before. Besides, his reaction would kill him before I could help.

"What can I do?" I crouched next to his body.

George's breathing was falling to something squeaky and weak.

"What the hell, Hazel?" a voice said from behind me.

I screamed and stood with my knife in one hand, my other arm hanging limp at my side.

"Joey?" I exclaimed.

"Who is that guy?" Joey asked.

"Joey!" I blinked at Trisha's wayward boyfriend, wondering if it was the drugs in my system conjuring him here. There didn't seem to be any other reasonable explanation—except that maybe Joey had been hiding, and there wasn't a much better place to hide than The Wild. My gummy brain keyed on Trisha's words: *Joey's allergic.*

I said, "Joey, do you have your EpiPen?"

"I . . . I don't. I'm sorry. What got him?"

"A rattler."

"Shit. All right." Joey slung the pack he'd had on his back off and onto the ground. "Damn, he's probably beyond helping, Hazel."

I watched, right there but from a strange distance, wondering what Joey was going to do. I crouched next to him.

Joey listened to George's mouth. "This guy looks dead as a doornail, but I think I hear some strained breathing. I can open a pathway in his throat." He reached into his pack for an ink pen and bit off the cap and then pulled out the innards tube with his teeth, spitting it away. He grabbed the knife from my hand and held up both tools. "Want me to try?"

I nodded because I didn't know what else to do.

Joey got to work, searching George's swelling neck with his fingers and then cutting a hole. "Everyone thinks this is called a tracheostomy, but that's not the right term. It's called cricothyrotomy. Trisha and I have been learning all about it on YouTube because I'm so allergic to scorpion venom, and those fuckers are everywhere." After he cut the hole, he slipped the ink pen's casing into the hole. Joey leaned in. "How about that? I hear air moving."

He looked like disreputable Joey but was behaving with the calm intelligence of a medical professional.

"What?" he said when he saw my expression. "Hey, it was Trisha's idea to learn this shit. First time I've done it. I hope it works." He shrugged.

"We need to get back to town," I said.

"That's not where I'm going. You don't look good, Hazel, but you can make it. Come back for him. He won't go far, dead or alive. I'll tourniquet his leg and watch him until I see someone else coming this way. I'll do CPR if he needs it, but I'm not sucking out any blood."

I didn't argue with him, ask him why he didn't want to come into town. I knew the way to Black Vulture, and I'd never wanted to be there so much in my life. I would not remember many details about my run back to town, except the sense that some distant voice guided me as my beat-up body stumbled the whole way.

CHAPTER 35

It had been three days since the ordeal in The Wild. I was going to be okay. The drugs George had injected into me—basically, a roofie—had messed with my consciousness as well as my memory, but I knew what had happened. Mostly. Though Rohypnol isn't a pain management medication, the drug had relaxed my muscles and made me not care about the pain I should have been feeling, which did hit me once the drugs and the adrenaline wore off. It was hideous for about a day and a half. I was fortunate to have Sonny help me at the house when I got home from the hospital. I was only taking Ibuprofen now.

My arm in a sling, I found my way to a booth at the diner, put my hat on the seat beside me, and sat across from Calloway.

I couldn't remember when it started, but this was our debrief station. No matter what the case—something local, or something I worked on for someone else, Calloway and I would meet here and talk about it when it was over.

Dixie dropped off two coffees and told us to let her know if we wanted anything else. She knew what we were doing. She also knew that we only had coffee, black, during these meetings.

"How are you, Hazel?" Calloway asked.

I'd been getting that question a lot over the past few days. "I'm going to be okay." I lifted my slung arm away from my body a little and wiggled my fingers. "I can work and drive again, so I'm in a better mood."

"You probably shouldn't drive."

I nodded. I was going to drive, but I wasn't going to argue with him. "I'm feeling better."

"Good." Calloway sighed. "George Clark is going to live."

Tears welled in my eyes. I should have wished him dead, considering what he'd done to me, but I didn't. Instead, I wished for more answers, and some way to make amends to him for what my father had done, though I knew that last part would be impossible, particularly since we still didn't know what happened to Wilmot Dylan. I believed what George had told me, but I sure would have loved to hear my father's side of the story.

Calloway continued, "He has lots of healing ahead, but he'll be okay. He'll stand trial and go to prison for life. He confirmed that the second set of bones belonged to Johnny. We can't find any dental records, but we could do DNA if we wanted to. We are confident that we have appropriate identification."

I swallowed and blinked away a swell of mixed-up emotions. "What else is he saying?"

Calloway wrapped his hands around his mug. "George moved away after Johnny was killed. For a long time, he barely got by, but when a professor at the university in Colorado found him passed out in some alley, George got some help. At least a roof over his head and food. The professor was the real Graham Kucero. When Kucero told George about his forensic specialties, George went to work for him and learned all he could. Kucero retired a few years back."

I remembered what George had said to me. I'd been some sort of inspiration to him. "He was educated a little like me."

"Well, an unconventional path, that's for sure."

"How long had he been planning this?"

"A long time, but he tracked down Silas in Tucson last year. He found him quickly in a shelter, apparently, followed him for a while and then went home. But he couldn't stop thinking about . . . well, all of it. He came back to Arizona a couple months ago and got to work. He purchased and then brought the barbeque fork, the pendant, and a few scarves with him. He said he threw one away behind the post office one night after Pearly left."

"Pearly sensed him."

"I think so, yes."

"I'm glad she didn't turn around."

"Me too. Anyway, when he got back to Arizona, he knew the first step was to kill Silas." Calloway paused and sighed again. "George says that he always wanted some sort of vengeance for his son, but until he ran into Silas, he didn't think it was possible. He says everything was set in motion then." Calloway paused and took a sip of coffee. "He regrets killing Silas, but once he did, he knew there was no going back."

"I guess not. Where did he deflesh the bones?"

"A hotel room in Tucson. Authorities up there are investigating, but . . . well, George cleaned up after himself pretty well."

"Jesus."

"Yeah, and he called me before I even knew to reach out to someone like him. When he did, I was just so glad to have help that I didn't put together the fact that, realistically, he wouldn't have heard about the bones yet."

I could tell by his tone that Calloway was beating himself up for that.

"Not your fault," I said.

"Well, I know that, but . . . I wish I'd been more on top of it. Anyway. There are no new leads on the guy who attacked you, and George claims not to know him. Keep aware."

"I bet he moved on."

"Maybe, but stay on your toes."

We were silent for a long moment, both of us wrestling with our thoughts, I presumed. Suddenly, Calloway waved toward the counter. I turned to see Jenna with a woman who must be her wife, Allie. Jenna waved back hesitantly, like she wasn't sure if she should come over. We didn't do anything to either encourage or discourage her. She stayed where she was. She smiled and then turned to place an order.

"I think Jenna will be good for Black Vulture," Calloway said.

"I hope so. What about Verro?"

"He's a good guy, Hazel, despite some stuff he's been through. He really is from Prescott."

"Your intel was incorrect?"

"My intel was good. I just didn't tell you the truth about it, exactly. Apparently, Verro got in some trouble up there. He was accused of theft. He was dismissed from his position, but never formally charged for any crime. Virgie knew about it, but was just so glad to have a police chief on board who actually understood police work, she didn't care, figured it was a win-win. The reason he was MIA from here for a day or so was because he'd had to run back up to Prescott. One of his former fellow officers picked a fight or some such thing up there. That's why he was beat up a little. Jenna knew what he was doing, but he'd asked her not to tell me. She'd been torn. He's apologized for putting her in that position."

I nodded. "Okay. Good."

I looked toward the kitchen, where Doug was working as hard as he always did. Virgie's hair made its way through and behind the cook. She was always around, even if you couldn't see all of her. I glanced at my finger. It was almost healed, though my broken arm would be in a sling for some time.

"I hope Verro and Jenna don't get bored," I said.

"They probably will, but it will be good for Black Vulture to have them around. Real police."

As Dixie passed the booth again, she refilled my already half-empty mug. "Where's Trisha?" I asked her.

"Day off." She winked and then walked away.

"What was that about?" I asked Calloway.

"Trisha is probably with Joey."

I hadn't imagined Joey out there with his ink pen and quick thinking, but he hadn't been there when the chopper arrived to gather George. I remember barreling into the diner and telling Trisha to call the police, but I didn't remember telling anyone where I'd left George and Joey. Later, when I'd awakened in the hospital in Tucson, I was informed that I'd been very precise. I guessed I'd been in The Wild enough that even my subconscious knew locations.

Like Jerry, I just wanted to get out of the hospital. Unlike Jerry, I didn't wait to be officially discharged. Once I was told that my arm didn't need surgery or setting but would just need to be stabilized at the shoulder to heal, I pulled out the IV and left.

Calloway continued, "Joey was hiding from some guys because of a gambling debt. I think Jerry and Trisha have convinced Joey to man up and be an adult. I figure that either Joey will be killed by some thugs, or Jerry will get things straightened out soon enough. I'm sure Trisha's helping with all of that."

Calloway would be protecting them if he thought they were in real jeopardy. He was confident in Jerry's abilities to get the problems solved. And probably Trisha's.

"Joey saved George's life," I said.

"You've mentioned that a time or two. By the way, Joey was the one to stop by his and Jerry's trailer to text Trisha that he was okay. Also, he wanted to grab an EpiPen, but he couldn't find any."

I remembered being irritated that Trisha wanted me to take her out to the trailer. "If Trisha hadn't convinced me to go out there and look, we might never have found Jerry in time."

"Yep."

"There's hope for Joey," I said.

"With good people in your court, there's always hope."

I was the living embodiment of that. I nodded. "I saw a cut on George's face. Was he the one to confront Jerry out in The Wild?"

"Well, yeah. Jerry saw someone digging through one of his piles of bones. It was George, who'd been camping out by the caves for about two weeks by then, apparently, getting the lay of the land, watching everyone, you mostly. George says he got the horse tail bones from one of the piles. Anyway, he ran off when Jerry came out to confront him. George took off on the ATV, but Jerry knew a way to cut him off down the path. Jerry just wanted to know what George was up to, but George wasn't going to tell him, of course. He coldcocked Jerry, hard enough that George thought he'd killed him, at least left him for dead. Then dehydration about got him, but Jerry's one of the toughest guys out here. Anyway, George got that small cut in the scuffle that took place before he went down. I noticed it when I first met him, but it didn't look like much of anything to me."

Whatever sympathy I had for George was diluted. Poor Jerry.

"Hazel, I have to tell you the rest."

I swallowed. "I'm listening."

"George's goal was to kill you, pose your bones, probably like a snake—"

"That's ironic."

"Isn't it. Anyway, the pendant was your mother's. He was going to use your knife to skin—"

"Deflesh."

"Deflesh you, and then leave the pendant around your neck. He wasn't sure when he lost the necklace, but he was going to use your knife, the one that killed . . ."

"His son."

Another long beat passed. "Yeah."

I nodded. "He wasn't going to go after Minnie or Thalia or the others?"

"No, he says he wasn't. Everyone is home. They weren't running. They were doing things in Tucson. Danielle moved in with a friend. She and her horses are happy and safe."

Calloway, seemingly relieved to get through telling me about George's plan to kill me, forced a smile. "How's the boyfriend?"

I sent him a withering look and then finished my coffee before I stood. I wanted him to know I wasn't really mad, so I moved and put my hand on his shoulder. "Thanks, Sheriff. For everything."

"Thank you, Hazel."

I put my hat on and made my way out of there, waving at Dixie, Doug, Jenna, and even Virgie (who frowned disapprovingly at me) as I left.

I took the short trip home, glancing at the time along the way.

CHAPTER

36

I POINTED. "IT'S ONE femur, twelve tibias, ten fibulas, lots of foot and toe bones. I thought it strange that there were no hand bones in the box, but there were plenty of arm bones."

Sonny whistled. "It feels highly inappropriate to give that description a hand, like applause."

I smiled. "Well, they belonged to souls who lived over a hundred years ago now, and they weren't murdered."

"Okay?"

"This is the box of bones from Missouri that I was telling you about. I've looked at them and sent off an email to Mr. Workman regarding my conclusions."

"Oh. Interesting." He looked into the box. "May I touch them?"

"Yes."

He reached in for the femur. "Can you share your conclusions?"

I nodded.

Sonny had been amazing, there for me at every turn. I was healing quickly, but he had met me at the hospital, keeping it together but still visibly distraught that I'd been so hurt. I'd been quite the sight, but he'd seen me at my worst and had still stuck around to help me in any way I needed.

At first I wanted to tell him that I would be fine, that I didn't want his help, but I did need a ride back to Black Vulture. Calloway offered, but seemed to disappear when Sonny arrived. I slept the whole way home. Then Sonny made sure I was comfortable in my own bed. He'd proceeded to stock the fridge and clean the whole place, including dusting the mounts in the museum. He slept in the smaller bedroom and made sure I took the prescribed pain pills and antibiotics on time.

He'd gone back to work this morning but had returned to my place by noon. I'd spent the morning working in my lab, and he'd wondered about the Missouri bones before everything else had happened. Since we had a few minutes, I shared the details.

I'd figured out their mysteries quickly.

"I called the city offices of Columbia, Missouri, first to ask what sort of building had been where a library is now located. They were able to quickly tell me that it had been a church."

Sonny's eyebrows lifted. "Religious sacrifice?"

I smiled again. "No, but that would make a great story." As he held the femur, I turned it and pointed at an ink spot. "Can you see that?"

"Barely."

"Right. I'm pretty sure it says '1864.'"

"Okay. I can see that."

"A note dated 1977 also came with the bones." I picked up the yellow piece of paper that I'd set on the worktable. "It says, 'These bones were found outside a library in Columbia, Missouri, when the foundation for a new wing was being dug. No one was called. We just put them away.'"

"1864, 1977?"

I nodded. "I don't know who put the 1864 there or how that happened exactly, but if you look at the ends of the bones, you can see how crudely the limbs were cut from the bodies."

"Oh." Sonny examined the end of the femur. "I see. So, what does all that mean?"

"Considering all the clues, I think that the church was used as a makeshift hospital during the Civil War. The limbs were cut off and thrown out a window to make a pile that was eventually buried. Again, I don't understand how one was retrieved and written upon, but there have always been people who thought it was wise to record events along the way. I think the bones were found and boxed in the 1970s, in preparation for the new construction."

Sonny looked at me. "Whoa. Really?"

"Yes, really. I've read about such a thing."

Sonny set the femur back into the box. He pushed up his glasses and peered inside at the old remains. "That's sad and interesting, and . . . I don't know. I feel like more should be done for them."

I nodded. "I know the feeling." I paused. I hadn't become jaded in my job, but I had become more accepting of the need to find answers and then keep going, be ready for the next mystery. "But maybe giving them this moment is good. We don't know who they fought for, but maybe we can thank them for following their heart and fighting for whatever they believed."

Sonny nodded and smiled at me, though it was a sad expression. "I can do that."

A moment later, I said, "Okay, I have a favor."

"Anything."

"It's a big favor, maybe more than I should ask."

"No such thing."

There could be no argument that we'd become close very quickly, and me getting injured was one of the reasons we'd spent so much of the last few days together. Maybe once I healed and we both got back to our regularly scheduled jobs, things would change. Maybe we didn't like each other as much as it seemed we did.

Though some might live in fear of people leaving them after their father disappeared like mine had, instead I'd somehow learned to enjoy what I could of the ride, and not be too worried about when it might change directions. I'd become resilient, I guess, even if I didn't quite realize it myself.

"Good. Could you drive me somewhere?"

"Absolutely."

"Thanks. I'll tell you about it on the way."

"That works."

I put the bones away and tapped the top of the box. It wasn't much, but it was my tiny way of sending respect to the people they'd once been a part of.

We made our way out of the lab, through the museum, and out the front door. I couldn't help double-checking the deadbolt Sonny had installed.

CHAPTER 37

I KNOCKED ON THE door.

"No one home?" Sonny asked a few moments of silence later.

"Maybe not." I knocked again.

David finally answered.

"Hazel. I heard about your adventures. Are you okay?" There was not a hint of snark in his tone, which surprised me.

"I'm fine."

"Who are you?" David asked Sonny.

"Sonny Riley." He extended his hand. "I'm a friend of Hazel's."

David ignored Sonny's gesture and crossed his arms in front of himself. "She's not available."

"She owes me," I said.

"How do you figure that?"

"Well, to begin with, I was alone as a kid. She could have taken me in."

"You know she couldn't have done that, Hazel. You *know* that."

"I don't."

David shook his head. "She's not available."

"David, let them in," Susan called from somewhere in the vast house.

I tried not to smirk, but my face beat out my good manners. Again.

David leaned toward me. "If she shows any sign of distress, I'll push you both out of here myself."

"Only if you can catch us," I challenged.

He sent me the best withering look I'd ever seen, and I had been the recipient of many, but I didn't let it deter me.

Reluctantly, he let us in and closed the door behind us, leading us back to the same room Susan and I had been in before. She sat on the same chair.

I walked in. "You know where my father is, don't you?"

"Sit down, Hazel. Please. Introduce me to your friend."

Sonny approached Susan and introduced himself to her. She shook his hand and smiled. "Aren't you adorable?"

"Thank you," Sonny said. "It's a pleasure to meet you." He looked at me.

On the ride, I'd told him who Susan was and what my goals were in visiting her again. He'd been supportive but had tried to talk me into giving myself a few more days to heal before throwing myself into a possibly contentious face-to-face. I told him I couldn't wait a day longer, and he didn't argue further.

I nodded at him. He let go of Susan's hand and took a seat next to me on a couch.

I said, "Just tell me, Susan. Everything."

"I can't tell you everything, but I can tell you enough."

"I'm listening."

Susan began with something that kicked me in the gut.

"Your father and I had been seeing each other."

"What?"

Sonny's hand went to my knee, which I only noticed somewhere in the back of my mind. He wasn't holding me down but reminding me that he was there if I needed him. I would thank him later.

She nodded. "Yes, Hazel. It started twelve years after your mother, my sister, died. Wilmot and I had frequently been there for each other. Shoulders to lean upon, ears to bend and such."

"I don't remember you at all." I had no doubt that I hadn't seen her around back then.

"You wouldn't. We didn't want you or anyone to know. I'm not well. I wasn't well then either, but I was functioning okay, and your father understood me. We were good at keeping it a secret. We wanted to see how it would go before we wanted you to even know we were good friends. We didn't want you to be further hurt if we couldn't be happy together. We thought that if we could . . . well, we thought that you and everyone would eventually understand. But what would be the point of putting anyone through that if we couldn't be sure?" She paused. "But in truth, I know we could never have gone forward. It would have been too much. I would have ruined it all at some point anyway."

"I . . ." Not only had I not expected to hear what she was telling me, but also I couldn't quite understand why she was telling me now. She read my mind.

"You need to know. It's important to the rest of the story, Hazel. There would be no reason for me to have been . . . around if not for my feelings for Wilmot."

I swallowed away the shock that was old news but brand spanking new to me. "Okay. Tell me."

"That class. Your father wanted someone else nearby because there were teenagers involved and he trusted me to help if needed. Only me, Hazel."

"Even if you weren't well?"

Susan didn't hesitate to nod. "Yes, even if I wasn't well. The responsibility helped me too. Besides, who else was he going to ask?"

I thought about it. The first two possibilities that came to mind were Jerry Smoot or Sheriff Calloway, and neither of those made sense. Neither did Susan, really, but if my father had feelings for her, perhaps he thought she could handle it.

"Okay," I said again.

"Right. So I was there during the classes, not in the room but the kitchen or upstairs." Her eyes suddenly seemed to shadow and then tears fell down her cheeks. "That day . . . was horrible."

"Susan?" David pleaded.

"I'm fine. Let me finish this, David."

He nodded.

Susan continued, "After everybody started freaking out about the . . . thing, and Silas threw that blood, I took the girls to the patio. I went back inside to ask Wilmot what we should do next. That boy . . . Johnny. He was so upset because Silas was so upset. The boys were more upset than anyone. Wilmot was trying to calm them down. I tried too, but Johnny just wanted Silas to shut up. Johnny was so much bigger. I can still see his fists balled at his side as he towered over Silas and berated him, calling him messed up, sick, a loser, those sorts of things. Silas grabbed a knife from the table—none of us even noticed it before that—and stabbed Johnny. He fell and hit his head on the edge of a table as he went down. We tried to stop the bleeding. We tried everything, but the boy was gone so quickly. We didn't know what killed him, the stab or hitting his head, but he was dead. Gone in an instant."

Susan took a ragged breath and wiped away some tears. "Wilmot told me to get myself together and take care of the girls, get them cleaned up and home, that he would take care of Silas and Johnny's body." She looked at me. "He left with the body in the back of that Jeep you still drive. He . . . took them home, I guess. I don't know. We didn't speak about it again. It was . . . too much."

I suddenly remembered seeing what I thought was dirt stains on the back-seat floorboard as he drove me to school a morning shortly before he disappeared. It wasn't much, but it got my attention. In retrospect it must have been dried blood. I'd asked Wilmot about it. He'd said he didn't know where it came from, but I didn't need to worry about it. The stains had been gone when I'd taken the time to look again later. That's what must have been trying to come back to me. Blood in the Jeep wasn't normal, even if Wilmot behaved as if it was no big deal, and even if it took me all this time to understand what it had truly been.

"Susan," I said, but I wasn't sure what I wanted to say. "Susan."

She nodded. "The day Wilmot left, he came to see me—"

"He left, of his own accord?"

She lifted a hand, asking for a moment. I gave it to her.

"I lived up in Sahuarita back then. He hitchhiked up to my house, telling me he was going to run away because of . . . it all. I told him to go home, go back to you, that it wasn't fair for you to lose both parents. I told him I loved him. He told me he loved me. I said that if he really did love me, he would face the consequences, he would be your father. He was stronger than that, I knew he was. He . . ." Susan let out a sob.

David ran to her side and put his hands on her shoulders, but she gathered herself and wanted to go on.

"He asked me if I would come with him back to Black Vulture. We would tell you about us and be a family." She sniffed. "I told him no, Hazel. I told him that wasn't fair to you either. That he should be the one to talk to you first. Maybe it would have been better for me to go."

"We can't know . . ," I said.

"That's true." She sat up straighter now. Maybe the worst of it was out now. "Anyway, he promised me that he'd go back to you, that he'd be the father you needed. I offered to drive him, but he said he'd hitchhike home."

"He lied to you?"

"I don't believe that, but I have no idea what happened to him." She nodded toward the freeway. "I-19 has seen bad stuff. Maybe something terrible happened to him on the way. He wouldn't have lied to me."

I wasn't so sure.

What I was sure of was that though I had a million more answers, some to questions I didn't even know until just now, and I still didn't know what had happened to Wilmot. No one did, including Susan, but it seemed like some cobwebs of mysteries had been wiped away. The truth wasn't completely clear yet, but it wasn't as murky.

The man who'd attacked me hadn't been found, and George claimed not to know anything about him. I'd managed to get a good read on the inside of the boot, and it hadn't been Wilmot's, but some guy named Frederick Renner. Frederick had died five years earlier.

Wilmot had claimed he would thumb it back home. He might have just gone north instead. Alternatively, I thought about what decision he might have made and then decided not to torture myself too much. I wondered if I'd ever know the full truth.

"Hazel, he loved you so much. He was scared that if he stuck around, you would pay the price for what he'd done, in one way or another. It was more about that than him paying any price, and I couldn't convince him to see it any other way."

"Huh," I said at the irony. "It appears that I'm destined to 'pay the price' no matter what." I'd once heard something like: the most ironic thing usually happens. I was living proof.

"Well, I hope not."

We fell silent, all of us working through our thoughts. I couldn't stir up anything inside myself for Susan. I didn't feel anger or sorrow toward her. I needed some time to process.

I didn't want to ask if we could be friends. Neither did Susan. That request seemed unreal, but maybe it could be possible as time went on. Not today.

I remembered something else. "Are you the one who sent me the dress when I was little, the one that looked like something my mother might have worn?"

She smiled genuinely. "Yes, that was me."

I didn't tell her I didn't ever wear it. That seemed mean, and I wasn't in the mood to be mean. Maybe later. But I wasn't grateful either. I had so much jumbled up inside me that I wasn't sure what I was supposed to feel. Next to me Sonny shifted, and I sent him a quick nod.

"I think we need to go," I said.

"I understand," Susan said.

"Excellent idea," David added. "I'll show you the door."

We let David lead us toward and then through the front door. He didn't tell us not to come back, but that was his vibe. He didn't slam the door, but his eyes told us that he wanted to.

"You okay?" Sonny asked as he took my elbow.

"I'm not sure.

"That makes sense. But you are going to be okay, Hazel. I'm sure of it."

I nodded again.

For a moment, I thought I smelled the same things I had when the man attacked me, similar to the scents from the javelina encounter. But it passed as we made our way to Sonny's car.

As he drove us back to my place, I put my mind to the future instead of the past.

I was going to go home and sit out on my patio with Sonny. Tonight maybe he would meet the other man in my life. Jack.

There was a lot to think about, try to understand, or maybe just accept. If Wilmot were here, if his essence or spirit had helped me veer away from the snake that had bitten George, I knew he'd say something like, just keep going forward, little bit. Don't look back.

I took a deep breath and let it out. Sonny sent me a quick smile.

The desert had tried to swallow me whole. But I'd won this round.

EPILOGUE

THE HOT WIND blew his long hair as he stood next to the cave's opening. His face was lined with deep wrinkles that came with age as well living outside.

He'd spent some of the time indoors, renting a room in a house in Tucson. He'd left Black Vulture with enough cash to pay cheap rent for a long time. But he'd missed the desert too much. He missed The Wild, his long-gone wife, and even Susan.

He missed Hazel more than anyone or anything. For a while, he'd kept tabs on her, but it became too painful to watch her from a distance, to see her living by herself, taking care of herself. Calloway would make sure his little girl was okay, but he spent a lot of time hating himself for not setting her up better.

It had all gone so bad so fast and without warning. A child had killed another child, on his watch. People might assume that he'd left so he wouldn't have to pay whatever price came with such neglect. But that hadn't been it. He'd run away to protect his little girl. He couldn't risk ruining her life. No one but Calloway would understand his reasoning, but he hadn't said anything to his old friend. He hadn't told anyone his plans.

In truth, he hadn't been so sure of them himself, except that when he left Susan that long-ago day, he knew that he couldn't bring himself to go backward. And after some time had passed, going back became impossible.

When he wasn't in Tucson, he was in the mountains, where the seasons flew by and nature taught him more about himself than anything else. He wished he could share those lessons with someone, but they were the kinds of things you had to learn for yourself.

Besides, he wasn't qualified to teach anyone anything. Hadn't he at least learned that much?

The old guy had stolen his dinner one night, grabbing it right off the firepit he'd dug and tended for so many years.

"I would feed you, friend," he'd said. "There's no need to steal." And when the old guy remained silent, he spilled his story, all of it, and then he wept, prompting the old guy to finally speak.

"What can I do for you?" he'd asked.

"Nothing. I'll be all right."

"I will check on your daughter for you."

At first he wanted to shake his head, tell the old guy that it wasn't necessary. Besides, there was something about the old guy that set off warning bells, an undercurrent of . . . violence maybe. But maybe not. He said, "You would do that?"

"I will. I will leave first thing in the morning. Meet me at the caves in ten days."

He'd wiped his cheeks and sniffed as something like a glimmer of hope ignited in his chest. Was this okay? Would he really like to know? Would it be like making a potential promise? Had enough time passed that it wasn't going backward anymore, that it just might be a new way forward?

Yes. Maybe.

Now, as he waited, his long-ago home in the distance, he became concerned that the old guy had lied or would not come, maybe because of some bad news.

The thing that had lit in his chest still burned. It might kill him if it was left unanswered. He didn't want to give up hope, but the sun was low, moving toward the horizon quickly now. Would he have to turn and go back to camp without knowing? Could he do that?

The smell came first. The man's stench was a welcome scent and probably a version of what Wilmot himself smelled like. A moment later, the old guy came into sight, waving as he approached, trudging over the desert floor. "I have much news, friend," he called. "Much news."

Wilmot Dylan smiled and wiped away some fresh tears. He waited and rolled the old phalanx over and through his fingers as a dust devil sprung up in the distance near his old hometown.

ACKNOWLEDGMENTS

THANK YOU TO so many people:

My agent, Jill Marsal, who is a champ.

My editor Denise Zaza and everyone at Crooked Lane. I'd heard about Denise and wished for the chance to work with her. I feel very fortunate. Everyone at Crooked Lane has been wonderful.

The people at the Tucson Forensics Lab. I have never been around a bigger group of people who love their jobs with such infectious enthusiasm. If I'd met you all when I was in college, I would want to be you. Shoot, maybe I still do.

Dr. Laura Fulginiti (Dr. Fulgi), forensic anthropologist, who let me name a character in the book after her and answered my bone questions with such intelligence and friendliness that I think I also want to be her. Here's the thing: I don't know what I don't know, so I have no doubt that I got some bone things wrong in this book. Those mistakes are mine only.

Jenel Looney, an assistant extraordinaire! Smart, insightful, funny, fun. A friend. How did I get so lucky to work with her?

Some author friends and I participate in a social media thing we call BookTalk. I cannot express how much I love these women (and their significant others): Jenel, Jenn McKinlay, Kate Carlisle, and Hannah Dennison. Without them, I would be a sad shell of a writer person, I'm sure.

My family is the best—Charlie, Tyler, Lauren, W. and C. I love you so much.

And to my readers: new books and new series are exciting and terrifying. Thanks for coming along on these rides with me. I hope there's lots more ahead.

When I decided to set this story in Arizona, I wanted to find the perfect spot to create a fictional community. Ultimately, and after visiting so many places that were *almost* perfect, I found Tubac, located on I-19 between Tucson and the Mexico border, west of the Tumacácori Mountains. Tubac is the cutest artist community in the world. Unfortunately, Black Vulture is not cute. So, to the lovely people of Tubac, forgive me for altering your lovely world in the name of fiction. Everyone should visit Tubac, by the way.

Also, I totally made up the Vulture Caves. There are no caves there. In fact, I made up a lot, but I sure did have fun creating this new world.